SYSTEMATIC SOUL SORTING

CLINTON CAMPBELL

Clinton Campbell

Disclaimer

This book contains some very mild sexual allusions, death, and many violent actions described within. It also contains a nongraphic description of suicide. If you find any of these things upsetting, I suggest passing this by

Mental Health is important!

If you are struggling with mental health, please reach out to your friends, your family, and seek out professionals, I know it is difficult at times, but you are not alone. Talk to someone.

SYSTEMATIC SOUL
SORTING

Contents

The Grey Room

Elliot cracked his eyes open to find himself in a room entirely made out of solid grey smoke.

He slowly pushed himself into a seated position, checking all four corners of the room, and found nothing at all; he was alone. There was a wooden pole in his hand—no, it was a spear with a long wooden shaft, and he could feel something warm situated right in the middle of his chest that he had never felt before.

Where was this? What was in his chest? Why was he holding a spear? How was he still alive?

Elliot gripped his shirt over where the alien sensation originated from, but nothing was under his shirt, the skin there perfectly unmarred. Elliot slowly stood up, dragging the spear with him, and the moment he completed the motion, someone appeared in the corner of the room. Elliot felt suddenly hyperaware of everything around him, and his heart thudded hard in his chest.

That was impossible. Where had he come from?

The man had just appeared in an instant, no accompanying effect or transition to denote movement or motion. The person, a man in his early thirties perhaps, glanced at him once before he immediately looked away without interest. Elliot stared at the man for a long moment as his adrenaline response slowly vanished.

The man did not attempt to approach him, so Elliot returned the favor.

Elliot made sure not to relax too much and started trying to figure out how to take the man down if he proved hostile. The man was shorter than him, if only just, but the man was wearing what looked like a full set of leather armor, and he was carrying a massive sword at his hip.

Why was he wearing armor? Why did he have a sword? What was this place?

Another person appeared on the other side of the room, and Elliot spun to keep them both in his sight. This time it was an older woman, somewhere in her fifties perhaps. Elliot took several steps backward until his back pressed against the solid grey of the fog wall in case someone appeared behind him.

Where were they coming from!?

Two more appeared in rapid succession on opposite sides of the room, both laying on the floor, seemingly unconscious. The woman had an Axe in her hand, while the man had a small sickle.

That was the same state in which he had woken up, not even a minute prior.

Is that how he had arrived here? Just appeared on the ground with a spear in his hand? Had he also teleported in with no explanation?

Movement on the right side of the room drew his gaze for a moment. A large red '57' along the fog wall immediately ticked down to '56,' then '55.' A countdown of some sort, just floating on the transparent fog wall with nothing around to project it there. Three seconds ago would be when the two people had appeared at once. The timer ticked down to

'29' before it suddenly reset to '60' again, right as someone else appeared in the room.

Elliot swallowed and did his best to figure out what was going on.

Every time someone appeared, the timer reset to 60 seconds. Some people arrived unconscious holding weapons, while others appeared in the room wholly awake and with much better equipment on their persons.

What would happen when the timer hit zero?

In a room full of people with weapons, and a countdown, his imagination provided several scenarios that didn't do anything for his nerves, and most of them involved everybody killing each other violently.

An older woman wearing fancy metal armor and wielding a long curved blade with lines etched across its surface smiled kindly at him, and he decided to risk it.

"Sorry to bother you," Elliot said evenly, "Do you happen to know what this room is?"

Elliot didn't make any move to step closer to the woman. He just turned to face her from his position against the fog wall. The older woman smiled pleasantly before she took a couple of steps towards him, and Elliot tensed up, thinking he had somehow made a mistake already.

The woman stopped a few meters away.

"Hello dear, my name is Anette." The older woman said kindly. "Is this your first time in the Grey Room?"

Elliot couldn't tell if she was genuine or if she was faking her demeanor, so he kept most of his focus on the wooden haft sitting in his grip, watching her intently for any hostile movement.

"It is nice to meet you, Anette," Elliot said evenly, "You can call me Elliot, and this is my first time."

Anette looked pleased with his manners and beamed up at him, entirely without fear.

"We don't have much time, so please excuse my brevity, dear." Anette said pleasantly, "You have died recently and have appeared in the Grey Room. Once the timer reaches zero, a door will open. We must defeat all enemies on the other side before we can leave this place. There will be monsters, horrors, strange beings, and other humanoids that are not quite humans. They will attack each other. They will attack us. Once all of the things outside of this room are dead, an exit will appear at the location of the last monster killed. Do not linger in the Dungeon for longer than ten minutes; else, the boss will spawn in response."

Elliot took in everything she said and didn't interrupt. Either it was the truth, or it wasn't; it didn't matter which. If she were lying and attacked him, he would have to kill someone. If she were telling the truth, he would have to kill something.

"Do not trust anything that isn't in this room right now, do not trust anyone in this room either. We may be on the same side, but there are no laws in this place." Anette said pleasantly, "You can activate the interface by placing a hand against your chest and saying 'Interface.'"

Anette followed her own directions, and an almost entirely translucent box appeared in front of her face, completely unreadable for him. Elliot moved to copy her, but he was distracted when the timer finally hit zero.

The numbers disappeared, leaving a perfect doorway behind. There was what looked like the dark wall of a tunnel beyond it.

There were more than twenty people here now, and almost all of the better-equipped people went straight through the door without fanfare.

The remaining five people who had all arrived unconscious moved slowly towards the entrance looking worried and terrified.

Elliot made sure he was the last one to leave.

The doorway led to a dark tunnel that almost immediately became a massive cavernous room filled with rocky formations that pierced out of the ground to reach for the roof hidden in the darkness. The cave walls weren't visible in the distance, too far away, and the light was too lacking.

Elliot thoroughly searched the immediate area with his eyes, and he could make out three tunnels that led away from the cavern while there was another in the ground five meters away from the door, angling down into darkness.

A cavern filled with tunnels that led in every direction. Tunnels that most of the equipped people had vanished into as soon as they had left the Grey Room. Only one armored guy stayed near the door to the Grey Room, seemingly content to wait whatever this was out.

"What is this place?" A man muttered nervously from in front of him. "Why would they just go into the tunnels? They're all going to get lost."

Elliot made no move to reply to the man, but one of the others did.

"None of them seemed very worried, and they were all wearing medieval crap too. Have they been here before?" Another man said harshly before turning towards the armored guy that had stayed. "Hey, asshole, what's in the tunnels?"

The 'asshole' glanced at him silently before walking further into the darkness without a word.

"Hey!" The man said aggressively, following him out. "I'm talking to you!"

Elliot lost sight of the armored guy in the darkness, and the aggressive guy stopped before looking down the tunnel on the ground. A long white hand suddenly emerged from the tunnel, followed by a long white arm and the rest of a tall white thing.

"Fuck!" The man shouted.

The thing grabbed him by the face and pressed him down onto the ground hard enough that Elliot could hear the crack from the door. The man screamed in pain as the thing started biting at his face.

Elliot stared at it in horror.

The nervous man immediately ran forward with his small sword and swung it desperately down at the thing's head. The creature lifted its arm up, and the sword hit hard enough to sever the too-long limb. The thing screamed in a pitch far too high to be human and lashed out at the guy with the sword.

He managed to get his sword up between him and the limb but was still sent stumbling backward across the cavern floor. The pale thing retreated back down the tunnel a moment later, and the guy with the sword dragged what was left of the other guy back over to the door. He needn't have bothered because the guy's face was missing entirely.

He was dead.

One of the others spun away from them and started throwing up violently against the wall, and the only woman in the group started crying quietly. Elliot stepped backward until his back was against the cave wall and watched the three tunnels to the left with a single-minded focus.

The thing had been twice as tall as him, with long thin limbs and long needle-like teeth, it had no eyes or ears, but it had a long forked tongue that had been dangling out of its mouth. It was strong enough to push a grown man to the ground with ease.

"What the fuck was that thing?!" Another man screamed in terror.

Elliot didn't take his eyes off the tunnels, and something moved right along the edge of the one furthest to the left. That guy had managed to cut its arm off, so their bones weren't strong enough to stop a metal blade, or maybe it didn't have them in the first place. Something moved close to the ground of the tunnel, flattening itself down as much as it could.

It was another one of the things.

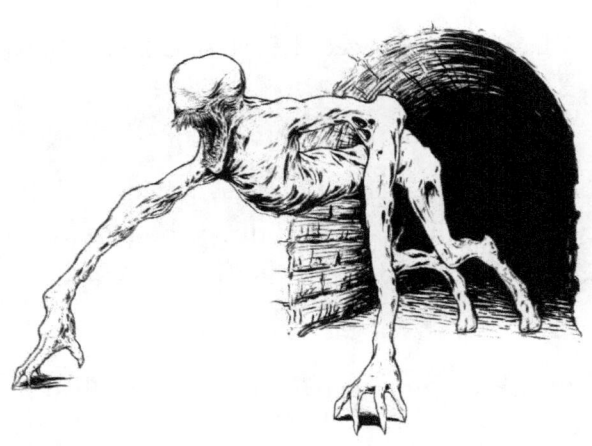

It stayed there against the floor in the darkness, waiting, and Elliot stared straight at it. It couldn't see him. If he alerted the others, would it attack, or would it run away?

"Fuck this. I'm not staying here!" The same guy snarled, "We need to find those other guys, or we're going to fucking die in here."

The thing twitched to follow the guy as he moved towards where the armored guy had gone, making sure to go wide around the tunnel, but nothing emerged to grab him this time, and he vanished behind some rock outcropping in the darkness soon after. The thing didn't move from its place by the tunnel.

It had some method of seeing movement in the dark. It didn't seem to register any of the noise the others were making, though. Elliot clicked his fingers on his right hand together, but the thing didn't even twitch.

"Everybody stay perfectly still." Elliot said quietly, "They can't see you unless you move, and there's one about ten meters away looking in our direction."

"Oh no," The woman said, terrified, from just behind him.

Elliot twitched, having not realized she was so close to him.

"How do you know that?" The sword-guy said nervously.

"It's only a guess, the thing tracked that guy leaving with its head, but as soon as he vanished behind a rock, it turned back to took at whoever moved behind me," Elliot said evenly. "Keep your weapon at the ready either way."

"That's why you clicked your fingers?" The woman sniffled.

"Yeah," Elliott said quietly. "A test."

The thing stared in their direction, unseeing and unmoving. There was a sudden piercing scream in the distance, along with the sound of a scuffle. It came from a completely different direction than the man had gone before.

"Oh, god." The woman breathed.

"What are your names?" The sword guy said nervously. "I'm Grant."

"Hannah," Hannah said shakily.

"Elliot," Elliot said quietly.

How could he kill the thing safely?

The thing couldn't see him unless he moved. It knew they were there, but it wasn't moving towards them, likely unwilling to expose itself when it didn't know our exact position. This was predator behavior, and this *thing* was patient. He could try and bait it into impaling itself on the spear, but if he failed, he would die gruesomely. What else did he have at his disposal? The 'interface' that the old lady had told him about, but he would need to move to touch his chest, and it might set the creature off.

Elliot didn't get the chance to figure it out because the thing suddenly started towards them slowly, crawling along the floor like a massive four-legged white spider.

"Don't move; it's coming towards us," Elliot said quietly.

"No." Hannah started crying again.

"Fuck," Grant said nervously.

Grant had already risked his life earlier to save that other guy; he seemed like a decent guy. Hopefully, he felt like being a hero again; they had one chance for this to work.

"Grant, here's the plan." Elliot said intently, "It will reach me before either of you. When I say the word, I need you to move suddenly to distract it, and I'll kill it."

Grant didn't reply, and Elliot took in a deep breath and let it out slowly as he prepared himself.

"Oh god," Hannah said in horror.

"If I fail, you'll have to take it down yourself," Elliot murmured as he stared at the thing that was only two meters away from him now, entirely visible in the torchlight.

It was just as alien as he thought earlier. Its flesh was mottled white with splotches of lighter grey all over it. Elliot clenched his hands tightly around the shaft of the spear, with the point still held up in front of him. The creature would run into his legs before the spear did anything where it was currently pointed.

He was out of time.

"Now," Elliot said evenly.

Hannah screamed as the thing snapped its head to the side to track Grant as he took two steps to the right, clearly into its line of sight, and it immediately started to raise its body up off the ground in preparation to lunge at him. Hannah grabbed the back of his shirt as Elliot drove the end of the spear straight through the back of its head and out the other side.

The thing went limp before it fell to the floor in a tangle of too-long arms and legs.

A small message appeared in the corner of Elliot's eye, written in neat gold font.

Loot Gained: 10 EXP, 10 Gold, 78 Bone Needles.

The bone needles sounded very much like it might have been the pale thing's teeth. The prompt vanished a moment later, fading from his sight, and he noted that Hannah still hadn't let go of his shirt.

"Thanks for not letting me die," Elliot said evenly. "You're a good guy."

"Don't worry about it," Grant said nervously.

"You two." Hannah sobbed, "I'm sorry, I didn't-"

"You're fine," Elliot said evenly, "There's still at least one more of these things running around, along with whatever caused that person to scream before."

"The one you killed is bleeding pretty badly," Grant said nervously, "The other one might have died already."

Elliot wasn't taking any chances with optimism here.

"Better we assume it's still running around, so we aren't surprised if it does show up again," Elliot said quietly.

"Yeah." Grant agreed nervously. "There was almost no resistance when I cut the other one's arm off, and your spear went straight through its head like it was a watermelon."

He'd noticed it as well. These things were fragile for something so physically powerful.

"Yeah." Elliot agreed. "We just need to keep a very close eye on anything around us."

"How are you-," Hannah said shakily, "Aren't you scared?"

"I'm terrified," Grant admitted immediately.

"Same," Elliot said evenly.

Hannah leaned her forehead onto his back and drew in another shaky breath.

"What should I do?" Hannah said quietly.

"The same thing as us," Grant said nervously, "Just keep your saber up in front of you and aim for the limbs if your slashing or the head if you want to stab."

He was starting to like this guy; they were like two different sides to a coin. Elliot was scared, but he was doing his best to compartmentalize the fear and pretend it wasn't there. But Grant was terrified, but he just pushed through the terror without hesitation and acted anyway.

As long as they stayed next to the door-

"Shit," Elliot said quietly.

They would have to move away from the door at some point. Anette said that the exit would open at the location of the last monster killed. They would eventually have to move to locate it. Would there be some kind of sign that they could leave?

"Is it another one?" Hannah said shakily, now standing between them and holding her saber up.

"No, sorry." Elliot said evenly, "A woman told me earlier that an exit will appear where the last enemy is killed."

"How do we know if they are all dead?" Hannah said quietly.

"She didn't say," Elliot said simply.

"So, we will eventually have to go look for it unless it's really noticeable somehow." Grant said, "It could open in one of the tunnels, and we wouldn't have any idea unless we checked them all."

"I don't think I can go into one of the tunnels," Hannah said shakily. "I'm-"

There was suddenly another high pitch scream from somewhere ahead of them in the darkness, and then abruptly, they could see, as a massive pillar of light appeared near the middle of the cavern that seemingly went through the cave roof far above them.

Dungeon Complete: 294 Enemies defeated.

"Dungeon?" Grant said nervously. "I guess that's the exit."

"Yeah," Elliot said evenly.

Hannah buried her face in her hands and sobbed. Elliot couldn't blame her; he felt like curling up into a ball himself. It took the three of them several minutes to gather the courage to move from the entrance, even with all the light given off by the portal.

They stuck close together as they approached the portal. Elliot made sure to keep an eye on every tunnel, rock, or crevice for any signs of movement. Just because some words said all of the enemies were gone didn't mean they were safe. Anette did say that there were no laws here—Any of the others could still attack them if they wanted to.

There was movement near the portal's light, the others appearing from different directions and stepping through it without bothering to talk to each other. Elliot caught sight of Anette for barely a moment before she vanished into the portal.

"Aliens, mysterious words, and now magic portals?" Grant said quietly. "Where the hell are we?"

Elliot didn't know, so he didn't respond, but Hannah had no such compunctions.

"Hell sounds about right—maybe this is it." Hannah said worriedly, "I died, and now I'm here."

Dying and then ending up in the Grey Room, the Dungeon, the monsters, and the exit portal—Anette's story grew more likely as everything seemed to line up.

"It might be," Grant said nervously, "That thing might have been a demon—it certainly looked like one."

"Did any words appear when you cut that thing's arm off?" Elliot said evenly.

Grant turned to look at him for a moment.

"No," Grant said immediately, "Are you saying that something appeared when you killed the other one?"

"Yeah," Elliot said simply, "It said I received gold, experience points, and bone needles for killing it."

"Like an RPG?" Hannah said hesitantly.

"I think so," Elliot said quietly.

"Seems more like a horror game to me," Grant mumbled.

They stopped next to the massive pillar of rising light.

"So, do we just step into it?" Hannah asked quietly.

Elliot noticed she was looking to him for direction, which he found distinctly odd. They had only met half an hour ago at most—now even *Grant* looked like he was waiting for an answer.

"Yeah," Elliot said hesitantly, "Let's go."

Elliot took a step into the light; everything flashed white for a moment before he appeared in the Grey Room once more. Hannah and Grant appeared beside him a moment later with no accompanying flash.

"Here again?" Hannah said shakily. "Are we stuck here?"

A prompt appeared, covered in writing, and judging by Grant's twitch and the gasp Hannah made; they could see their own versions of it as well.

Loot Gained: 1204 EXP, 220 Gold.

The writing that appeared on the prompt was an exhaustive list of information about the Dungeon, and it was all woven together to produce a score. Completion time, dungeon difficulty, personal kill contribution, total enemies killed, *boss kills,* and more—each of those contributed to a multiplier that rewarded you with experience and gold.

If he was receiving gold, that should mean there was somewhere to spend it, and If he was gaining EXP, there should be some use for that as well, probably in the 'Interface' that Anette had mentioned.

Elliot refocused on the present—he could figure that stuff out once he was safe. A white rectangle of fog had appeared on the other side of the Grey Room.

"Where did that come from?" Grant asked. "It wasn't here when we arrived."

"When the writing appeared, the white-wall did as well," Hannah said shakily. "Is it the exit?"

"Most likely," Elliot said evenly. "We should leave this place in case we get stuck in here again."

Hannah noised out a terrified squeak in her throat at the idea of going through all of that again.

"You're right, Elliot," Grant agreed, "Let's go."

Grant stepped forward towards the wall; both Hannah and Elliot followed a moment later. Grant placed his hand against the wall; it slid through to the other side before he pulled it back and stared at his hand for a long moment. Grant turned to look back at them before he stepped through the wall, leaving Elliot and Hannah alone in the room.

"Do you think he's alright?" Hannah said shakily.

"There's no way for us to figure that out without going through first," Elliot said evenly, "Come on, Hannah, we can go together."

Elliot offered his hand, and Hannah gripped it tightly before Elliot led them both through the wall. The transition was instantaneous; as soon as his eyes passed through the wall, they were suddenly outside in the daylight.

"Oh," Hannah breathed in relief.

There was a massive wooden arch above them, painted red, it looked like the gates Elliot had seen in Japanese villages, but he couldn't remember the name. Golden bells were hanging from each side of it, and a small set of stone stairs led down towards a city. Grant was standing on the stairs waiting for them patiently, and he looked relieved that they had both appeared.

Elliot stared around for a long moment, taking in the land that stretched out seemingly forever in front of them, and then he turned around. Behind the gateway, there was nothing but twinkling lights in the distance and inky blackness.

Elliot walked around the gate and looked downwards, staring at the end of the world.

"What is this place?" Hannah said quietly as she came to stand beside him.

Grant appeared on her other side, joining them in staring into what could only be an endless river of stars.

"Some kind of flat landmass floating in space," Grant said slowly. "This shouldn't work at all, but then again, nothing about the last hour has made much sense."

"Yeah," Elliot said, "Its turtles all the way down, huh?"

Hannah started laughing, and they both turned to look at her curiously.

"You're very clever young man, very clever." Hannah giggled, cheeks slightly warm at the attention.

Elliot smirked before turning away again.

"That totally went over my head," Grant said, bemused, before glancing over his shoulder. "Should we go down to the city?"

"Maybe someone down there knows what this is all about?" Hannah said, hopefully. "We might be able to get home somehow!"

Grant looked optimistic as well, but Elliot wasn't so sure about that. He absolutely knew that he was dead, and he shouldn't be walking around on some endless plane floating in space. Hannah had let slip earlier that she had died as well, and Anette had outright stated that he had died.

"Yeah," Grant said firmly, "We should try to find a way home."

Elliot didn't bother speaking up; he had nothing to say that would make them feel any better. Elliot took that adage seriously. If he didn't have something nice to say or at least a valid reason to say something mean, he wasn't going to. All this *we* business was strange, though. They had only known each other for a little while. They were practically strangers.

Hannah took his wrist and tugged him back towards the gate. Elliot stared at her hand for a moment before glancing up at her eyes.

"Come on, Elliot!" Hannah said brightly.

Elliot was forced to follow along in her wake or be dragged, so he fell in step beside the two.

They took the stairs that led down to a dirt road and started up the path towards the city. He could see people milling around the stone buildings in the distance, murmuring to each other. The closer they got, the darker the place seemed, people were sitting on the streets in ragged clothes, and there was an air of tension in the air.

Elliot noted that there were others wearing clothes in perfect condition if simple ones. Some people were wearing armors, and nearly everyone carried a weapon of some sort, bows, knives, swords, spears, and giant weapons that looked unwieldy, far too heavy for someone to carry so casually.

There was a flash of movement on the flat top of a building to his right, and something blurred over the street onto the opposite roofs. The figure disappeared barely a moment later, moving impossibly quickly.

"Did you see that?" Hannah said, shocked.

"Yeah!" Grant said, amazed.

This place was filled with superhumans, likely a result of using the 'EXP' and 'Gold' they had supposedly gained from completing the 'Dungeon.' It also made him realize that they had a problem.

Anette had known about the Grey Room well enough that she could explain it to someone in a very brief but effective way, almost as if she had done it many times before. Probably because she had, she had been in the Grey Room before today. Which meant you could go back into the Grey Room, likely through the gate.

Nobody would choose to go back into that horror show without a solid reason of some type. This meant that it was either incentivized, through the need for Gold and EXP, to go into the Dungeon regularly.

Or you were somehow forced to.

"Excuse me!" Grant said politely, "Can I ask you some questions, please?"

The words snapped Elliot out of his thoughts for a moment. He glanced over at the man that Grant had flagged down. Short, stocky with a massive beard, full plate armor, and a Warhammer on his back.

"Aye," The man said smoothly, "What do you need, laddie?"

Grant fumbled for a moment, having not prepared any questions in advance to ask the man, and trying to figure out how to start, so Elliot came to his rescue.

"We just completed our first Dungeon and have arrived in the city. What should our short-term and long-term goals be? Are there any threats we have to worry about now that we are here?" Elliot said at length, tone calm.

The man scratched at his beard in thought for a moment before nodding.

"Short-term, you need to find a place to stay, there's inns, taverns, hotels all over the city, but they cost gold," The man said smoothly, "Long-term, you either are looking to save up enough to buy a reincarnation token from the shop or a house to establish yourself somewhere permanent here, you could try to set up your own shop, maybe join one of the factions."

Elliot listened carefully, doing his best to commit his exact words to memory to think over later.

"You'll reappear back in the Grey Room after exactly a week if you don't walk through the Torii before then, unless you can afford a skip token, but they are expensive." The man continued. "Apart from that, buy whatever armor and weapons you think you can use for the next Dungeon and hope you get an easy one next time. Good luck, you three."

The man patted Grant on the arm as he passed and continued down the road heading towards the city's gates.

"Fuck," Grant said quietly.

"We have to go back?" Hannah asked, horrified.

Find a place to stay for the night, investigate the Interface, work out a long-term plan.

"I'm going to go find somewhere to stay for the night," Elliot said evenly.

Hannah immediately grabbed him by the wrist again.

"We should stick together, Elliot," Hannah said shakily. "Please."

Elliot floundered for a moment. She hadn't even put an argument forward for *why* they should stick together. Grant didn't say anything and just watched as he failed to find a response. How was he supposed to respond to that?

"Elliot," Hannah pleaded.

"Fine," Elliot said quietly. "Let's go find somewhere to stay."

Hannah's smiled brightly at him, and he averted his eyes, embarrassed.

"Yeah," Grant said, amused, "Sounds good to me."

They moved along the street and studied the buildings; most had simple wooden signs hanging above the doors. Elliot felt uncomfortable with how close Hannah was to him, but he did his best to ignore the feeling. Elliot noted three places of interest along the way, 'Weapons,' 'Armour,' and 'Servants,' before they found an 'Inn.' Elliot made a note to visit all three to see what more he could learn about this place.

The inn was simple, a small entrance room with a long counter, a slightly bigger room off to one side with tables, benches, and a wooden railing separating it from the entrance, and a staircase on the right of the counter leading upwards.

A woman, perhaps in her forties, was operating the counter, reading from a bunch of loose papers that had been tied together with twine, and she looked up as they approached the counter with indifference.

"Hello—" Grant started politely.

He didn't even get the second word out before she cut him off.

"Don't care," The woman said briskly, "One room left on the top floor, single bed. Ten gold for the night."

The woman pushed a small glowing brick across the counter and stared at them expectantly. Grant looked completely lost, and the woman blew air out sharply through her nose to express her annoyance.

"Touch the stone, say how much Gold." She said in annoyance.

Grant quickly reached out and touched the stone.

"Ten gold?" Grant said nervously.

The brick on the counter flashed with gold light for a moment before the woman yanked it back. She tossed a key at Grant, who fumbled for a moment to collect it before abruptly ignoring them again.

Grant mumbled out a thank you and moved towards the stairs, glancing back at them. Elliot had to plant a hand on the wall to stop himself from tripping up the stairs as Hannah pulled him along behind her.

He noted the brick the owner had used to collect payment—The bearded man from earlier had stated that you could start your own shop. That was obviously what this woman had done.

If you were forced to go into the Dungeon every week, why would you start a business? The incentive had to be the skip tokens—if you could earn enough gold here to skip the weekly Dungeon, that was most likely the safest method.

The room Grant had purchased was tiny, and as the woman said, the room had a single bed sitting against the side of the room. It was covered in white sheets, a fluffy pillow, and a surprisingly thick mattress.

There was enough room on the floor for perhaps two people to lay comfortably. However, the stone floor didn't look very comfortable.

"Uh, maybe we should go somewhere else instead," Grant said sheepishly. "I kind of got caught up there for a moment."

The woman had forced an immediate and rapid purchase out of him—that was for sure.

"It's fine!" Hannah said happily, sitting on the edge of the bed. "We can find somewhere else tomorrow night, and I'll pay for the next room."

Grant sat down on the bed near where the pillow was while Elliot just moved to sit against the wall on the floor opposite them—he wasn't going to sit between them on the bed.

That would have been far too awkward.

Ten gold for a room for one night and a maximum of seven nights until he would be forced to complete another dungeon—so seventy gold for a place like this for one week.

Food would most likely become the most expensive drain on his funds, depending on how much a simple meal cost. The Dungeon said he had received two hundred and twenty gold which he needed to last him at least a week.

If a room for a night here cost ten gold, a meal would most likely cost less than that—but it really depended if foot and water were scarce here or not. Highballing it at ten gold a meal would put him at seventy gold in food expenses a week.

That was a total of one hundred and forty gold for a single week, which left him eighty gold to buy some armor, a different weapon, or other equipment he could use to increase his odds of surviving the next Dungeon.

This wasn't nearly enough, and it was also a massive waste.

The optimal strategy would be to spend the gold on equipment first and immediately head back into the Grey Room. If he survived, he would have more money immediately, and if he died, he wouldn't be going hungry.

If the dungeons were random like the man had implied with the comment about hoping to get an easy one next time, then going back today wouldn't be any more dangerous than going back in seven days. Except then, he would have less money, less equipment, and the possibility of being weaker from lack of proper food if this place didn't have a good low-cost meal.

It *was* possible that if he went back inside the Dungeon today, he would die—but there wasn't any indication that the odds would change in a week. If he would be forced into the Dungeon every week until he died, it was probably better to go willingly, frequently, and with very specific goals in mind.

Killing that thing in the room had given him an additional ten gold and seventy bone needles—he still had a suspicion that they would end up being the creature's teeth. If he could sell them for more gold, like some monster drops from a game, he could try to specifically go into the Dungeon looking to kill many weaker monsters.

The Dungeon had only taken thirty-two minutes to finish, and while it had been the most terrifying 32 minutes of his life, he couldn't sit around because he was scared. He didn't even technically have to kill anything to make more money either—he could hide at the start again, wait for the other participants to kill everything, and then leave.

That could be another two hundred gold in his pocket.

Half an hour of life-threatening danger for a safety net that would keep him fed and rested for another week, it wasn't exactly a good trade in his mind, but surely it was better spending the entire week worrying about the next Dungeon and going in under-equipped for whatever monsters might be inside.

There were only two things left for him to deal with; first, he needed to tell the other two what he planned on doing, and then after that, he was going to open the Interface.

The Interface

Elliot studied them both for a moment.

Grant was a seemingly thoughtful guy when he wasn't in life-threatening danger; he had light brown hair cut short and pale green eyes. He was neither tall nor short, sitting somewhere right in the middle, well-groomed, and he was still currently wearing a set of leather armor over the top of his black suit.

Hannah was the opposite; she seemed to show everything she felt at the exact moment she felt it. It made her seem incredibly open. She was quite short, sitting somewhere around the five-and-a-half-foot mark. Her eyes and hair were both dark brown, hanging down between her shoulder blades, and her face was covered in a smattering of freckles.

"I'm going back to the dungeon today," Elliot said evenly, ripping the band-aid off in a single go.

Hannah looked horrified.

"Why?" Grant said seriously. "You seem pretty smart, Elliot. Why does this seem like a good idea to you?"

"Optimising resources," Elliot said easily, "If I wait a week, I will drain enough of my money with food, lodgings and end up only being able to afford cheap gear or none at all. If I spend the entire two hundred on equipment and go back in today, I can make sure I am as well equipped as I can be given the circumstances."

Grant threaded his hands together and seemingly thought it over. Hannah was biting her lip and looked distinctly upset.

"What if you go back in, and you die?" Hannah said shakily.

"I'll be forced to go back in seven days from now, and I might die then as well," Elliot said quietly. "Hannah, picture this."

Hannah nodded hesitantly, willing to hear him out.

"Two worlds, in one, you have a full set of armor and a good weapon. In the other, you have a helmet and a sword." Elliot watched her quietly. "Which of these two worlds gives you a better chance against equally unknown odds?"

"I know what you're saying, Elliot." Hannah swallowed nervously, "But it's dangerous—That *thing* was in there, and who knows what will be in there next time?"

Hannah's argument wasn't very moving, and she seemed unable to think much beyond the sheer horrifying visual of that creature. Elliot sighed to himself. It's not like he wanted to go back in there with the monsters, but it was the best use of resources, and anything less than that increased the risk of not being prepared enough.

Hannah buried her face into her hand and drew in a long shaky breath before she fell silent.

"You're right," Grant said resignedly after several minutes. "The only thing I can think of is that there might be an unbeatable monster in there today, but maybe not in seven days, but I have no way of knowing that, and it could just as easily be the other way around."

Hannah curled her knees up onto the bed and buried her face in them, crying quietly.

"Yeah," Elliot said quietly. "I'm trying to model this like a game. I need upfront resources to afford a business, and then I need to use that business to regularly pay the price for however much a 'Skip Token' is, and then earn enough for a 'Recarnation Token.'"

"It's a safe strategy, as far as I can see," Grant said easily. "I wish we knew more—we don't even know how those tokens work. There might be an unknown factor that unravels that strategy."

There very well might have been—he wasn't wrong there.

"Why does it have to be monsters?" Hannah cried quietly. "I need to get home. The bus—my little sister, was waiting for me at home."

Hannah cut herself off with a sob and cried quietly again. Elliot sighed before standing up. He walked over to the bed, sat down beside her, and pulled her into a one-armed hug against his side.

"Was there someone around to look after her?" Elliot said quietly.

Hannah buried her face into his arm and shook her head; Grant looked pained, most likely thinking about his own situation. Elliot tried to estimate Hannah's age—she was in her early twenties at least.

"How old is your sister?" Elliot asked quietly. "Can she look after herself?"

"Seven." Hannah cried. "I've been looking after her since mum died. She—"

"She will almost certainly be taken in by social services and looked after a while you aren't there," Elliot said evenly. "She will be okay, and then once we've figured out how to get out of here, you can go find her, alright?"

Hannah sobbed louder and buried her face in his neck, clinging to him tightly. Elliott pushed down the horribly awkward feeling rushing through him at the closeness to a complete stranger and rubbed her back calmly.

"Hannah," Elliot said quietly, "It's going to be alright—it helps if you say it out loud."

Hannah sniffled loudly into his neck and blew out a shaky breath.

"It going to be alright," Hannah said quietly.

Elliot patted her on the back more firmly and then pulled back away from her, feeling like he had overstepped his boundaries by about a million miles. Hannah let him go slowly but kept her hand fisted in the front of his shirt as she slowly managed to find some measure of calm.

Grant swallowed, his own eyes looking slightly wet before he sat up straight and let out a slow breath.

"I left my partner behind." Grant said nervously, "When I died, a car accident on the freeway, by the way, I bet he's—my partner would be pretty upset right about now."

"We can go see him too," Hannah said brightly, her face still a mess of tears and snot. "When we get out of this place."

"Yeah," Grant smiled, "We'll go see them."

"Elliot, did you get in a car accident too?" Hannah asked curiously, wiping at her wet cheeks with her sleeve. "Do you have someone you want to see when we get out of here?"

Elliot thought about the question for a moment before he patted her on the shoulder gently and headed back to his place on the floor.

"I don't have anyone to go back to, really." Elliot said quietly, "I jumped off a building."

The horrible silence he knew was coming washed over them, and he forced himself to focus on the other task he had left to do. Elliot lifted his hand up to his chest and placed it against the warm spot.

"Interface," Elliot said clearly.

His body thrummed for a single moment as something rushed through him and then vanished as quickly as it had come, leaving behind a simple, transparent box floating in the air in front of him, filled with words.

Status, Ability, Inventory, Shop.

"Elliot?" Hannah said quietly.

He didn't reply as he tried to interact with the panel—and the second he made the decision, the panel changed to show his Status.

He was listed as a Level 1 with 1 Strength, 6 Speed, 1 Magic, and 1 Defense. There was also a Current EXP tracker and a place he could spend his exp towards a level. It cost one thousand EXP for a level, and each additional level rewarded him with 1 Strength, 6 speed, 1 magic, and 1 defense.

That seemed incredibly lop-sided towards speed, and he wondered what kind of stat spread other people had and if it was possible to change it somehow. Elliot was distantly aware that both Grant and Hannah were opening their own Interface by following his example but returned his focus to his own.

He dumped all of his exp into a level up, which immediately updated to show 'Level 2,' but the next level requirements were the same. That meant there was no scaling, at least at this level, just a flat rate of 1000 EXP per level.

Elliot watched as his Strength, Magic, and Defence all increased to 2, while his speed jumped all the way up to 12. That was a *massive* disparity in overall stat distribution. If he continued to live long enough to see himself rise to higher levels, it was only going to get worse.

He moved onto the ability menu next—of which he had two. The first was a passive skill called 'Explorer' that suggested he would be able to find hidden things in the world around him. The second was an active skill called 'Swap,' which would allow him to swap places with objects, people, and enemies.

Detecting hidden things was interesting, but he wondered how it worked in practice. Would he just know that there was something hidden nearby? Would he be drawn towards it? The active ability was strange as well; figuring out how to use it was going to be something he would need to do very soon.

The only things inside his inventory were gold, a set of common clothing that he currently had equipped, and 78 bone needles—yeah, they were definitely the things teeth. It was more or less what he expected to see.

The last menu was simply a rather straightforward shop interface: health potions, water, food, basic equipment. The further down the list he scrolled, the more interesting the items became and the more exponentially expensive they grew.

Skip Tokens for bypassing the weekly Dungeon were 10,000 gold each. Shop and House tokens were 100,000 each and allowed you to purchase the respective property. Revive Tokens were 1,000,000 gold each.

Random Exotic, Legendary or Unique items sold for 1 million, 10 million, and 50 million gold, respectively. Right at the bottom of the list was a final item—a Reincarnation Token – for 100 million gold.

One-hundred-million gold for a Reincarnation Token—it was absurd.

He only received 220 gold from that Dungeon. To reach that kind of insane threshold, he would need to do something like 100,000 dungeons at 1000 gold per Dungeon. The only way you could possibly do that in a sensible amount of time was if you were somehow able to get a large amount of bonus gold through a multiplier of some sort.

You could sell items to the shop as well, which might be a secondary way of making money if you were lucky enough to find something that was worth a decent amount. Elliot slotted the Bone Needles into the sell screen to check the price, 78 gold, which meant 1 gold per needle.

He canceled the trade and stared at the other items in the store list, thinking. Full leather cost 100 gold—would *leather armor* have stopped that thing in the Dungeon from killing him?

Elliot didn't think so. It had torn through the flesh and bone on the front of that man's head without any difficulty. Chainmail *might* have stopped it, but he couldn't be sure without testing it something he wasn't willing to check.

The fact that it said 'Common' was a reference to its quality, a term used in many RPG systems he had seen before. It implied that higher levels of item quality existed, and the Exotic, Legendary, and Unique items at the bottom of the shop were probably only some of them. Unique was a strange quality to be used as the rarest though, it was often designed as simple and weak filler gear.

Jumping from common straight to exotic was likely *not* how the system worked. You could probably receive equipment drops from the monsters in the Dungeon then, items that had quality above common that could be sold for more gold.

"This is like a video game." Grant wondered aloud before his eyes opened wide in shock. "One-hundred-million!"

"For what?" Hannah said distractedly.

Elliot couldn't help but notice that she kept on glancing at him, and it was making him feel more uncomfortable by the second.

"Check the shop," Grant said evasively before falling silent.

"Oh," Hannah said, disheartened. "How are we—it's so expensive."

Elliot didn't reply. Instead, he thought over his decision. He had enough money for leather armor and a bunch of health potions. Was it better to save his money or spend it? If he went back in with nothing, he could potentially have enough for Chain or Plate armor the next time.

If it was a game, he would have just gone in again blindly without issue and saved his money, but it wasn't a game. There would be no restarting if he died in the next Dungeon. He had to play this as if it was a hardcore mode, which meant spending his money on the best gear possible for each Dungeon until he was confident he could survive without spending money.

A slow and steady climb to 100 million gold—he was just another turtle, figures.

Elliot reopened the shop, selected the common leather armor and four health pots, leaving him with only twenty remaining gold, he switched back to the inventory, and they listed there.

Elliot selected the armor, and some options appeared. Equip, Salvage, Destroy, and Drop. Seeing as he didn't want any of the others right now, he equipped it, and then suddenly, he was wearing a full set of thin leather armor over his clothing.

"Wow!" Hannah said suddenly. "How did you do that?"

"That would be the common leather armor?" Grant said thoughtfully before focusing on his menu again.

A few moments later, he was wearing his own slightly different set of leathers over the top of his clothing.

"Hannah, go to the shop and buy the armor," Grant said easily, "Then go back to the inventory and select the armor to equip it."

A few moments later, Hannah was wearing her own, slightly smaller variant of the thin armor.

"This is so strange," Hannah said, bemused. "How do you take it off? Oh, there's a new option when you select it in the inventory."

"Unequip," Grant said out loud, reading the option. "Interesting that it's a full set and not just the torso piece."

"Yeah," Elliot agreed, "The Chain and Plate is likely a full set as well in that case."

"Did you buy any Health Potions?" Grant asked distractedly.

"Four," Elliot said evenly.

"I'll buy some too," Hannah said quickly.

They fell silent for a while, just investigating the Interface for anything they might have missed. Eventually, Elliot found himself trying to drum up the courage to leave the room. It was a harder decision than he had made it seem to the others.

He really didn't want to go back into the Dungeon.

That pale thing had been so unnatural, so different from anything he had ever seen before, and from what Anette had said, there were plenty of other things just like it or worse. She had mentioned that there were things that were not quite human and others that were straight-out monsters. He couldn't help but wonder which classification the pale one had come under. It had two arms, two legs, and a head, just like a human, but it couldn't have been further from one.

Were there monsters in there that had different numbers of limbs? The pale one had teeth, claws, and a yawning maw filled with needle teeth, but were there things that made it look cuddly by comparison?

He really, really didn't want to go back in—but he was going to do it anyway.

"I'm leaving soon," Elliot said evenly.

It was more of an attempt to force himself into action than a narration of his actual actions; he still couldn't bring himself to move.

"Is this really the only way?" Hannah asked quietly. "There's nothing else we could do?"

There was plenty of things they could do, like try and get a job out in the city, beg for money—prostitute themselves for it even. None of it mattered—they weren't finding 10 thousand gold each in a week. They would be pulled back into the room and forced to fight for their lives.

This was the only way that ensured they had the equipment needed to survive.

"We don't have enough money for a single skip token, and at 10 thousand gold, it's impossible," Elliot repeated his thoughts out loud before slowly pushing himself to his feet. "You don't have to come, Hannah—I'll be fine on my own."

Hannah just stared up at him with wide eyes.

"I'm not going to let you go back in on your own," Grant said firmly. "We would have died if *all of us* weren't there last time."

"I didn't do anything," Hannah said shakily.

Elliot really didn't want to convince either of them to come with him, but he wasn't one to let an untruth hang in the air when he knew otherwise.

"It was comforting having somebody at my back; I'm sure Grant felt the same having you there with us." Elliot said honestly, "You helped as well, Hannah."

"He's right," Grant said firmly. "If I was on my own, I probably would have run. Together we were able to be brave, and we are all still here because of that."

Elliot glanced over at the older man; he really was a good guy, a much better person than *he* was at least.

"Um. Thanks," Hannah said, a little embarrassed before she visibly steeled herself. "I'm coming too."

Elliot thought about telling them not to follow him because he knew the course of action he was taking was risky. If they came with him, he would be taking a measure of responsibility then to make sure they all survived—but Elliot hadn't even been able to keep *himself* alive.

That's why he was in this place.

"I can't promise you two anything if you come with me," Elliot said evenly.

They knew the danger as well as he did, but it was better to have all the cards on the table.

"Yeah," Grant said easily. "But we can do our best to protect each other when we are in there, alright?"

That he could agree to.

"I'll do my best to make sure nothing happens to either of you," Elliot promised honestly.

Grant smiled at him.

"Me too!" Hannah said firmly before grabbing him by the wrist again.

Elliot did his best to ignore the sudden physical contact.

"Make sure you both buy whatever you think you will need before we leave." Elliot said evenly, "Let's spend a little while thinking up some strategies for when we get inside as well."

"Good idea," Grant said easily.

Hannah continued to stare up at him with bright eyes, still holding onto his wrist, and he couldn't help but look away embarrassed—she was so touchy.

The discussion of strategy stretched, and eventually, he realized what she was doing.

"What should we do if—" Hannah said quickly.

This time Elliot didn't reply.

Instead, he pushed himself to his feet and gave her a tight smile. Hannah had continually come up with new and insightful situations that could arise, bringing them back into discussing the latest potential threat. It had become obvious that she was stalling, hoping to push the trip back to another day, another time.

He could understand her reluctance, he didn't exactly want to go either, but he had already locked himself into the path through the power of pre-commitment. It was something that helped him solve countless issues in his life—but it had also driven him into some very bad situations. It wasn't willpower. He doubted he was exceptional in that regard.

Elliot had simply trained himself to do exactly what he said he would do every single time. It was the one talent he'd had in his life to keep going until he had either accomplished what he said he would, or it became impossible to succeed. He would mindlessly follow through on his promises, on his threats, on his goals, and through the consequences that would come after.

"Sorry, Hannah," Elliot said quietly, "You don't have to come, but I'm leaving now."

Hannah's hands were tightly wound in the linen on the bed, and Grant pushed himself to his feet before placing his hand on Hannah's shoulder.

"I'm coming," Hannah said quietly.

Elliot had already stepped out into the hallway and felt the clarity of his goal set itself firmly in his mind. He started down the stairs and silently made his way past the woman at the counter.

Thirty minutes, that's all it would take for his circumstances to better themselves—Thirty minutes in a cavern filled with monsters, but thirty minutes nonetheless.

Elliot could already see the Torii in the distance, towering above its surroundings with its large wooden legs planted firmly in the stone foundation beneath it. The spread of stars beyond it glittered, beautiful beyond his ability to describe.

It was an interesting trick of the mind that he felt no fear approaching the gate, despite knowing what horrors lived inside. The abstraction of the Grey room being somehow inside the simple wooden gate was enough to create a strange *distance* from the threat, at least enough for the fear to be missing.

Similarly, he felt no fear at the idea of standing inside the Grey room, but when he thought of the door, where the smoke had been erased in a perfect rectangle, he could feel the terror there, hiding just out of perspective.

Elliot found himself stepping around to the side of the Torii, and staring out at the end of the world, the million twinkling lights, the patterns, and the inky void behind it all.

The still moment stretched on endlessly until he heard the quiet crunch of feet on loose stones.

"Elliot?" Hannah called out.

Elliot closed his eyes for a moment before taking a deep breath and turning back around. He stepped around the Torii to find them both standing beside the steps. Grant looked nervous again, while Hannah looked determined.

He smiled at them both before stepping back through the portal.

The Grey Room hadn't changed much in the last couple of hours. It was still grey, and it was still lined with smoke-filled walls. There were also people already inside, far more than the last time he was here.

Elliot moved to the closest wall and kept his eye on the one thing that *had* changed in the room. There was a glowing white outline on the other side of the room, surrounding the countdown timer.

The outline was the same shape as the door that had appeared there last time, a tall rectangle that reached the floor. Was this a result of his passive? Is this what hidden places or at least invisible doors looked like?

They would be hard to miss if they all looked like that.

"Hey," Elliot said evenly as the two approached him.

"It's not so bad here this time," Hannah said curiously, looking around at all of the people. "It feels different."

"It's because there are more people. It brings a sense of security to be in a crowd this large when facing the unknown." Grant said slowly, "Most of them have armor as well, and weapons. They look strong."

Elliot agreed, but there were also many people here that *didn't* have armor, which likely meant it was their first time here. Some were calm, some were terrified, and many looked lost or confused.

The strong, the weak, and the ones that didn't know anything, respectively.

The timer almost reached zero before it was abruptly reset again, but this time he couldn't see who had appeared; there were just too many people now. Elliot wondered why there were so many this time.

Did that mean anything for the Dungeon?

"It might be harder this time," Grant said nervously, voicing his own thoughts. "If there's this many people."

"Maybe it's easier!" Hannah said brightly.

There had been 294 enemies last time, not including the people from the Grey room, of which there were less than twenty. If there was a correlation between how many people were in the room and the Dungeon's difficulty. That would mean that twenty people here equated to a dungeon difficulty rating of 'D' and an enemy count of almost 300. So somewhere between ten and twenty monsters per person?

There was a couple of hundred people here right now. Did that mean the Dungeon would be harder in response? Would it be rated a C or worse? Would there be 2000 enemies this time? 3000? *More*? It could be the opposite, and the enemy count stayed the same regardless of the number of participants in the grey room, and this time it would be far, far easier.

He couldn't tell with only a single data point, and he certainly didn't share Hannah's optimism.

"We don't know the rules of how this works yet," Elliot said quietly as he watched the timer tick downwards. "More people here might mean more enemies in the dungeon, or the enemy count could stay the same."

"Exactly what I was thinking," Grant admitted, "Although both guesses might be wrong as well."

"It could be something else entirely," Elliot said in agreement, "More people here means more powerful monsters there, or more people here increases a hidden quota of some sort that the system decides on."

"Hidden quota?" Hannah said curiously.

Grant looked thoughtful as well, so he elaborated on his thought.

"Everyone gets pulled back here after a week of not going into the Grey Room. Whoever designed this place is forcing people to be in the Dungeon regularly." Elliot said quietly, "That means they have a *reason* for us to go inside and that it serves some purpose that we haven't been able to determine yet."

Hannah had scrunched up her face in thought.

"So if the system is built to derive some unknown value from us when we complete the dungeons, the number of people being drawn into each dungeon is equal to whatever that is." Elliot finished evenly, "Something like this costs some form of energy to run, all the teleporting and space warping that is going on has to be expensive, and they wouldn't do it for no reason—it might simply be an energy quota of some sort."

The others had to have noticed already that the room was slowly increasing in size the more people appeared, it had started as barely more than a small warehouse, but now it was larger than a football field.

"It could be entertainment?" Hannah said suddenly, "Hidden camera's set up to watch everyone, like a reality-tv show!"

"It could be," Grant said thoughtfully, "You level up here, so we the contestants get stronger with every success? Draws in more people to cheer for their favorites, like a gladiator arena?"

Something felt off about that idea to Elliot.

"They fought lions and other things," Hannah said squeamishly. "It's kind of like the monsters inside?"

"Gladiators fought other gladiators as well," Elliot said slowly as the thought began to nibble at the back of his mind.

That pale thing in the room had been patient, far more patient than he would have expected an animal to be. The other one had used his limb to try and block Grant's sword as well. What if they were right, and it was a gladiator's arena of some sort—only the pale thing didn't represent a lion in their analogy.

What if they actually were fighting *other Gladiators*?

What if that thing had been a *person*, from a different place, perhaps with a different body, but a human *mind* equivalent? Did it have its own Grey Room? What if it was stuck in the same system they were in? Had it died and woken up there—in a room with others like it? Forced to fight strange creatures that might even look terrifying from *its* perspective?

The countdown ticked back to '60,' but it was getting closer to zero with every iteration.

If there were two Grey Room's in opposition, one for the pale things and one for the humans, how would it work?

They drew in people after one week, and the timer started when around five people were inside. Was the reason it was taking in so many people this time because the grey room it was opposed with had pale things coming in at a far faster rate, which meant that the human side's portal remained open to match it? Some kind of balance system to keep the 'teams' equal? What if there were *more* than two grey rooms? What if there were a thousand?

Elliot swallowed at the thought.

The timer hit zero, the door was revealed, and the glowing white outline vanished without fanfare. All of those with armor headed towards the door immediately, and those who still looked lost fell in line as part of the crowd, not unlike a herd of sheep to the slaughter.

"There's light outside the door!" Hannah said, amazed, "It's not the same cave?"

"Trees—it's a forest." Grant said nervously, "We might be fighting animals."

Elliot wasn't so sure, but he didn't reply. The crowd had grown noisy as they spread out through the forest, seemingly searching for different things—the new 'players' looking for buildings, some kind of civilization to show where they had been taken, unaware of the danger they were in.

The others were already hunting.

"Come on," Elliot said evenly.

He moved to follow one of the heavily armored people as they strode through the crowd and further into the forest with purpose. Hannah and Grant both followed closely on his heels as they stalked the man's trail. They made sure not to approach too closely, and soon they had cleared the crowd. A couple of people from the crowd broke off to follow them, no doubt thinking that if they were moving so quickly that they somehow knew where to go.

The forest was dense, but the trees were tall and thin, leaving just enough space to pick your way through. The floor was carpeted in fallen leaves, sticks, and dying branches, while small spiderwebs were threaded between every other tree.

"Oh my god," Hannah said shakily, clamping her hands onto the back of Elliot's shirt. "Did you see that spider?!"

Elliot had, it was the size of his hand easily, but more or less a regular spider, nothing monsterlike about it other than the size it had managed to grow to. Hannah was clearly terrified of the things, and Grant didn't seem much better off if his pale face was anything to go by.

He had never cared about things like that himself; if it tried to bite him, he would kill it; if it didn't, he would leave it be.

"Elliot!" Hannah squeaked out, terrified, "There's another one!"

Elliot just hummed out an acknowledgment and kept his eyes on the armored man's back. The guy must have already known they were following him—they weren't exactly quiet about it—but he made no move to communicate with them.

Something large moved in his peripheries, and his eyes glanced over in that direction—another large movement near that location but behind a different tree, and then another, then another. Short, squat things with rough skin textured like tree bark and large wild eyes stared at them from the forest. They had sharp talons at the end of three stubby fingers and no teeth in their mouths.

A weird pressure thrummed in the back of his mind, corresponding with their presence, something he had pushed to the back of his mind after he had first unlocked the Interface.

"Incoming," Elliot called quietly to the armored man, who also existed as a faint pressure in his mind.

The man immediately stopped and glanced back at them before he started searching around. He found the creatures after a moment and started heading towards them at a walking pace. The creatures fanned out into a large semi-circle and started coming at him from all sides.

Elliot readied his spear and moved to flank the right side of the creatures, and a small portion broke off from encircling the man to block his path. Grant stepped up beside him with his sword drawn and followed him when he stepped towards them.

The one on the far left started scurrying into a wide circle around them and towards Hannah, who let out a noise of terror as she waved her saber at it threateningly.

Elliot took two steps forward before stabbing his spear straight at the one in front of him. The creature darted to the side with a surprisingly deft movement, avoiding the attack before it jaunted forward to slash at his legs with its clawed hand.

He dragged the haft of his spear between them and bodily pushed the creature away from him before stabbing at it again, this time making sure not to overshoot it. It took three rapid stabs before he managed to land a hit, and the creature screamed in pain before its nearby allies all turned and rushed towards him.

They weren't quick enough, and Elliot staked the creature to the ground without mercy. That same golden lettering flicked into existence.

Loot Gained: 2 EXP, 2 Gold, 1 Rough Hide, and 1 Sharp Talon.

He didn't have any more time to think about it as the creatures approached him.

Elliot could feel them—in that same strange sense that seemed to imprint a blueprint of everything around him into a map within his mind.

The creature that was still attacking Hannah hadn't turned at the noise of his comrade's death. Grant was rushing towards the back of the same group that had abandoned him. Elliot tugged on that feeling, directing it at the creature that was attacking Hannah.

Elliot suddenly stood next to Hannah, with seemingly no transition.

"Elliot!" Hannah said, terrified.

He ignored the fact that she was pointing her sword at him. Instead, he turned, rushing towards the back of the creature he had just swapped places with. The creature turned at the noise of leaves crunching underfoot, but he was far too late, as the spear went straight through the unsuspecting creature's back and out its chest with a spurt of thick black liquid.

It shrieked desperately as it died.

Loot Gained: 2 EXP, 2 Gold, 1 Rough Hide, 4 Sharp Talons.

Grant reached the group, pincering the rest of them between the two humans, and Elliot took stock of the situation as Hannah completed the triangle around them.

Of the five creatures that had broken off from the larger group to attack them, two were already dead, and one of the remaining three was missing its right arm. Hannah screamed and buried her saber into one of the creature's heads, and it split all the way to the neck.

The last two tried to flee.

"Grant," Elliot said evenly. "Think fast."

He swapped with one of the running creatures, depositing it in front of Grant, who acted immediately when he realized he was looking at one of the creatures and killed it with an overhand slash.

Elliot appeared next to the other creature, taking its ally's place before he buried his weapon in its side, pinning it to the ground with the spear. A moment later, quiet descended upon them as the last of the monsters died.

Loot gained: 2 Exp, 2 Gold, 1 Rough Hide, 3 Sharp Talons.

"Not bad." The armored man said easily. "You're still pretty new, huh?"

Elliot turned to study the man, every creature around him was in pieces, and he didn't have a scratch on him.

"Second dungeon." Elliot said evenly, "These things are a lot weaker than the other ones we fought. How many Dungeons have you done?"

Hannah and Grant kept their silence as they came to stand beside him. The armored man scratched his chin at the question, bemused.

"No idea," The man said honestly, shrugging, "It would have to be in the thousands by now, I guess."

Elliot stared at him for a long moment, fitting that piece of information into his growing understanding of this place.

"A couple of thousand dungeons, does that get you any closer to the end items in the shop?" Elliot said quietly.

"I guess?" The man said, amused, "I just enjoy killing monsters, so I spend all my money on better gear, you know? If you survive long enough, you're more likely to find something in one of the dungeons than buy it from the shop—as far as weapons or armor anyway."

Elliot simply nodded.

"Thanks for helping us with the weak ones, then," Elliot said evenly.

The man laughed at the comment.

"It's all the same to me really, don't mention it." The man grinned toothily before he turned and walked away.

They watched him go quietly and spent several long moments just staring around at all the dead creatures on the ground. Elliot couldn't help but think about the noises they'd made as they died and swallowed.

He really hoped these things weren't intelligent, but he was starting to think they might be. They moved far too well to be wild animals, like a well-practiced group chittering and pointing as they fought.

"I think these things are like us," Elliot said quietly.

"They are," Grant said uneasily.

"What do you mean?" Hannah asked quietly, "Like us?"

"They aren't Lions, Hannah," Elliot said evenly, using her previous metaphor. "They are other Gladiators."

"Oh god," Hannah said, voice shaking.

"They were talking to each other," Grant said nervously, "I can understand them; it's my passive skill."

He turned to look down at the one he had killed at the end of the fight—It was a creature who thought, planned, and lived. He felt like it should have been an earth-shattering moment, that he would realize what he'd done and be disgusted, or alarmed, or horrified.

Elliot felt nothing.

It was too different from him. His mind had unconsciously slotted it into the category of 'a monster,' and he would have had to drag it out of there by force to be able to feel any of the things he would if it had been human.

Elliot had always found it hard to care about things the way most people did. Most of his empathy had been entire constructed through repeated effort and introspection. He'd asked countless questions as he'd grown and done his best to internalize the things that most people simply took for granted.

He'd never actually managed to reach that genuine feeling of empathy for others. What he had was closer to a code of conduct or a ruleset, maybe. He knew he could do something similar here with time, reinforce the idea that these creatures were humans in all but appearance.

The exact specifics might have been off earlier, but the general idea was still sound.

These beings had their own Grey Room, in opposition to the one that existed for Humanity. They had a civilization somewhere, a society with people, traditions, and culture. Perhaps it was on another world or in another time—it could exist within another reality entirely for all they knew.

Even if everything that made up their lives was different, there were two commonalities that he knew they shared with these beings. They were capable of high-level thought, and when each of them died, they were placed into this system and forced to kill each other—that was enough of a base to start with. The question he was left with was whether he *ought* to train himself to see them as more than the monsters they appeared to be.

Elliot stared down at the creature he had murdered and wondered if he was actually the monster here in the end.

Interlude: Elliot Archer

Apartment, Saltwall City.
September 3rd, 2019, 9:04 PM

Elliot felt the stutter of vibrations through his pillow as his phone began to vibrate. Rather than answer it, he curled himself tighter into the bed and dragging the sheets high to cover his face.

He wondered if it was going to be like this forever. It seems as if everywhere he looked, and everything he did was a reminder that Dimitri Lawrence was gone. There was no way for Elliot to lose himself in any of the things he had once enjoyed. Every last thing was tied to his friend in some way, and all of it was a sick reminder of the man's absence.

He'd stopped using his computer entirely, the task reminding him of the stupid comments they'd make to each other. Watching movies meant he had to suffer through it without the silly critiques they'd invented in an attempt to one-up each other. Last night he'd found himself copying a link and even gone as far as to paste it into the group chat before he'd felt that sick realization rear up once more.

Elliot couldn't even be in the same room as May without feeling like his chest was going to burst; there was too much shared history between the three of them for it to be separated. In-jokes, quips, and callbacks that got caught in his throat.

Even if he could have learned to suffer through it, May had already left—moved back to stay with her parents in the aftermath of her brother's death.

Elliot tightened his grip on the sheets as the vibrations started up again, pulsing through the pillow with a pattern of short bursts that meant an incoming call.

Dimitri had always been the unacknowledged fulcrum in his life that pushed him to keep going forward. They'd had each other's backs for years, and when one of them had begun to falter, the other would be there to spur them both onwards.

His death had been the herald for everything to start falling apart.

Elliot was starting to get comments at work now—that he was looking pale or disheveled. That he wasn't as focused as he normally was, and all of the little missteps were crashing around him like hammer blows instead of the minor mistakes they actually were.

His work life had always remained separate from his personal one—not out of choice, so much as it was a result of his personality. He'd always been the quiet one in their group, and large swathes of his life had been built from that foundation.

He'd left the comments unaddressed or brushed them off with weak excuses—Elliot couldn't bring himself to tell them what had happened. They hadn't known Dimitri before, and he didn't think they deserved to know now.

The vibrations began anew, and white-hot anger boiled in him—his arm lashed out, sliding beneath the pillow and sending the phone spinning out across the room. Elliot found himself sitting up, glaring at the floor, furious that someone would continue to ring after he hadn't answered.

Elliot caught sight of the still vibrating screen, lit up with three white letters, and found himself choking back a sob as the sudden rush of emotion left him. He climbed off the bed and did his best to compose himself before picking up the phone.

"Hello, May," Elliot murmured. "Sorry I didn't answer; my phone was in the other room."

"It's okay, Elliot," May said, sounding just as wrecked as he did. "How are you holding up?"

Elliot closed his eyes in shame—he should have been the one to call her.

Rooftop, Saltwall City.
February 6th, 2020, 9:18 PM

Elliot felt like he had discovered something of the underlying nature of the world.

It wasn't cruel like everyone was always want to say, and it certainly wasn't conspiring against them—there wasn't some personification of nature that watched from above, feeding on their pain. The world didn't hate; because, in order to feel something as visceral as hate, you needed to be able to feel something in the first place

The world was indifferent to the misery that continued to accumulate on its surface, clinging to the lives of the people. All of it beneath the world's notice, and yet somehow, it had still managed to infect us all.

Three weeks was all it had taken before the world had forgotten about Dimitri Lawrence. Elliot hadn't heard his friend's name in over a month now, not since he'd stopped answering May's calls. It had started to feel as if she had slowly begun to move on from her brother's death, and Elliot had felt something growing in him.

Elliot couldn't stand the thought that what he'd always felt for her was slowly transforming into a sick resentment, and so he'd stopped picking up. Months had passed him by after that, but nothing had gotten better, and he began to feel as if he was slowly being crushed—he reached out in a moment of weakness and then wished he hadn't.

May had gotten married.

Elliot hadn't even known she'd been seeing anyone, but he'd been the one to cut himself off from her, so he was the one to blame. One of the other elements from their high school days, left in the past entirely until she'd gone back to her hometown. He'd created a hundred and one excuses to avoid going to the wedding and then gone anyway because, in the end, May had asked him to come.

Seeing all of the people he'd grown up with all in the place he'd spent his childhood had only made it worse. Elliot cut all contact again after that, letting the calls ring out, and eventually, she stopped calling.

Office Floor, Saltwall City.
March 6th, 2020, 8:04 AM

The world had become too mechanical to him; he did the same things every single day. He'd stopped going out entirely and avoided all out-of-work contact with his co-workers, simply moving from his apartment to the office and then back to his bed. It was like he was playing a role, following the steps and keeping up the façade.

His phone vibrated for the first time in a long while.

Elliot finished typing the next entry, saved the document, and then reached down to his phone. He wasn't supposed to be taking personal calls at work, but he couldn't really find it in himself to care.

"Hello, May." Elliot said, "It's been a while."

"Hey," May said quietly. "I didn't expect you to pick up."

"No calls during work hours!" Sarah snapped, glaring at him on her way past.

Elliot didn't respond to either comment, but May had heard the voice.

"You're at work?" May said, abashed. "I'd offer to call back if I thought you'd answer."

He deserved much worse than that, honestly, but May had never been cruel.

"I was about to take a break," Elliot decided, standing up. "How have you been, May?"

"I've been good; I—" May said before catching herself. "Elliot, why did you stop talking to me?"

Elliot stepped out into the stairwell, ignoring his co-worker's call for an explanation from across the room, and her voice was cut off entirely as the door swung shut behind him.

"It wasn't really something I consciously decided to do," Elliot said, leaning against the railing. "But if I were pressed to give a reason, it would be that hearing your voice reminds me of how everything was before."

Elliot's uncharacteristic bluntness took her off guard, and it was several long seconds before she managed to respond.

"I understand; you know that I do, Elliot." May managed, straddling the line between sympathetic and hurt. "But that isn't fair to me."

Elliot stepped away from the railing and started up the steps, the movement taking some of his focus off the shakiness in her voice.

"I wasn't thinking about fairness either," Elliot said quietly. "I was just trying to get away from everything."

"There are so many times where I find myself thinking about Dimitri," May murmured, "We should be sharing those memories, Elliot, not hiding from them."

The name should have elicited something in him, but he was too tired now and far too detached from it all.

"I know, May." Eliot sighed. "I didn't handle any of this as I should have; I'm sorry."

"If you know, then stop avoiding me," May managed, drawing in a shaky breath. "Idiot."

Some of the tension in May's voice had washed away, and he closed his eyes.

"I thought I was the smart one?" Elliot said.

"Nope, that was definitely me," May said, and he could almost hear her smile. "Who was the lady that was shouting before?"

"A co-worker," Elliot said, opening the door. "We all need to work late today because someone quit—she's a bit fired up."

There was barely a cloud in the sky, which wasn't exactly unusual for Saltwall City.

"What are your plans for when you do get off?" May asked.

"I don't have any," Elliot admitted.

"Well," May said, working to keep the conversation moving. "I've been playing Inexorable Melody."

That was a name he hadn't heard for a while, and it took him a moment to dredge up what he recalled about the game.

"Is it any good?" Elliot wondered.

"It's actually really fun," May said, warming to the topic. "It might be uh, Forty hours? Sixty if you take your time?"

Elliot hummed in response, tracing the curves of her voice.

"I've only done the single-player stuff so far, but the multiplayer is supposed to be amazing." May said, "Have you seen any of the full release gameplay yet?"

"No," Elliot said.

"What?" May said, bemused, "You were the one who told me about it last year, remember?"

"Yeah," Elliot agreed. "I remember."

"Sean was looking forward to playing it with us," May said, "We could make a team—just the three of us?"

Just the three of us.

"Elliot? Are you still there?" May asked after he fell silent. "Did I do something wrong?"

"You didn't do anything wrong, May," Elliot said genuinely. "I'm really glad I got to talk to you."

"You sound strange," May said, concerned. "Do you want to meet up in the city? I'll drive up tomorrow, and we can hang out for a while?"

"Sorry, May," Elliot said quietly, "Maybe next time."

"Elliot?" May said.

Elliot stepped off the edge of the building.

The Conflict

They didn't stay near the bodies for exceptionally long; instead, they moved even further away from the entrance. Hannah had been quiet since the revelation, wringing her hands together in an attempt to distract herself from everything. Grant had remained calm but nervous and held his sword at the ready as he searched the trees for movement.

Elliot stopped to stare at a massive boulder, one of the many that were littered through the forest. There was so much visual noise in the woods that he had still almost missed it—it had a glowing white outline that he could see was hovering on the other side.

It was obviously a hidden chest or a crate of some sort.

"Elliot?" Grant said as he suddenly turned off the path.

"There's something hidden behind that rock—It's showing up as a white glowing shape." Elliot said quietly. "My passive ability allows me to see hidden things like this apparently."

A smooth metal box sat on the forest floor, covered in leaves, Elliot reached down and flipped the latch open, and the lid sprang up. There was a moment where his heartbeat thundered in his chest, and he realized too late that it might have been trapped somehow, but nothing happened.

Secret Found: 1/100.

Loot Gained: 500 Gold, 1 Uncommon Long Sword, 1 Uncommon Kite Shield, 1 Uncommon Hide Armor.

"Really?" Hannah said from the other side of the boulder. "I can appraise things or something. I don't know how to use it yet."

"Appraise items, maybe?" Grant wondered, "My Active is 'Assess,' which tells me how strong something is in comparison to myself, I think."

Hannah made a noise of interest as she spotted the chest.

"A chest?" Hannah said curiously, "Anything in it?"

Elliot stood up and opened his inventory, finding where the three items were located and selecting 'drop.' All three of them appeared on the ground in a heap, startling the other two.

"We can work out what to do with them later." Elliot said evenly, "Grant, you should equip all three for now."

Grant slowly bent down and picked them up, and after a long moment, they vanished from his hands into his inventory. A moment later, his armor suddenly changed color and size, a shield appeared strapped to his arm, and the sword at his side became suddenly longer.

"Cool!" Hannah giggled.

"You can have the next stuff we find, Hannah," Elliot said evenly. "There is apparently one-hundred 'secrets' in this Dungeon, and that was just the first one."

"You don't have to give me anything, Elliot," Hannah mumbled embarrassedly, but he'd already changed the subject.

"So, we search around for some more until the portal appears?" Grant asked thoughtfully. "We have to be careful. There's still an unknown number of monsters here."

"Yeah," Elliot said calmly, "Let's go."

They moved back to the small dirt path, but Elliot now had a pattern he was looking for. Anything white drew his gaze, including the clouds peeking through the treetops. There was a tree covered in white papery bark that had drawn his attention for a moment, but nothing of note.

"Another group of those bark-things," Hannah said. "Over there."

Elliot turned his head around to locate them, having been tunneling his vision to look for white and not paying attention to his surroundings, and slowly crouched down behind the nearest tree. The other two followed his example a moment later, and they studied the group for a while. Only seven in this group and one of them was gravely injured.

There was another body on the ground near them, but it definitely wasn't human. The body was tall, slender, and pale green, covered in claw marks and bleeding freely, with dark red blood. The face was hidden behind a tree and out of sight from their position. Three different races inside a single dungeon, Humans, Bark-things, and Green-humanoid-things, the multiple Grey Room theory was growing more plausible by the second.

"Can we kill them on our own?" Grant asked nervously.

"We could just leave," Hannah said.

Elliot had no intention of leaving.

"You can stay here if you want," Elliot said evenly, "I'm going to sneak attack one of them with Swap."

"Swap?" Hannah said hesitantly. "Is that what you did in the other fight, where you just appeared?"

Grant looked interested as well.

"My active skill," Elliot said quietly. "Swap places with things or enemies."

Elliot picked up a couple of stones that fit into his hand and placed them in a line behind the tree before he stood up quietly, nodding at the other man. Grant seemingly got the idea and looked at the group of bark things for a moment, pulled out his sword, and turned to face Elliot.

Hannah looked alarmed.

"Wait!" Hannah whispered, "Tell *me* what we are doing first!"

Elliot paused for a long moment and then averted his eyes.

"I'm going to swap with the one at the edge of the group. Grant is going to kill it as soon as it appears." Elliot said calmly, "I'll swap with the first stone. I'll walk back into place in front of Grant and then swap with the next one."

Hannah stared at him with her mouth open for a long moment, unable to think of anything to say.

"I'm going, don't scream," Elliot said evenly before turning to nod at Grant.

Grant readied himself again and then nodded firmly.

Elliot swapped with the Bark-Thing that had wandered off from the group. He appeared in another part of the forest, staring at the group of Bark-things. They hadn't noticed him yet, and he could hear the sound of something fall to the floor some distance away.

The bark-things turned to face the noise, and Elliot frowned before taking a step forward on the leaves. The things immediately turned to him at the sound and started scuttling around towards him, so he swapped places with one of the stones by the tree. The body of the Bark-thing lay on the ground dead with Grant standing over it determinedly.

"They heard the body land," Elliot said quietly, moving to stand over the bark things body. "Ready."

"Ready," Grant said quietly.

Elliot switched again, this time with the one at the back of the group, and immediately switched out with another stone, he arrived just in time for Grant to pull his long sword out of its face, and it tumbled to the ground.

"I hate this place," Hannah whispered.

"So do I," Grant said uneasily.

Elliot just stepped forward and swapped with another of the bark-things, but this time he stabbed the nearest one in the chest with his spear, and the remaining three bark-things turned to him and screamed.

Loot Gained: 2 EXP, 2 Gold, 1 Rough Hide, 4 Sharp Talons.

Two of them ran at him, while the third turned to run away, and Elliot swapped with the runner, took two steps towards the others, and stabbed one of them in the back again.

Loot Gained: 2 EXP, 2 Gold, 1 Rough Hide, 5 Sharp Talons.

The things turned, and he swapped with the one that tried to run again and repeated it, this time the bark-thing almost managed to spin fast enough to avoid his attack, but not quite.

Loot Gained: 2 EXP, 2 Gold, 1 Rough Hide, 2 Sharp Talons.

The last bark thing stared at him in horror, and Elliott stared back at it feeling nothing at all.

"Hey," Elliot said quietly, "I'm not enjoying this, and I don't want to do it either. Sorry, man."

The bark-thing turned to run. Elliot swapped with a dead branch in front of it and staked it to the ground as soon as he appeared. The thing grasped at the spear in its chest for a long moment before going limp.

Loot Gained: 2 EXP, 2 Gold, 1 Rough Hide, 5 Sharp Talons.

Elliot could feel the others moving towards him now, no doubt investigating after he hadn't immediately returned. He realized after the second swap that his plan meant that Grant had to kill everything and dropped it immediately. The guy didn't deserve that on his conscience.

"Elliot!" Hannah called out.

Elliot switched with one of the many branches on the ground near them.

"I'm here," Elliot said evenly.

"Oh, thank god," Hannah said, relieved but shaken.

Grant was looking around for movement, which is what Elliot should have been doing; he chided himself for allowing his attention to slip for even a moment; he really was useless in the end. Elliot could see a flicker of the white glow back through the trees in the direction they had already passed.

"That's all of them," Elliot said quietly. "I can see another secret."

Grant glanced in the same direction he was looking for a moment before going back to scanning the area. Hannah stepped towards him suddenly and dragged him down into her arms, and Elliot froze at the utterly unexpected hug.

"I thought you died." Hannah said quietly, "Stop running off on your own."

Elliot patted her on the back gently and didn't respond. After a long moment, she finally released him, and he gripped the back of his neck awkwardly, staring over her head to avoid her gaze. A massive light erupted in the distance, bright enough to be seen through the trees and spearing up into the sky high above.

Dungeon Complete: 1278/1278 Enemies Defeated.

"That's a lot more than last time," Grant said quietly.

"They weren't as strong as the pale things." Elliot said evenly, "Only two-exp as opposed to the ten-exp I got last time."

"So weaker but more of them?" Hannah said thoughtfully, "But there were so many people this time; I thought it was going to be harder to make up for that."

Elliot started towards the secret, mind racing about numbers, and the other two followed once more. If he could figure out a baseline system to rate these things compared to himself, he might be able to use that to come up with a better idea of how this worked.

"Grant," Elliot said evenly, "You can feel how strong something is with your skill?"

"Yeah," Grant said easily.

"If I was the equivalent of two units of 'power,' how strong was one of those bark-things," Elliot asked quietly, kneeling down to the chest and flipping the lid.

Secret Found: 2/100.
Loot Gained: 500 Gold, 1 Uncommon Dagger, 1 Uncommon Warhammer, 1 Uncommon Leather Armor.

"If you were two, each of them was a two as well." Grant said quietly, "It doesn't make much sense, though, because they were so much weaker than us."

"Two-exp for a level two, ten-exp for a level ten?" Elliot said evenly in return.

Grant's eyes widened a little bit, and he looked thoughtful.

"How do you know that?" Hannah asked, bewildered.

"He's guessing, but if the next thing we beat fits that pattern, then we can use that to make some rough estimates on how this system works," Grant said slowly.

"Very rough," Elliot said quietly, "There was a third type of monster here."

"The dead woman?" Hannah said uneasily, "She almost looked human if she wasn't so green."

Elliot emptied the items onto the ground in front of him.

"Hannah," Elliot said evenly before stepping backward.

Hannah smiled brightly at him before bending over at the waist to snag the items.

"What are you thinking, Elliot?" Grants asked curiously.

Elliot quickly dragged his eyes away from where he had been looking down Hannah's shirt.

"I think there's an unknown number of Grey Rooms working at the same time, drawing beings from either different planets, alternate realities, or something else," Elliot said distractedly, keeping his gaze locked firmly on the tree to his right. "I think the sides might be matched together with an algorithm based on the level of power or experience on each side, and the winner plays on."

"That's..." Hannah said quietly, "Horrible."

"Yeah," Grant managed. "What made you think there was another Grey Room?"

Hannah had equipped her new armor and the dagger. She couldn't actually lift the Warhammer, so it stayed in her inventory.

"It was the timer, right?" Hannah said suddenly.

Elliot glanced over at her, surprised that she had figured it out, but Grant looked lost.

"It was the timer," Elliot said evenly, "It resets every time someone enters on our end, but it starts counting down as soon as there are five people inside. Each person appearing means that if the conditions inside the Dungeon stayed static, all you would need to win would be to have a couple of thousand people enter each time just to roll over the opposition."

Grant scrunched up his face in thought.

"There are more enemies in this one, but they are all weaker." Grant said slowly, "There were a lot newer or second-timers here as well."

Elliot nodded.

"The thing in the first room was too patient to be an animal, and these things were too organized not to be intelligent," Elliot said evenly, "You said they could speak to each other. That was the next piece of confirmation."

Grant started nodding.

"Intelligent enemies, other 'Gladiators,'" Grant said thoughtfully, "With their own room, and every time someone enters over there, the algorithm has to adjust by resetting all the timers and pulling someone else in to even it out again."

"When the timer hits zero, the 'dungeon' starts, and all the sides fight until one is left," Hannah said quietly. "How many rooms are there?"

"There's no way to know." Grant said gravely, "It could be less than one-hundred, or it could have been more, minimum of five creatures per room equals something like two-hundred and fifty teams at a maximum this time at least, but it could be less, we don't know where they are drawing them from either."

"It could be every iteration of every alternate reality for all we know," Elliot said morbidly, "This might just be some kind of automated factory."

"Like a recycling system for those who have died?" Grant said quietly. "Input dead, output what?"

"A slaughterhouse for the gods," Elliot said evenly. "Souls, meat, or memories? Who knows."

"That's..." Hannah said weakly before shaking her head. "No more of that, let's get out of here!"

Elliot blinked at the sudden change of direction, but she was right that they shouldn't linger here for long. Elliot wondered what a boss looked like, but he had no intention of finding that out any time soon, not that he was sure *how* to go about finding out exactly.

"Yeah, let's go," Grant said firmly.

Elliot followed them as they made their way through the forest towards the light of the portal, thinking about everything that had happened and the things that might still come to pass. If this was some kind of automated system, the only way they were getting out was through their own actions.

The armored man had been in *thousands* of dungeons, enough that he had lost count. If he ever wanted to get out of this, he was going to need at least that many behind him. Which meant he had a long path ahead of him, and he was only going to survive to see the end of that path if he put all of his mind towards that goal.

As Elliot stepped through the portal, he promised himself that he would become strong.

The grey room was just how they had left it.

Loot Gained: 2192 EXP, 1128 Gold.

It was a lower difficulty score than the first time, which lent some credibility towards the Bark-creatures being lower level than the tall-pale-things. It had been evident given both their presence and apparent physical capabilities, but the confirmation was useful, nonetheless. Enough exp for two more levels as well, something he would do later once they returned to the room.

There was a noticeably less amount of people returning to the room, and Elliot waited outside the Torii until people stopped emerging. Hannah and Grant both watching the edge of the world and pointing out stars to each other.

Elliot was reasonably sure they weren't the first people out of the room, but out of the two-hundred or more people that had been in the place, less than fifty had emerged. Even doubling that number left him with a possibility of almost a hundred dead from that E-rank Dungeon. They had been lucky to have gotten a lower difficulty, and they were even more fortunate that they hadn't been near whatever had wiped out most of the group.

Elliot wondered how long their luck would hold out.

They returned to the room without detour, Hannah and Grant talking quietly amongst themselves while Elliot busied himself with checking over the system menu. He silently used all of his gained exp to increase his level twice, leaving him at level four. His attributes were updated to show 4 strength, 24 speed, 4 magic, and 4 defense.

Elliot studied it for a moment; Speed was going to be his highest stat, his strength was lacking in comparison; he would have to increase his ability to deal damage purely with equipment. He hadn't picked up a weapon in his entire life before he woke up in the Grey Room, but the spear seemed like a reasonable enough weapon to stick with, he could attack from a safe range, and it dealt damage to a small area which would hopefully alleviate the need for more strength.

Elliot would have to see if he could buy a better spear at that weapon shop he had spotted on the way back to the room. There weren't any spears in the system shop, although it *was* possible that he could get one from the random options. Unfortunately, the cheapest was one million gold.

He found his way to the inventory menu and checked it over.

Inventory: 1168 Gold, 4 Small Health Potions, 78 Bone Needles, 7 Rough Hide, 24 Sharp Talons, 42 Small Stones.

With only just over a thousand gold, he was a long way off any of the system shop weapons at present, so the weapon store he had walked past on the street outside would be his next stop, and if he was still unable to afford anything, he could always try to sell the other things he had picked up along the way.

"Grant," Hannah said curiously, perched on the edge of the bed. "How old are you?"

"I'm twenty-eight," Grant said easily.

"So am I!" Hannah said excitedly. "How old are you, Elliot?"

Elliot glanced up at them from his reclaimed place on the floor and hesitated for a moment.

"I'm twenty-three," Elliot said evenly.

"I thought you were older." Hannah smiled brightly.

Elliot turned his thoughts inward for a while, avoiding being drawn into the conversation again. It was pretty obvious now what was going to happen, now that he'd had some time to think about it all. Whatever this place was, it wasn't going to just stop; they would have to go back into the Dungeon, potentially tens of thousands of times, until they finally made enough to buy a token.

It wasn't plausible. They would die long before then. It was better to play the long game here. He would aim for better gear first and incrementally increase his level until he was able to handle everything that came his way.

He needed to go find that weapon shop.

"I'm going out," Elliot said quietly, pushing himself to his feet.

"Are you going back to the dungeon?" Hannah said worriedly.

"No," Elliot said simply. "I'm going to check out some of the stores."

Elliot stepped into the building he had spotted earlier and immediately turned to look around.

There were weapons *everywhere.*

There were things he had never seen before, like the long needle-like rapier that was longer than his spear or the length of chain with a dagger on one end. The one that he couldn't help but glance at twice was a massive bladed circle on the end of a metal pole.

Who would even *use* that?

"What are you looking for?" An old man said calmly from his seat by the counter.

Elliot turned to look at him, having missed him in his fascination with all the weapons.

"I'm looking for a spear." Elliot said politely, "Better than a starting weapon, and with a metal haft."

His spear had a series of gouges in the haft already, and a thin metal spear would be preferable to a wooden one. The old man stood up easily and headed over to the far corner, to the right of the entryway. Elliot turned to see a series of spears lined up next to each other on a wooden mount, not unlike a pool cue holder.

"Starting weapon, huh?" The old man sighed, "How much have you got to spend? Hundred gold?"

"A thousand," Elliot said evenly.

The old man blinked and glanced back at him over his shoulder.

"Huh," The old man said curiously, "I've got an uncommon one here, all-metal, a little bit shorter than most spears though, I'll give it to you for seven-hundred."

Elliot studied the shorter spear the man pulled off the rack, not quite as long as his current one, thinner and all-metal. The point was a tight spiral, almost like a drill. He had no idea how to tell the price appropriate for weapons, so it would have to do.

"Check the quality first, if you want." The old man said easily before tossing it to him lengthwise. "I don't think you're the type to run off with it."

Elliot managed to catch it with little effort and immediately placed it into his inventory. He opened the menu and checked the quality as the old man pulled out his trading stone.

Inventory: Uncommon Drill-Tip Spear.

He checked what it was worth as well—730 gold.

"Thanks for the discount," Elliot said evenly and reached out to the payment stone. "Seven-hundred-Gold."

The stone flashed, and the man inventoried the brick once the transaction was complete.

"No worries," The old man said easily, "I've got some rarer stuff stashed away for when you get some more cash, and I'll keep an eye out for any spears in the meantime."

"I'll be back to buy one of them then," Elliot promised. "What's the price range for the next tier in quality above uncommon?"

He hummed thoughtfully.

"I've never seen a rare weapon below ten thousand, and they can range anywhere from that, up to a million." The old man explained.

"Interesting," Elliot said evenly, "Thank you, I'll see you around."

"Name's Aestus." Aestus said easily, "Don't die down there, kid."

"I'm Elliot," Elliot said quietly, "and I won't."

There was one other shop Elliot was interested in checking out, and it was more for information purposes than anything else. As he stepped over the threshold, he looked down the street and spotted the other sign, 'Servants.'

It hadn't escaped his notice that non-humans were running around the city, doing their best to remain unobtrusive but still standing out easily. He had even caught a glance of a bark-thing before it rounded a corner, scurrying after a tall woman. This store was very different; it was a small room with a counter and a door behind it that led to somewhere else. A woman with sleepy eyes watched him as he stepped inside before she stretched her arms above her head with a long yawn.

"What can I do for you, handsome?" The woman said, amused.

Elliot averted his eyes from the woman for a moment before glancing back at her.

"Sorry to interrupt your nap." Elliot said, "Can you explain what this store's purpose is?"

The woman leaned forward, bodily over the counter, and rested her chin on her hand before she smiled up at him.

"We buy anything that gets captured in the dungeons and then sell them to those who want them." The woman giggled. "You're new, huh? Bet you don't even know *how* to capture them."

The woman swayed her hips from her position poised on the counter, and he did his best to keep his eyes on her nose.

"I didn't even know you *could* capture them," Elliot said quietly.

"I'll tell you how, but the first monster you sell here takes a fifty-percent discount my way." The woman giggled. "Sound fair?"

Elliot just nodded, and the woman grinned up at him.

"My name is Kara, by the way," Kara said happily.

"Elliot," Elliot said in response.

"To capture something, you just need to knock them unconscious, or otherwise have them vocally submit themselves to you for capture, and then place your hand on their head." Kara planted one of her hands on the counter firmly, "Claim."

There was a flicker of blue light beneath her palm before it fizzled out. Elliot immediately placed his hand out in front of him and repeated the word, and blue sparks fell from his hand onto the countertop before vanishing.

"Easy, huh?" Kara giggled. "You can bring those you've claimed back through the portal, and once you've claimed something, it's counted as 'defeated' to the Dungeon."

"Easy." Elliot agreed quietly. "I'll make sure to bring you some interesting ones then."

Kara laughed at the comment.

"I'll look forward to it, handsome." Kara said, coyly, "Don't be a stranger?"

Elliot nodded as he retreated from the dangerous woman and back onto the street again. Claiming monsters and then selling them. Why did people *want* them though, did they help you fight? The monsters probably didn't want to be claimed, that was for sure, especially not the intelligent ones. Elliot would make sure to only claim those who seemed evil or without much in the way of higher intelligence.

Now he had a decision to make.

He could return to the room, where Hannah and Grant were waiting, or he could go back into the Dungeon. Going back to the room seemed like the more uncomfortable decision to him, as being stuck in such proximity to other people held a strange intensity to it that he wasn't used to at all.

Elliot turned and headed for the Dungeon.

The others would probably be upset with him, but he knew that they wouldn't want to return to it again, at least not three times in a single day, and he knew they would attempt to convince him not to if he returned to speak to them first.

Stepping through the Torii felt easier than before, the unknown shrinking as his knowledge of the dangers increased. The grey room was empty this time, and he had to wait almost three minutes before someone finally appeared, but like a pebble falling down a mountain, it started an avalanche of people following quickly behind.

A boisterous laugh rang out throughout the room, and Elliot turned to study the source. It was a red-haired woman with a massive grin on her face, standing tall in the middle of the room with her hands on her hips. Tens of copper bangles lined both of her arms, hanging in a large stack around her forearms, rattling with each movement, but no weapon in sight.

"A week, Tsunami." The woman laughed, "I'm *finally* back! Kaoru can be so mean!"

The shorter Asian woman she was talking with looked resigned and brushed a straight lock of her dark hair over her ear before responding reservedly; a bow sat on her back, made of some kind of dark wood carved with an intricate design.

"Amber, you're lucky it wasn't *longer*. I would have banned you for a *month*," Tsunami said simply.

The boisterous woman looked horrified at the thought.

"A month!?" Amber squawked, "You monster!"

Tsunami just sighed again.

Elliot watched them for a while with interest.

They were obviously involved in some kind of larger group. Being 'banned' from going into the Dungeon seemed strange on its head. Did they force them to buy skip tokens? It also seemed like something that could only be enforced by someone with authority over them, so a larger organization of some sort.

Whoever this Kaoru was, she had to of been either the leader or the person who dealt with punishing dissenters. The man from earlier had mentioned 'joining a faction'; perhaps this was one of them; its purpose was still unclear.

The timer continued forever downwards, in between flickering back to its starting position now and then, drawing his thoughts back towards the current situation once more.

The best use of his time in this Dungeon would be to secure more money to buy better equipment as soon as possible, and the best way he had discovered to find the money was the secrets. Even a single one would double his 'mission' income and provide another week's worth of resources to survive on the outside.

There was nowhere near as many people in this Dungeon, only eleven total, a stark contrast to the last time. There were no noticeable new people either; everyone seemingly had armor of some kind on; he was likely the weakest person in the room. This would be another data point for figuring out how the system worked.

Last time had been hundreds of low levels and a small number of stronger ones. This time seemed to be a small number of more powerful people, and him. What would the opposition be? A massive horde of weak enemies? A small but elite group? A mixture?

Elliot would do his best to avoid them entirely with liberal use of his ability and try to cover as much ground as possible, looking for secrets. If he ran into something he couldn't handle, he would lead it in the direction of the stronger-looking people so they could deal with it, but if it was something he could handle, he would deal with it himself.

Amber's loud voice drew his attention again for a moment.

"Let's make a bet!" Amber laughed. "How many runs do you think it will take to find one?"

Elliot listened curiously as Tsunami seemingly thought it over for a long moment.

"Three?" Tsunami said thoughtfully. "What are we betting?"

"Seven!" Amber cheered, "Dungeon winnings?"

"That's fine," Tsunami agreed simply. "They are pretty common though, why choose such a high number?"

"Because I'm an optimist!" Amber laughed loudly.

Elliot watched them intently. They were looking for something inside the Dungeon, something common enough to appear in less than ten attempts. Were they hunting monsters? Capturing them to sell, perhaps? Or maybe they killing them for the materials they dropped?

Some kind of organization that hunted specific monsters?

They also seemed extremely comfortable with the idea of going into the Dungeon, looking forward to it even, which spoke of great confidence.

The timer was already reaching the single digits before each reset now; it was almost time. Fourteen people, including himself, now stood in the room, but Elliot found his eyes drawn to the white glow of the hidden doorway.

What was behind the door this time? Pale predators that hunted with endless patience, or bark-goblins that co-operated to take down bigger threats, or was it something worse than either? Maybe it would be more of those tall green women who he never managed to see any more of.

If he did see one of those three species again, should he try to capture one? The idea of a pale thing with needle teeth following him around was far too spine-chilling to consider, and he had trouble with the thought of capturing something so human-looking like as the green woman had been.

The bark-goblins he only felt a little better about, but still not fully settled. Their less than human appearance made it easier, but they were intelligent enough to have conversations so it still felt wrong.

Perhaps none of them, Elliot thought as he moved towards the door as the timer reached '3' before it reset once more. This would likely be the last countdown, at least judging by the previous ones.

Sixteen people in total.

Elliot felt excitement blossoming in him alongside the ever-present fear, something he'd long since stopped feeling back in the other world.

The feeling seared through him, lighting his senses up at the thought of becoming stronger, becoming faster, of conquering an obstacle, and being rewarded for it.

Was this what the world felt like to everyone else? He'd forgotten it, somewhere along the line. Life had beaten him down, and it had all flat-lined into a monotonous existence that lacked any joy, but it was coming back now—He could *feel* it.

Despite the fear, Elliot found himself smiling quietly as the timer reached zero, and the white rectangle that only he could see vanished as the door appeared.

He followed the group into the hallway beyond, feeling a warm rush of air push its way into the grey room. It was a jungle this time, and it was *hot*, the middle of summer standing in the sun hot and pretty humid as well.

Elliot stared around at all of the trees with wary eyes; he would need to be very careful here. There was so much visual noise to pick through; it would be easy to miss any green or brown creatures. On the other side, there was seemingly an infinite amount of things to swap within his range, twigs, sticks, branches, rocks, large clumps of dirt, and leaves, along with other more vague things.

Elliot watched as Amber and Tsunami strode off through the jungle seemingly without fear, so he moved to follow them surreptitiously, at a great distance, but making sure to keep them within his swap range.

There were bugs everywhere, on the trees, and crawling through the vegetation, the plants included things he had never seen before, like massive yellow mushroom-like things that stuck up in tall clumps around the bases of the trees, and he could faintly hear the sound of a river in the distance. It all felt so alien, despite having never been inside a jungle, the bugs were all unrecognizable, the trees were strange, and the color and shape of the mushroom seemed so off it was jarring.

A flicker of white in the corner of his eye drew his undivided attention for a moment, and once he had located it, he spotted the chest behind a couple of layers of trees and bushes. Elliot headed towards it, and sensing nothing large moving around within his range; he swapped places with a lump of dirt next to it.

Secret Found: 1/100
Loot Gained: 500 Gold, 1 Uncommon Combat Bodysuit, 1 Uncommon Truncheon, 1 Uncommon Heater Shield.

Elliot frowned at the items, two items were useless to him, but the bodysuit might be better than what he had on. He checked and found that to be the case and quickly equipped it in place of his leathers. It was black, relatively thin, and made of some kind of stretchable fabric that clung to him tightly.

He felt pretty uncomfortable wearing something so form-fitting if he was honest, but the stats were easily better than the leathers, and functionality over aesthetics was the order of the day, at least in this case.

Elliot still hadn't run into any of the creatures in this Dungeon yet, but he had felt the two women from earlier fighting with two roughly human-shaped things—most likely monsters of some kind.

Nothing was coming his way, and he hoped it would stay that way, so he could just loot the area in peace.

The Split

Elliot knelt down beside the chest, running through the now-familiar process of flipping the latch.

Secret Found: 4/100.
Loot Gained: 500 Gold, 1 Uncommon Dagger, 1 Uncommon Amulet, 1 Uncommon Ring.

"Oh, come on," Elliot muttered. "That's the third dagger."

Elliot pushed himself to his feet, unable to help the spark of annoyance that rushed through him. He did his best to shake it off and moved on, switching places with a loose rock buried in the leaves some distance away.

The small jaunt had brought him back in range of the two high-leveled people he was keeping track of—There was another signature moving towards him from the north, and it was moving at an alarming speed.

Elliot turned to face the direction, searching the trees furiously for anything, but he couldn't see through the jungle well enough to locate whatever it was. He swapped with a broken branch much closer to the two women—Somehow, the thing turned and started towards his new location with barely a pause.

"How?" Elliot murmured. "Can you see me or hear me? Tracking by temperature? What is it?"

Elliot saw a flash of red behind a distant tree and swapped with a branch on the edge of the large clearing the two women were standing in. Once more, the creature adjusted its direction to continue heading straight for him, slipping between the trees inhumanly fast.

"Incoming! It's an extremely fast red humanoid, coming from the northwest!" Elliot called out. "I can't track it, so it's all yours!"

After he'd finished the warning, he swapped with a rock on the other side of the clearing, placing the two high-leveled women in between him and the red thing. It was cowardly sure, but from what he had observed since they had been here, these two had already killed something like roughly fifteen already, and they still looked completely uninjured.

Surely they wouldn't mind *one* more.

Elliot watched the backs of the women as they visually searched the location where he had shouted from. They tensed, staring through the foliage, looking for the creature as the sound of breaking branches and crunching leaves moved towards them.

Elliot tracked it with his swap-sense right to the edge of the trees before he finally caught sight of it, but it was nothing but a blur of red and black as it cut across the clearing at almost untraceable speeds.

Amber started towards it immediately, and he noticed that she didn't have a weapon at all; she wore simple cloth wraps around her fists. He could easily see that the red creature was much faster than she was, and she was very, very quick.

Tsunami—still in the center of the clearing, held her dark-colored bow up at the ready, and he watched as she spun quickly to target the creature. She fired three arrows that practically vanished from the bow, and one of the trees behind the creature shattered into a hundred pieces as the projectile hit it, and the other two made it further into the jungle before felling two more trees out of sight.

Amber, who had been attempting to engage the creature in hand to hand, was suddenly on the ground, lying on her side. The creature dove towards the woman, and Elliot made a snap decision—he swapped places with Amber, depositing her in his previous position within the trees, and then immediately swapped places with a branch on the other side of the clearing, barely escaping.

The creature kept moving and started circling Tsunami's position with its vanishing speed, and the archer steadily turned with it, firing methodically in front of the creature but landing no hits as the arrows shattered the forestry behind her target.

Amber reappeared from inside the treeline and managed to intercept the creature, slamming bodily into it from the side—there was a brief moment where the two of them were locked in a savage physical struggle, and for the first time since the battle had started, Elliot could actually see the creature properly.

Two thin arms and legs, five fingers on each hand all tipped with claws, mottled red and black patterned skin, two long ears that speared straight downwards from the sides of its head tapered to a point level with its neck. It had a large wide mouth, filled with perfectly white, flat teeth.

There were no eyes or nose, as the creature's head abruptly ended above its mouth. Elliot felt a tingle in his spine at the sight of the thing. It looked so distinctly *almost* human he could barely look at it without feeling revolted.

The struggle kicked back up into higher gear again as they started smashing small craters in the ground around them with each strike, and arrows continued to fell trees when Tsunami could safely manage to take a shot.

They just couldn't hit the thing—Elliot couldn't even see it properly, only able to keep track of it in short bursts. Amber was looking more and more injured the longer the fight went on, with blood beginning to coat her skin from the numerous claw marks that had shredded her thin armor.

Tsunami was doing her best to stay out of range of the creature, but Elliot was soon forced to swap places with her when the creature began targeting her. When he swapped himself out of danger, he felt searing pain flash up his right arm. The cut was shallow, barely a nick compared to how injured Amber currently was.

The fact that the red thing had managed to *touch* him that time was chilling—it was far too fast, and he was suddenly very aware that unless they figured out a way to kill it, they were all going to die.

Elliot's mind raced as he considered his options.

Anything they tried to attack it with, it would more than likely dodge with its superior speed. They couldn't contest it in melee, and they couldn't outrun it. They needed to remove its ability to dodge, to corner it somehow.

An earth-shattering crack rang out as another arrow left Tsunami's bow—Stronger than her previous attacks, it downed a series of trees in a line of terrifying destruction. Elliot was reminded once more that right now, he was nothing a speck viewing a battle between gods.

Elliot caught a glimpse of a distant cloud-filled sky through the new gap in the forestry, and the flash of blue brought with it the solution as everything clicked into place within his mind.

"Tsunami," Elliot said seriously, striding towards the woman. "Shoot me."

Tsunami spun towards him warily—and when Elliot broke into a sprint towards her, she brought her bow up, arrow notched. Elliot's foot came down as she pulled the string taut, and then he swapped with the red-creature.

Elliot found himself in the creature's previous position, in a full mount over Amber and a knee planted on each side of her chest. Amber stared up at him with wide eyes, her shredded and bleeding arms raised defensively over her face. A screech washed over them, and he spun back around, dismounting the woman in the process.

The creature dragged itself towards Tsunami with a massive bleeding hole in its torso, right above the hip.

Tsunami shot it again without mercy, and a cloud of detritus was sent away from the impact zone showering the woman in dirt. The creature screeched in pain, stretching its hand out towards the archer, and the next arrow passed through its fingers and vanished the rest of its eyeless head.

Dungeon Complete: 73/73 Enemies Defeated.

The world lit up in that same blinding light of the portal—they were consumed by it as it opened up directly on top of them. The light faded, and then the three of them were once more inside the grey room.

Elliot took several steps away from the still downed and bleeding Amber, backing up to the fog wall behind him to keep them both in his sight. He'd almost gotten them both killed, and he had no idea if they were the type to seek revenge.

Loot Gained: 1973 EXP, 6300 Gold.

Tsunami quickly made her way over to her friend, where Amber was fighting to bring herself back to her feet. A red vial appeared in her hand, pulled from her inventory, and she tipped it all into Amber's mouth. Some of the wounds littering her face and arms vanished before she went on to help her consume two more.

"Thanks," Amber croaked, her pale skin growing warmer.

He used the moment to go over the dungeon statistic—The dungeon reported its difficulty rating as a C-rank, and Elliot stared at it aghast. That thing was strong enough to fight the three of them at once and was winning handily.

What kind of monsters would be present in a B-rank dungeon? Or an A-rank?

The amount of gold he'd gained was also far higher than the other ones he had participated in, and after searching through the information, he figured out a few things. For one, the lowest rating he received overall was the rating that decided the multiplier for gold rewarded. This dungeon had only lasted for just over twenty minutes, and the quick clear time had dragged the multiplier up.

"Well, that wasn't as fun as I imagined," Amber said belatedly, with an uneasy grin. "Who are you anyway?"

Elliot wasn't sure what to expect; she wasn't anywhere as angry as he thought she should be.

"Elliot," Elliot said evenly, studying them both.

Tsunami still hadn't put away her bow—that was a reaction that made a lot more sense to him.

"You're the one who was teleporting us around?" Amber said easily.

Elliot just nodded.

"Thanks for the save, man. That thing had me dead to rights." Amber laughed, "Been a while since that's happened."

"Thank you for saving me as well." Tsunami said calmly, finally putting away her bow. "Oh, and for the kill-shot setup—I couldn't land an attack with how fast it was moving."

Elliot inventoried his own drill-tipped spear to match the goodwill they were showing.

"Thanks for killing it," Elliot said in response. "I wouldn't have been able to do that on my own—all I could do is play support. Sorry, you got so badly hurt."

Amber planted her hands on her hips, her bangles jingling together and her stance practically broadcasting confidence now that she was once more unharmed.

"Nah, it's not the first time I've got my ass kicked. What level are you anyway?" Amber asked curiously. "Thirty? Forty?"

"I'm level four," Elliot said evenly, feeling vaguely embarrassed. "What level are you both?"

Amber blinked at him like he was the strangest thing she had ever seen.

"Level *four*?" Tsunami said, bewildered. "Such terrible luck to be pulled into the dungeon while so many stronger people are around—my word."

"I wasn't pulled; I chose to come back in." Elliot said, wondering, "You didn't tell me your levels."

"One-hundred-sixty-eight." Tsunami said, bemused.

Elliot forced his face to remain still, but it still took most of his effort, and he felt the muscles in his jaw tighten.

"One-ninety," Amber laughed, "I can't believe you're level *four*. That's hilarious."

He had somehow wandered into a dungeon with people so far above him that the reason he was still alive was purely that he hadn't encountered anything. If he hadn't had an ability that allowed him to run away and if he hadn't been keeping track of where they were, he would have been killed by that creature. It had been faster and stronger than both of them—It must have been at *least* level two-hundred, if not higher.

"So the average level of the monsters in there was above one-hundred?" Elliot said evenly.

Tsunami tilted her head at him curiously, clearing, seeing that he was fishing for information.

"Not really?" Amber said cheerfully, "It's more like the strongest person in the dungeon would be within a hundred levels of the highest monster, maybe? Something like that?"

Tsunami sighed.

"Nobody really knows if that's how it works, but the general consensus is that it has something to do with the total level of everyone in the grey room." Tsunami said clearly. "Standard practice is to take a rough estimate of how strong the ally group is and then apply that to the enemy as well."

Elliot frowned, immediately seeing a problem with that, the dungeon with the bark-goblins had something like twelve hundred enemies, but there had only been a couple of hundred allies. There were clearly lopsided team sizes involved somehow that would skewer the level distribution massively.

"If you added up the total level of everyone in this room at the start, what was the assumption you made?" Elliot said evenly.

Amber grinned at the question.

"Sixteen people, nobody looked like they were in the two-hundreds, so we were probably the strongest here, so around a thousand total levels max?" Amber rattled off again, and Tsunami nodded in agreement.

Both of them had no problem with answering a few questions, apparently, so he pushed his luck.

"What level was that red-thing at a guess, two-hundred?" Elliot asked evenly.

"Ugh." Amber groaned, "That thing was an outlier, maybe like three hundred?"

Level *three hundred?*

A thousand total levels minus *that* was seven-hundred leftover, divide that amongst the rest of the enemy creatures in the dungeon—how many was that? Seventy-three? If that was all of the enemies in the dungeon, the average level for each of them was only about level ten.

Was that how this worked? Or were there a bunch of level one monsters in the other grey rooms—Ones that were as new to this system as he was? It was purely speculation, but everything he learned would help him.

It hadn't escaped his notice that nobody else had appeared in the room during their discussion, despite the portal having being opened inside the dungeon for almost five minutes now. Elliot had a sinking feeling that the red thing had killed all of the others. Amber and Tsunami thought they were the strongest people there, and that red-thing was twice Tsunami's level.

None of the others would have stood a chance against it.

"Everyone else is dead," Elliot said evenly. "Aren't they?"

"Yeah, that thing would have gotten them all before coming after us." Amber said honestly, then blew out a frustrated breath."Fucking outliers, man."

It was the second time she used the term, but the meaning was clear with the context. Sometimes monsters appeared with a greater portion of the total levels, and they destroyed everything in their path. It might have been what had happened to the bulk of the group in the last dungeon as well.

If there *were* other grey rooms for each of these monsters, Amber and Tsunami were probably considered outliers to most of *them* with their absurd levels.

"I overheard you both talking earlier. You were hunting something," Elliot said quietly. "Are you a part of a larger group?"

Tsunami raised a thin eyebrow at him, but Amber just grinned again.

"Naughty! Don't you know it's rude to eavesdrop?" Amber laughed, "We're part of a monster-hunting faction, Lion's Arc."

Elliot simply nodded, but Tsunami must have guessed he hadn't known about it because she expanded on the statement.

"We hunt specific monsters for materials and common drops," Tsunami said pleasantly, "We get paid to run multiple dungeons a day and fill quotas for the shops in the city."

"Which is code for going into the dungeon over and over again, hoping we run into the right type of monster." Amber laughed before shaking her head again. "A fucking outlier on my first one back, how unlucky!"

Tsunami nodded in agreement.

"If you're still alive when you reach level one-hundred, you should look us up. That's the minimum requirement to join Lion's Arc," Amber said happily before stepping forward to pull him into a hug. "Thanks again for the save."

After a frozen moment where he couldn't believe she was touching him so casually, he swapped positions with Tsunami, leaving the shorter girl trapped in the tight hug. Elliot quickly made his way to the exit.

"Hey!" Tsunami cried in surprise.

Amber's laughter followed him through the gate and back to the endless plain.

Elliot sat down at the edge of the world and watched the stars—He didn't think he would ever get tired of this view.

He wondered how people could be confident enough just to walk up and hug a stranger. The idea of doing something like that made him shy away from the thought. They seemed like interesting people despite Amber's apparent lack of physical boundaries.

He'd learned a lot this time—The existence of outliers was terrifying, random creatures of a high level that got matched against far weaker ones. It was like a broken match-making system in a video game, where you fought the top-level players at level one.

It was also something he could strive to *become*.

If he raised his level enough, would every dungeon he entered result in him being the outlier? Or would the system adjust and match him with higher-level creatures instead? The word 'outlier' meant something that was outside of the normal expected range, and they had treated it like it was quite rare.

If that was the case, then the system probably adjusted to match you against what is considered to be an equal playing field, in total levels if nothing else.

A thousand total levels and a thousand level ones seemed unlikely, but a thousand total levels with an average of level twenty? Or thirty? That was something like fifty people—that seemed like it might fit the situation.

Elliot heard the footsteps and felt the distinct signature of the two women as they appeared, but they were only outside for a few seconds before they stepped back through the Tori.

If the system did work at least somewhat like that, the existence of a level three-hundred was daunting. What was the range of levels *it* had usually been matched against? Three-hundred to four hundred? How high did it go? If the level system didn't scale with experience and it was always a flat thousand exp to level up, the only limiting factor on how strong you could grow would be either a level cap or that you were eventually killed by something else.

How long had this system been in place? Were there ancient, undying creatures with levels in the thousands? Even higher? Things that had chosen to stay in the system rather than escape it with a token? Who was the strongest being at the top?

Elliot felt his skin tingling at the thought; it was almost like a hidden ranking system in, one that you could climb, fueled by the deaths of monsters. Despite the fear and high possibility of death, he couldn't help but feel excited at the prospect of climbing it.

Elliot had always wanted to be something, something that didn't feel like he was only *pretending* to fill a role as if he had only *tricked* people into thinking he was capable of it without having the skills to back it all up.

Everything in his life had felt like that to an extent.

He'd somehow tricked his friends into liking him back in the old world because why would someone choose him to spend time with? He had no sought-after qualities that they couldn't find elsewhere. Elliot felt as if he had tricked his teachers into passing him, that he'd tricked his boss into hiring him despite his complete lack of skills.

Elliot couldn't bring himself to think the next obvious thing he had tricked himself into and how that had fallen apart entirely. It hurt too much to think about, even with his flattened emotional spectrum—all of it just brought him back to that ledge that lingered, everpresent in his thoughts.

Maybe he could actually be something here if he climbed that death ladder to power. If he could become the strongest being in this system, then nobody would be able to say he tricked his way into power—maybe he would even believe it.

Elliot closed his eyes, took a deep breath before he let it out slowly over the course of a minute, feeling his shoulders drop as the breath slowly left him, and when he had no air left to give, he opened his eyes again and looked at the stars below.

That would be his primary goal, for now, to become the strongest being in this system, and he wouldn't settle for anything less than that—because he had nothing else.

Elliot returned to the room, and he spent a long minute at the door firming his resolve. Less than a second after he had knocked on the door, it was swung open from the inside, and Hannah stuck her head out.

"Elliot!" Hannah said happily and dragged him inside by the arm. "You were gone for a while."

Most of his focus went to the hand encircling his wrist before he stepped back towards the wall—Hannah let him go, and Grant sat up on the bed swinging his legs over onto the floor.

"I went back into the dungeon," Elliot admitted

"You actually went back in again?" Hannah said quietly.

Grant studied him for a moment.

"I thought you would," Grant admitted, "Hannah thought you wouldn't."

"Yes," Elliot said simply, sitting back against the wall and rubbing at his eyes. "I've learned some things about this place, but I can tell you that afterward, I need to sleep."

"Alright," Grant agreed, "I can wait."

"Elliot, you *shouldn't* go in there without—" Hannah said worriedly before she cut herself off. "We would have come with you."

"I didn't want to have to convince either of you to go in again," Elliot sighed before he lay down facing the wall. "It seemed easier to just go in by myself; I'm not used to being around others anyway."

There was an awful period of silence that followed his comment, and he gritted his teeth to help weather it; he should have just stayed silent.

"*Elliot—*" Hannah said quietly.

The bed rustled slightly, and she cut herself off. The invisible social pressure slowly faded away from him over the next couple of minutes and disappeared entirely when the other two began to talk quietly amongst themselves about the old world.

Eventually, Eliot fell asleep to the sounds of Hannah's quiet laughter.

Some amount of time must have passed while he was asleep, but he couldn't tell how long without access to a clock. Eventually, something rustled for a moment on the bed, followed by a squeak and he pushed himself up into a sitting position.

Grant was still asleep on the floor, one arm and leg sticking underneath the bed with his head on one of the two pillows in the room. Hannah, on the other hand, was sitting on the bed with her feet curled up beneath her. He noted that her shirt was askew and currently showing an alarming amount of her chest as she rubbed at her eyes with her hands.

"Morning," Hannah managed through a yawn. "Elliot."

Elliot managed to drag his eyes away from her mostly bare chest long enough to force himself to meet her sleepy gaze and fought back a yawn of his own, the gesture almost contagious.

"Morning," Elliot mumbled, averting his gaze from her entirely when he failed to keep his eyes from drifting downwards again.

"I feel bad that I was the only one who got to sleep in the bed," Hannah admitted. "How bad was the floor?"

Elliot huffed out a quiet laugh.

"About as comfortable as you would expect," Elliot said quietly, "I don't mind, though."

Hannah giggled.

"We decided on bed rotation last night after you went to sleep," Hannah said, smiling, "We can take turns with the bed, so it's fair."

Elliot just nodded at her; he didn't mind either way. He would probably just rent another room when one opened up here anyway. Hannah crawled forward across the bed, and her shirt hung open at the front, so he turned to stare at the door since his self-control was apparently nonexistent this morning.

Hannah climbed off the bed and stretched, with her arms high in the air.

"What's the plan for today, Elliot?" Hannah yawned again, distorting the words, but he got the message well enough. "Dungeon again?"

Elliot wondered if this was going to be the start of another rift between the three of them.

"Yes," Elliot said evenly, "I plan on going in several times today. I want to reach level ten as soon as possible."

"Level ten?" Hannah said curiously before she sat down next to him on the floor, shoulder to shoulder. "What level are you now?"

Elliot barely managed to avoid leaning away from her and felt uncomfortable by the pressure of her arm and leg against his own.

"Six," Elliot said nervously.

"Six?" Hannah said curiously, leaning closer towards him. "I'm still level four."

"O-okay," Elliot said in agreement, unable to think of what he was supposed to say.

"You're so shy," Hannah giggled. "It's strange that you're so brave as well."

Elliot didn't think it was that strange, and he knew that he wasn't brave either. There were things he wanted, and he knew the ways to get them. This was just forcing himself to carry things out; there wasn't a hint of bravery involved in the process.

"I'm not brave," Elliot said quietly, "You and Grant are brave. I'm just..."

Elliot trailed off, unwilling to complete the sentence and unsure which word was the most fitting.

"Well, *I* think you're brave," Hannah teased and nudged him roughly with her shoulder. "You calling me a liar?"

Elliot glanced down at where Emma's hand that had slipped down to grip the top of his thigh.

"No," Elliot said flustered, "Just mistaken."

"You're blushing!" Hannah teased, "Are you sure you're level six? That seems more like something a level four would do."

Elliot scoffed at the silly comment before looking away entirely, staring determinedly at the opposite wall again. All that accomplished was a small squeeze of her hand and another giggle at his expense.

"Stop picking on Elliot, you scarlet woman," Grant said tiredly as he pushed himself into a sitting position. "Unhand that man."

Hannah started laughing.

"You're just jealous I'm not picking on *you*," Hannah said impishly.

Grant laughed brightly at the comment.

"Sorry, sweetie," Grant said confidently, "You've got the wrong parts to tease *me* like that."

"Hmph," Hannah complained, but it was easy to see that she was trying to fight down her smile.

Elliot did his best to ignore the playful banter, but the hand that was still resting dangerously on his thigh was making it very difficult to dis-associate himself from his surroundings.

"What were you guys talking about?" Grant wondered as he stretched, his back let out a large satisfying crack at the motion, and he groaned.

"Going back into the dungeon again today." Hannah said quickly, "Elliot says he's going several times."

"You sure that's a good idea?" Grant asked distractedly, looking under the bed for his missing shoe. "The reasoning you gave for going again so quickly was for resources, but you must have gotten some yesterday."

Elliot nodded, a topic he was more comfortable speaking about. Hannah still hadn't removed her hand, and every little movement was pulling at his attention—was she doing this on purpose?

"Yesterday, there were two high-level people in the dungeon I went into, Amber, a level one-hundred-ninety, and Tsunami, a level one-hundred-sixty-eight." Elliot said quietly, "They fought and killed something they described as an 'outlier' with an estimated level of three hundred."

Grant gave up on his shoe and turned to face him, looking much more serious than a moment ago. Hannah just tightened her grip on his thigh.

"It was fast enough that I couldn't follow it with my eyes," Elliot said gravely, "I'm not comfortable remaining this weak for an extended period of time when I could be working on getting stronger *now*, which means I'm going to be doing several dungeons a day until I don't feel as vulnerable as I do right now."

"I'm scared too," Hannah said quietly, and he felt her thumb brush his leg. "But I don't think I can go in that many times; I really don't want to go back in at all."

Elliot understood how she felt because this place was definitely terrifying; he could easily agree with that. That wasn't enough to put him off his task because he had already pre-committed to this decision. He wasn't going to go back on that unless there was an extremely valid reason why he should.

"An outlier," Grant said thoughtfully, "Did you learn anything else?"

"They were part of a faction called Lion's Arc, for level one-hundreds and up that hunt specific monster types in the dungeon for profit." Elliot recounted, "They also mentioned that the dungeons have some kind of equality to them, in that the total levels of the 'sides' are roughly equal."

Grant looked interested in that, while Hannah looked more interested in the first part.

"Can *we* join a faction?" Hannah asked hopefully, "Not that one obviously, but there must be others, right? That guy from yesterday mentioned them as well."

Elliot was already thinking of creating one himself, eventually at least, but it was dependant on him being strong enough first and to afford the token as well, at a hundred thousand gold. It wasn't *that* far off; he was already a tenth of the way there. He didn't feel comfortable with the idea of joining another group whose aims he didn't know either.

"That's a good idea," Grant said thoughtfully, "We should definitely join one of them. It would be a source of additional information as well."

Elliot found himself once more in disagreement with them both. These factions decided upon their own rules and enforced them upon the members. Amber had been a prime example of this, with her words implying that she had somehow been pressured into staying out of the dungeon for a period of time as a punishment of some sort.

He wasn't ready to give up his relatively little freedom and autonomy to someone just because they managed to save up for a token. Elliot didn't mind helping them find somewhere to join, and they were perfectly within their rights to make that decision for themselves, but he had no intention of joining himself.

"Mm!" Hannah said happily, "We should ask around about the factions."

Elliot kept his silence instead of starting another argument.

"I'm going to get something to eat," Elliot said quietly.

With a final brush of her hand, Hannah finally removed it, and he quickly pushed himself to his feet.

"I'm hungry too!" Hannah smiled.

"Hold on; I still can't find my shoe—" Grant said in alarm as he scrabbled under the bed.

Elliot waited out in the hall for them both to emerge.

The roads were as full of life today as they were the day before, and his first goal was to head for food stalls he had seen during his previous passes through the city. Elliot studied all the fruits, vegetables, and other more prepared meals, wondering idly if this place had a name.

Each of the stalls had a separate owner, and each of them had a trading stone visible. Elliot wondered where all the variety of foods had come from—apples were available in the system shop, but everything else here wasn't.

Were they growing these somewhere outside the city? or maybe they were taking them from the dungeons?

Elliot bought a bunch of bananas, six apples—somehow cheaper than the system shop price, which was more evidence towards other of obtaining food existing—and four skewers of some unknown, cooked meat, stashing all but one of each in his inventory.

He waited nearby as Grant and Hannah both searched through the stalls and bought their own preferred foods. He turned to look at the massive Torii in the distance, easily visible even from inside the city.

While he had refined his long-term goals slightly, his short-term goals were still all over the place; Elliot wanted to create his own faction, which would cost one-hundred-thousand gold—he needed to stop spending more money when he didn't need to.

That was short-term goal number one, earn a hundred thousand gold and buy a faction token.

Goal two was to find better equipment, but it was a much muddier task because of how broad the price range was for weapons. Aestus had told him that the 'Rare' classification could range from Ten-thousand gold at a minimum to one million gold at a maximum.

He could break that down to a weapon upgrade every hundred-thousand-gold, plus the resell value of the weapon if he could find a vendor to take it. There was always a chance he might find something better in the dungeon as well.

He needed to make sure to keep his weapon as relevant as possible because his strength score was basically nonexistent, so the only damage upgrade he was going to get was from a better weapon.

The armor situation was a more difficult decision—his attributes and skill were already starting to lean heavily into a natural speed build, with a focus on evasion rather than outright defense or damage reduction. As he'd seen with the horrible red creature, the problem was that even a glancing hit could be debilitating. So a decent set of armor was probably a good investment even if he didn't plan on getting hit if he could help it.

All three of these goals required that he started farming gold, and the best way that he knew how to do that at present was to open the secret chests. At five hundred gold per chest, it would end up being a non-trivial amount.

If he were lucky, the other people in the dungeon would kill everything; then, he could remain relatively undisturbed.

If this had been a game and the risk of danger hadn't been real, the optimal way would have been to actually kill everything as soon as possible and *then* run around the dungeon to find all the chests to maximize the completion time multiplier effect. But this wasn't a game and killing things brought with it the risk of being killed in turn, which was a failure condition for obvious reasons.

Anette had also mentioned that if you stayed too long in the dungeon afterward, a boss would spawn, and he had no intention of testing that out anytime soon.

Elliot shook his head; there was still so much he didn't know. He would stick with finding the hidden chests for now.

They stopped to eat, lingering in the marketplace before slowly making their way back to the dungeon. Almost the entire time, the conversation centered around factions, and Elliot had done his best to remain out of it.

He would have been content to listen until they managed to make a decision on what they were going to do. But in the end, Hannah managed to drag him back into the conversation as they reached the edge of the city.

"Elliot," Hannah said nervously, "We should find out about the factions first. There might be an easier way to do this that we don't already know about."

Elliot tilted his head at the comment—it seemed much more structured than how she normally spoke, almost like something Grant would say.

A glance over at the guy showed him conspicuously looking away from them and studying a building that was entirely uninteresting.

This was getting old very quickly—Looks like this was where he would have to speak up.

"I have no intention of joining a random faction and subjecting myself to whatever rules they've decided on." Elliot admitted quietly, heart thudding in his chest at the social confrontation, "I completely understand why you would want to look into them, and that's fine. You should go ahead and join one if you think it's the best decision for you, Hannah. Nothing is tethering you two to me, and you certainly don't need my permission to make the decision or to go off on your own. More than that, you don't need me to come with you while you do it—because we barely know each other...."

Grant turned back to watch him, openly frowning. Hannah herself was wringing her hands together and looked upset.

Elliot *hated* things like this—he always felt pressured by others to explain himself, as if just having an opinion that ran counter needed to be justified. He'd noticed over the years that most people didn't share that problem; they seemed to be able to just say what they thought and leave it at that.

Elliot's anxiety levels continued to creep upwards, a thousand counters to his own argument spilling through his head and a sudden realization that they must think him so stupid—he forcibly pushed everything to the back of his mind and locked it all away.

He opened his eyes a moment later, and the color had once more fallen away from the world.

"Different goals, different experiences, different mindsets, it's perfectly normal for us to come to different solutions," Elliot said evenly, feeling nothing at all. "I think by now, it's become pretty clear that I'm not good at dealing with social stuff or interpersonal conflicts like this, so this is where we are going to part ways."

Elliot crushed the tiny spark inside of him that told him he was making a terrible mistake.

"It's probably better this way anyway because if you stick with me, I'll only end up dragging you both down with me." Elliot said quietly, "So... thanks for sticking with me this long when you didn't have to—it was almost like having friends again."

Hannah had started crying quietly at some point during his over-explanation, but Grant just watched silently.

"Hannah, Grant." Elliot said quietly, forcing himself to say their names, "Sorry, I'll see you around. Don't die."

Elliot turned around and walked away.

His death grip on his mind broke down as he left, and the color bled back into the world. Elliot clenched his eyes shut to try to lessen the stinging. His willpower was tested further as Hannah let out a sob behind him, but he forced himself to keep on walking.

He walked the long winding pathway at an even pace, and the Torii grew larger as he came closer. He climbed the stairs and stepped through the pane of white without pause.

The Grey Room looked much the same as it always did, and he moved towards the fog wall to distance himself from the quickly growing crowd of people that were already inside. Elliot studied the people there, trying to find patterns in the group that might tell him what the future might hold for him.

There were a substantial amount of people without armor, which he thought might skew the dungeon towards having a lot of weaker enemies, but it could always tilt the other way, with a smaller amount of higher-level elites on the enemy side.

Elliot counted them all several times but had to keep readjusting his numbers as more appeared. There was something like thirty people who must have been level one, fifteen people with what looked like non-system-shop equipment. The standouts were the seven much better equip people spread out across the room.

There was one bald man in the corner with a massive glowing Warhammer on his back who looked almost gleeful—he must have been another of the ones who enjoyed killing the monsters.

All the first-timers and the non-shop equipment probably landed at a minimum of somewhere around level one-to-five, so one-hundred total level there. The seven better-equipped people he had no idea about but put them at level fifty each for an estimation. Which brought him to the last guy, who looked about as well equipped as Anette had in that first dungeon, so somewhere in the multi-hundreds.

That left him with an estimate of seven-hundred-and-fifty total level as a minimum and one-thousand total level as a maximum.

The existence of the out-of-place guy with the Warhammer meant he was potentially an outlier, so the enemy teams would either have an additional three hundred total levels to divvy up, raising the average level of the enemy team or it could just mean that the enemy teams had their own multi-hundred level monster running around.

If there were roughly a thousand total levels per team and less than a hundred people here, he should be able to work out a rough estimate of how many teams were participating in the round once the dungeon was complete.

Once the dungeon reported how many enemies there had been—for instance, six hundred enemies defeated would mean far fewer teams than fourteen hundred enemies defeated; if he did this for multiple rounds, he might be able to establish at least a minimum amount of teams that participated in each round.

It wouldn't be *accurate*, but it would be helpful as a guideline, regardless.

The timer was finally starting to wind down, so he had to adjust his total-level estimate slightly with each addition, merely adding a number that seemed likely for the new person.

Each time someone entered, the timer got closer to zero before resetting, and the man in the corner became more eager. Even from across the room, Elliot was beginning to think there was something deranged in the man's expression.

Elliot tried to piece together why the man was acting so openly bizarre. The man had no one with him that looked like a companion, and people had actually begun to move away from him as they noticed his laughter.

It had become quite obvious that the man was obviously the strongest person in the room, likely on the entire field if there wasn't a matching outlier. He didn't seem excited to leave the room, or he would have been closer to the hidden door.

He wasn't even looking in its direction; he was watching those near him. His twisted expression brought back to Elliot the warning that Anette had given him.

Don't trust anyone outside of this room, and don't trust anyone inside it either.

Elliot tensed as he realized something terrible was going to happen. What benefit was the man deriving from being present in this dungeon while also being the likely most powerful?

Nobody would try to get in the man's way—Was he planning on making everyone fight the boss by force or something?

When the timer finally reached zero, the man tore out the tunnel with a ferocious speed as he dragged a person along with him, and it became clear what he intended to do. He was planning on killing every single person in the dungeon—including his allies.

Because there was nobody here that could stop him.

The Lonely

A brave few of those who had been standing closest to the crazed man tore off after him in pursuit. None of them looked prepared for what they were about to face. The seven remaining higher leveled people looked worried, far more informed of the danger they were currently in. The newest amongst them began pushing their way out the door after the guy, hoping to help.

Six of the seven high-level people stayed exactly where they were, staring around at each other with wary eyes. The seventh, a man with a greatsword, moved to stand in front of the door before turning to face them.

"He's going to kill everyone." The man said seriously, "I'm going to need your help, or he's going to kill us afterward."

"Fuck that," A man snapped, holding a pair of ill-matched scimitar, "I'm not stepping a *single* foot outside of this room while he's out there. We wait him out in here; he won't stay forever."

"It's true—we can't take damage in the grey room, so he can't kill us while we remain in here." A woman said hesitantly.

She wore a long black dress split at the thighs, a matching wide-brim hat, and held a pole with a complicated assembly of metal at the top—a staff perhaps? Elliot shook his head and focused on the situation—he hadn't known that you couldn't take damage inside here.

It didn't matter, though, because he'd already shown that you could carry someone outside by force—just because he couldn't damage them inside the grey room didn't mean he couldn't *harm* them.

"He can simply walk in and take you back outside when he's done with everyone else unless you're strong enough to stop him ." Elliot said evenly, "And there are far worse things he might do to *you* in particular if it comes to that—he wouldn't even need to leave the grey room first to do it either."

The woman fell silent at the words, looking stricken.

"It'll assist you in killing him," Elliot said quietly, moving towards the man at the door.

The woman cursed under her breath before stomping over to join them. None of the others moved for a long moment before the other woman sighed, this one equipped with a thin rapier at her side; she stalked forward, her black leather coat swishing about her thighs.

The man with the greatsword reached out and clapped Elliot on the shoulder gently and waited a moment longer, but none of the other three men in the room made a move to join them.

"My name is Arte," Arte said easily. "Level One-hundred-fifty-three, Strength, defense, speed, magic."

Elliot frowned; his estimate had been wildly off on the strength of this man. He had him pegged at around level fifty. The introduction was strange but informative, and the woman with red hair in the dress spoke up quickly.

"Meri," Meri said quickly, "Level one-hundred-twenty-nine, Magic, speed, defense, strength."

The rapier woman spoke up next.

"Sara," Sara said calmly, "Level one-hundred-forty-six, Speed, strength, magic, defense."

Arte turned to look at him, and Elliot sighed. The pattern had coalesced into what was obviously their individual attribute growth spread, and he appreciated the conciseness. Arte was a tank, Meri was a mage, and Sara was an evasion-based fighter.

"Elliot," Elliot said deadpanned, "Level six, Speed, and then the rest."

Meri turned on him in disbelief, but he simply stepped past the three of them and into the tunnel. Unwilling to deal with the questions about his low level—how come this kept on happening? Elliot stepped out onto the sand and was blinded for a long moment before he was able to take in his surroundings properly.

Sand dunes were all that existed as far as he could see; they were in a desert. The bodies of the unaware littered the sand, body parts crushed or torn off entirely. Uproarious laughter could be heard over the dunes to his left, but it was mostly muffled by the screaming.

People were fleeing in the opposite direction, but the man would get to them eventually, Elliot knew.

Elliot swapped with a lump of sand to his left and almost let a sigh of relief out that it worked. He could feel the sand as a continuous mass beneath him, but it felt different than the forests he was used to. He wouldn't be bereft of his power after all—it was probably more effective here than anything.

The voices of Arte, Meri, and Sara echoed up behind him as they rushed to catch up. Elliot stared down at the chaos beyond in horror. The bulk of the people had to of come this way... because there was even more dead here than at the entrance, and the killer was slaughtering them without any apparent effort on his part.

The bald man spotted them in passing, acknowledging them with the eyes of a predator before he went back to work, prioritizing killing as many of the lower leveled people first.

Elliot swapped within twenty meters of the man and pulled his drill-tip spear from his inventory.

"Listen, this is your only warning," Elliot said evenly, already committing himself to what he was about to do. "You need to stop this, now."

The man let out an insulting laugh before he spun on his foot and pushed off the sand towards him—the particles were sent away from the man at the force.

Elliot could feel the adrenaline surging through him, and everything seemed slower than usual. The bald man was somewhere around Amber in terms of speed, and he already knew he wouldn't be keeping up with the man as he was now.

Elliot swapped out of range the instant the man had turned and sat crouched in the sand as the man swung his head around to locate him once more. He noticed the others coming down the dune first and started moving towards them.

Sara, the woman with the Rapier, was actually *faster* than the man they were fighting. He watched her flittering to the side of each strike. She slashed and stabbed at his wrists and fingers, trying to dislodge his grip on the Warhammer, but her attacks merely glanced off his armor, doing no real damage.

Arte was struggling to keep up with the man's speed, desperately blocking and swinging in an attempt to slow him down. He did seem to be able to at least deflect the man's attacks with his greatsword, but it was clear he fell far below the man in physical strength.

Meri suddenly exploded.

Elliot swapped positions far behind her and realized quickly that she hadn't actually exploded. She had unleashed a massive ball of fire at the man, and it was growing the further it traveled. When it reached the man's position, he came rushing through it with no visible damage, fire tearing uselessly at his grinning visage as he pushed through the flames.

Elliot once more smoothly slid into the role of support as he switched out with his temporary allies, pulling them out of danger and then evading the man's attack by swapping places with more of the never-ending sand.

The man was getting angrier by the second as he failed to land a killing blow on anyone continually robbed of every finishing blow. But Elliot could see that he wasn't slowing down at all, and after his frustration had reached its peak, his Warhammer was lifted up high into the air.

The man roared and smashed it down on the ground; a wave of crushing force created an intricate design in the sand, and then it exploded—All of the sand in the area was immediately sent high in the air obscuring everything from sight.

Elliot lost track of the man with his eyes but could still feel him moving with his swap-sense—the man was almost upon Meri, who was still stationary, waiting for an opening to attack. Just as the murderous man cleared the outer edge of the still falling sand, he found her missing once more.

Elliot deposited her at the top of the dune and then swapped next to her.

"Thanks!" Meri said, panting from fear.

Meri gesture down at the killer with her staff, and the twisted metal prongs at the end of it crackled with Lighting. A runic circle appeared in the sky, far above them, and then Lighting tore through the air to slam into the man below—the first solid hit of the fight.

It seemed to do some damage this time because he leaped screaming and blackened toward her from the bottom of the dune, with his weapon raised high above his head. He twisted and then flung it forward in a vanishingly blur, directly at Meri.

Elliot swapped with the weapon in mid-air, reaping its forward momentum and arresting his own, and for a moment, he was left spinning in mid-air. He swapped again, appearing beside the massive weapon as it tumbled out of the air and onto the sand.

Elliot reached out and inventoried the Warhammer. The man roared, armor blackened and his fury running hotter then the fireball that decimated his landing zone. He swapped places twice more, using the moment to move Arte behind the now weaponless man just as he landed on the sand.

Arte looked bewildered at his sudden positional change but wasted no time in lashing out with his greatsword. The thick blade, more of a slab of metal than a sword, carved a massive rent into the back of the killer's armor.

He followed through on the swing, rotated, and went in for a second attack at the same location, but the man turned, pushing forward into the attack before it could land, and tackled Arte to the sand.

They grappled for a moment before the larger man snatched his wrist in hand. Arte tried to disengage, but the man clamped down on his wrist and squashed the armor flat against his skin.

Arte screamed in pain—and then Sara was suddenly within range of them both. She unleashed a series of vanishing stabs at his face, and the man staggered backward, covering his face with his gauntlets and weathering the attacks.

Elliot watched it all with intent eyes.

The only place he had bothered to guard so far was his face, no doubt because his armor was far stronger than whatever bonuses his defense gave to his bare skin or his eyes. The man's desperate retreat changed suddenly, and he moved the palm of his hand in front of the next attack from the Rapier.

It pierced straight through the less armor section of his gauntlet and out the back, puncturing the metal. It lodged there, and he clamped down on it, shattering the weapon with a cry of triumph and pain.

Sara had no option but to disengage from him now, no longer able to deal damage without her weapon, but she easily got out of range of the man, her speed far greater. Left without an immediate target, he turned to face Arte, where the man was furiously trying to rip the mangled bracer off his arm.

Elliot swapped next to Meri again and spoke quickly.

"I'm going to get him up in the air." Elliot said concisely, "You hit him with that lighting spell again."

"Go," Meri said worriedly, her staff already crackling with Lighting once more.

Elliot appeared just in the killer's line of sight, a dark blur in his peripheral vision. The man turned quickly and found nothing as he vanished, appearing behind him in a crouch. He stabbed forward with the spear, and it glanced off the armor with a shower of sparks, leaving nothing but a scratch in the finish.

The man blurred, but Elliot had already swapped further away again and dug one of the many stones he had pilfered from the forest out of his inventory. Elliot appeared next to Arte, who had finally managed to get the bracer off and was three potions deep in an attempt to heal the terrible wound.

"Arte, throw this up as high in the air as you can," Elliot said seriously, "I'm counting on you."

Elliot swapped back within range of the killer and had to swap again to avoid the sudden mad dash as he came after him.

"Stop running away, you thieving fuck!" The man raged, "I'm going to fucking *skewer* you on that assholes sword—I'm not going to leave until every single one of you cunts are dead!"

Elliot could feel the stone leave Arte's hand, surging up into the sky with unnatural strength.

"No hard feelings," Elliot said quietly.

The man stepped towards him aggressively, more in the act of intimidation than anything else, and Elliot swapped places with the stone far above them.

The world spun lazily around him, pulling at his clothes as the air dragged against him, and for a moment, he could see that the desert stretched on seemingly forever. In the distance, he could see the remainder of the lower levels that had run away, chasing a group of neon orange things too distant for him to make heads or tails of.

Just an endless plane of sand and a massive runic symbol burned into the sky, shuddering with unreleased energy. His viewpoint continued to spin, he saw a spread of scattered glints amongst the dunes, and then he saw the fighting far below him—Arte desperately avoiding the man who was now armed with his greatsword as Sara played interference as best she could without a weapon.

Elliot swapped places with the monster that had tried to kill them all.

He appeared on the sand next to Arte and immediately had to swap away from him to avoid the man's committed attack.

"Sorry!" Arte called out, panicked.

Elliot turned to stare up at the top of the dune where Meri stood.

Yellow light was surging around the tip of her staff, and the circle above them flickered as Lighting began pouring out.

The man, still falling, was struck in mid-air, and after almost five seconds of continuous blinding light, the spell finally faded. The blackened remains fell limply through the air and crashed headfirst into the sand with a crunch of metal and bone.

Elliot made no move to check on him; he wasn't falling for any of that pretending to be dead shit—He turned, intending to advise Meri to strike him again, but she called out first.

"I got the drop!" Meri cried happily, "He's dead!"

Elliot felt like that couldn't possibly be true, with the amount of buzzing energy in his system and how his eyes were still flashing around the battlefield, finding locations to swap with next. He realized that his hands were shaking, his grip around the spear white-knuckled and painful. Even his breathing was labored, and when he took a breathe, it felt like the first he'd taken all day. He tried to still himself, to force the shakes away, to reach some measure of co-existence with the world, but it only grew worse.

The adrenaline and panic overwhelming him, and his vision blurred for a terrifying moment—he spun away as Sara came towards him, and he forced himself to lower the shaking spear he'd brandished at her.

"It's alright, Eliot." Sara said calmly, "Breath, you're hyperventilating."

It took most of his effort to listen to her, taking in a series of deep breathes and letting them out as slowly as he could. He could feel the humiliation and shame of having something see him like this—in the midst of what had to be a panic attack.

He almost reflexively swapped again as Arte and Meri reached them.

"Holy shit!" Arte said, amazed, "We're *alive!*"

The man let out an ear-ringing shout of excitement, stabbing his fist up into the air.

"Did you see that light show!?" Meri cried in amazement. "I've *never* charged anything up that much before."

Elliot let the voices wash over him and finally felt himself start to calm, their happy energy taking away the edge of hysteria he was feeling—So much had just happened in such a short amount of time...

"Level fucking *six*, you are *amazing!*" Arte said, amazed, as he clapped Elliot on the shoulder. "Thanks for the saves, man."

Elliot still flinched at the touch despite seeing it coming, but Arte seemed to take it in stride and patted his arm once more before removing his arm.

"I thought I was *dead* when he got near me. I fucking *love* you," Meri confessed as she flopped backward onto the sand in relief. "Oh my *god*, all the shit I've gone through to be almost killed by *that* degenerate, I can't believe it."

"Keep breathing," Sara insisted quietly, and he realized that he'd gone back to holding his breath.

Elliot followed her quiet advice as he listened to the three of them talk, and eventually, he got himself under control enough that he could manage to speak.

"Is your arm alright?" Elliot asked quietly.

Arte's mangled bracer was covered in blood, and it still hung from his arm, partially attached to another plate. Arte clapped his hand over where the wound was to show it was undamaged and flexed his arm.

"Good as new, just had to get the armor out of the way for the potion to work properly, gotta love those things," Arte said, relieved, before glancing down at his arm. "I might buy armor that's more easily detachable in the future, though—that's definitely near the top of my three most painful experiences."

Elliot managed to hold himself back from asking what had topped it and found himself remembering the reason he had come here in the first place. Along with the events that preceded it... At least Hannah and Grant hadn't been dragged into this mess, even if they probably hated him now.

He'd spotted several chests when he'd been in the air, and he turned to face the direction he thought the largest spread had been. His gaze landing on the top of a distance mound—he opened his mouth to state his intentions and found Sara staring at him steadily with a glint of worry in her eyes.

Elliot couldn't deal with the pity anymore—he fled, appearing on the distant dune before glancing back at them. The three of them moved to locate him, but he turned and orientated himself before swapping out to the next dune. He kept going until he spotted the flicker of white light through a distant dune.

A few swaps later, and he was standing next to the chest and staring down at it thinking.

If he'd gone with Hannah and Grant to investigate the factions in the city, what would have happened here? Would everyone in the dungeon have been killed? Would it have gone unreported, with the only survivor keeping the dark secret to himself? Arte, Meri, and Sara probably would have all died, but why did the thought bother him so badly? They were strangers whose existence was even further distant than Hannah and Grant.

Why did he feel like he had developed a connection with all of these people—when he had barely spent any time with them? Elliot had closed himself off from a lot of people in the last year, as everything that had brought him any joy had just fallen away.

He found in his possession a complete lack of interest in creating any new connections with people he *had* tried despite it, on the advice of others but in the end, he had let it fade away like everything else in his life.

He had spent a grand total of one day with Hannah and Grant, but he felt like he was closer to both of them than anyone from his old life. There was a similar connection already forming with Arte, Meri, and Sara now as well.

Was this how it was going to be for him now? Would he meet someone amid terrible atrocities and then develop a one-sided connection with them before they wandered out of his view once more? Elliot wiped at his eyes for a moment and kneeling down to open the chest.

He couldn't think of anything that sounded more lonely.

Secret Found: 1/100
Loot Gained: 500 Gold, 1 Uncommon Rapier, 1 Uncommon Horned Helmet, 1 Uncommon Horned Pauldrons.

"So there were individual armor pieces after all," Elliot murmured, staring at the word *Rapier* for a long moment before he sighed.

Elliot slowly made his way back to where he left the three and found them missing, so he made his way back towards the entrance instead. He found Meri sitting by the door, fanning herself with her hand and sweating profusely in her far too tight dress.

He averted his eyes.

"It's you!" Meri cried before fumbling for his name. "Uh."

"Elliot," Elliot said simply, "Where did the other two go?"

Meri looked embarrassed to have forgotten his name already, but strangely enough, he couldn't find a part of him that cared any longer.

"They went to look for the others. All the tracks led that way," Meri said flippantly, gesturing in the direction he had seen the distant group. "I'm *totally* done for today, *fuck* this dungeon; I'm going to go get drunk instead."

Elliot found himself amused by her attitude despite himself.

"I'll go speed things along then, so you can get out of here quicker," Elliot said wryly before turning to look at where the tracks led.

"Oh, you are *such* a sweetheart!" Meri cooed as he vanished.

Elliot appeared up on the hill, doing his best to ignore the warmth in his cheeks, and scanned the desert before swapping to the next high point. Movement on his far-left caught his eye, and he found what looked like Arte, cresting a dune and vanishing.

A moment later, and he was looking down at him and Sara.

"Sara," Elliot said quietly.

Sara spun around with blinding speed and then paused when she realized who it was, while Arte stumbled two sinking steps into the sand in his attempt to spin around. Elliot opened his inventory and removed the Rapier before staking it into the ground in front of him.

"I don't know if you had a replacement, but you can have this if you want." Elliot said evenly, "Are you still following the tracks?"

"You came back!" Arte said happily, "I was wondering why you suddenly ran away, but yeah, this desert is really big though, it's going to take forever to find whoever's left, and we haven't even *seen* another team yet."

Sara moved forward to take the Rapier and inventoried it before humming and retrieving it once more.

"Thank you, it will do for now," Sara said pleasantly.

Elliot just nodded and removed another stone from his own inventory, holding it out to Arte.

"Aerial view?" Elliot suggested.

The man blinked before the realization hit him.

"I fucking love you, man." Arte laughed.

The aerial view did provide him with a visual of the missing group; they were still following after the distant group of Neon-Orange things, apparently too slow to catch them. He also spotted another flicker of white in the vicinity and made a quick detour to flip the latch on the chest.

Secret Found: 2/100
Loot Gained: 500 Gold, 1 Uncommon Horned Bracers, 1 Uncommon Horned Chest Piece, 1 Uncommon Horned Leggings.

Elliot swapped back to his original position next to the others.

"Anything?" Sara asked quietly.

"The only group I can see is following several orange things in that direction," Elliot said, gesturing in the direction he had spotted them. "They can't seem to catch up to the monsters."

"Let's go then before they get any deeper into the desert," Arte groaned, trudging up the dune.

Sara and Elliot both fell in step beside the man as they ascended.

"Does this kind of thing happen a lot?" Elliot said quietly. "The man with the Warhammer, I mean."

Sara glanced at him out of the corner of her eyes.

"People killing their own team?" Sara asked steadily, "It's not uncommon; I've seen it happen three times since I found myself in this place."

Arte let out a noise of effort as he stepped onto the top of the dune and scanned the area.

"Six times for me." Arte said distractedly, "None of them were anywhere near as strong as Svent, though."

Svent, Elliot thought quietly, the name of the man he had helped kill.

"You knew him?" Sara said carefully.

Arte noised out an affirmative before beginning his descent down the next hill, and they followed him once more.

"He's actually a pretty famous member of the Crushers," Arte admitted. "They are a bit of an infamous group."

"What type of faction are they?" Sara said thoughtfully, "I don't usually keep up with faction politics."

Elliot found himself intrigued at the direction the conversation was headed.

"High-level group who runs dungeons for profit, more or less." Arte said simply, "I suppose they fall under the Dungeoneer classification, but it's really just a group of really strong melee guys."

"Why was he soloing?" Sara murmured to herself.

It seemed obvious enough to him why—Svent had found a disturbing niche where he could farm gold and items. Elliot stared up at the dune in front of them with resignation; he was getting sick of sand already.

He swapped the three of them up to the top in a series of quick exchanges.

"Whoa!" Arte said, amused, "I suppose that beats walking."

Elliot scanned the desert and then moved them all to the next dune and then once more before stopping.

"You should start a delivery service!" Arte laughed, "That would be hilarious; I don't think I've seen a faction like that yet."

Sara snorted at the comment.

"That would be a terrible waste of such a useful ability," Sara said, annoyed, before gesturing. "That must be the remaining group."

Elliot watched as the group sat in the shade of the dune, looking tired and sweaty. One of the people spotted the three of them, and then they were all moving to get their weapons out.

"Don't come to any closer, assholes!" The woman closest to the front shouted, waving her ax at them.

Arte stepped forward without fear, with his hands held up placidly.

"We managed to take down the bald guy who was killing everyone; we aren't here to fight you," Arte said easily. "Which way did the monsters go?"

"I don't give a shit about what you're saying, dickhead." The woman said angrily. "Stay over there!"

"Fine, fine!" Arte laughed, "Relax."

"The monsters went that way." Another man near the side of the group said helpfully. "We were hoping we could kill them and make the portal appear before that guy found us, but they were too fast to catch."

Elliot nodded at the man; it was a good idea given the situation; Svent had been classed as an 'ally,' so killing all of the monsters in the dungeon should have spawned the portal; that's what he would have done in their position as well.

"How many did that murdering piece of shit get?" The woman at the front said darkly.

"There's three left in the room and our group." Arte said simply, "We'll go take care of the monsters; you should stay here until the portal appears."

"Fine," The woman said forcefully, "Hurry it up."

Arte laughed again at the order.

"Sure, sure," Arte said easily, "Elliot?"

He obliged and moved them all to the top of the dune, leaving the group behind them to let out cries of surprise at their sudden disappearance. Elliot was glad that there was apparently no cost associated with his swap ability because the number of times he had used it in this dungeon alone was ludicrous. Another series of swaps and another two dunes brought them in range to see the group of orange beasts clamor up the side of a dune.

They had the general shape of a bovine with clawed feet, but their faces were large bulbous things and with very human expressions on them. Wide mouths and large flat teeth lined their mouths, and two large round eyes sat close together in the center of their faces.

"I've seen these things before, their pretty common actually," Arte said easily. "Defense and speed are the primary stats; these seem relatively low level, though."

"I fought some in my last run as well," Sara said simply in agreement. "They attack by biting and will try to pin you down with their feet."

Elliot took the information in thoughtfully; what would high-level versions of these creatures be like? Incredibly fast and durable sounded like a horrible combination to come up against.

"I'll bring one of them over here, get ready to kill it," Elliot said evenly.

Arte immediately yanked his greatsword off of his back, and Sara's new Rapier appeared in her hand as they both turned to face him.

"Man, can I hire you?" Arte said, impressed, "This is so much easier than normal, except for the whole Svent thing I mean—"

Elliot swapped out with the one that was at the back of the herd and then moved up to the top of the next dune to get a better angle on the rest. He could see Arte cut the beast in half with his massive sword, and once they were ready again, he swapped a new beast near them before vanishing again.

It barely took them two minutes to kill the last of the creatures this way, and when Sara pulled her Rapier out of the last one's head, they were all unexpectedly swallowed by the light of the portal, dumping them in the Grey Room.

Dungeon Complete: 697/697 Enemies Defeated.

"Well, that was both the hardest and easiest dungeon I've run in a while," Arte said, honestly. "What the hell happened to the other enemy teams, though?"

Elliot nodded at the question—two hundred or so humans, and about half that in bovines. Where were the other four hundred enemies?

"There should have been at least five total teams, but we only saw the beasts and us," Sara said, sounding troubled. "The other three must have either killed each other or died because of the environment somehow."

Elliot took note of her comment about total teams; that was an important fact to file away for later consideration. Dying by the environment, however, hadn't even passed through his mind before this dungeon—they could have died in the desert without a source of water.

Were there other environments unsuited for humans that existed as a biome in this mess? Elliot turned his attention to the dungeon statistic.

Loot Gained: 2297 EXP, 2200 Gold.

Despite Svent's presence in the dungeon, his status as an outlier the fact that he had almost killed them all, there was *nothing* in the results screen to indicate it in any way.

Elliot stared at it intently; the lack of acknowledgment spoke of automation; a thinking mind would have noticed the massive spike in difficulty that had occurred and increased the rewards surely. The system either didn't think what had happened was a noteworthy event or was incapable of registering that it had occurred at all.

It made him smile—there were blindspots within the system, and while this one wasn't immediately useful to him, the existence of mistakes or weaknesses that hadn't been ironed out was a good thing because he might find one in the future that he *could* take advantage of.

People began appearing in the grey room eventually, the groups moving towards the portal at their own pace. Most of them hurried out of the room without even a backward glance—no doubt glad to be free of this strange place.

Another ten minutes passed before Meri appeared, looking tired and sweaty.

"Ah, there you are," Meri said tiredly as she came over to join the three of them.

"Managed to finally get off your butt, huh?" Arte grinned.

"If I never see a desert again, it will be too soon," Meri whined, ignoring the comment entirely. "Do you three want some of the loot?"

Elliot blinked at the question before his mood took another dive. All the equipment and money of the people Svent had killed, he didn't want *any* of it. Arte and Sara both didn't share his issue, and they divided it up between them, and when they offered him a portion, he just shook his head.

"You sure?" Arte said curiously, "You were pivotal in taking him down."

"Don't be shy," Meri said happily, "Things like this happen all the time here."

Elliot just shook his head again.

"I already took his weapon, remember?" Elliot said evenly. "That's more than enough for me."

Arte blinked.

"I'd forgotten about that—damn, you are one lucky guy." Arte laughed, "You should be able to make a massive chunk when you sell that."

He hadn't even considered what it was worth; he hadn't even checked his inventory to see what it said—not that it mattered.

"Once I sell it, I'll give you all a share." Elliot promised, "You know that tavern with the badly drawn dragon on the sign, near the city gates? I'll meet you there afterward."

Arte raised an eyebrow at him, but Meri looked pleased.

"Are you sure about that?" Sara asked quietly, "It will be worth a *lot* of money; you might want to rethink your decision to share."

The look of pity in her eyes had vanished at some point, and he simply nodded.

"I'm sure." Elliot answered, "Where is a good place to sell it quickly?"

"There's a place near the food stalls; the sign just says 'Weapons,'" Arte said bemused, "The guy there, Aestus, deals with some pretty top tier stuff."

Elliot nodded; it was the same shop he had bought his spear in; he knew where it was.

"Then I'm going there now," Elliot decided, "I'll meet you at that dragon place afterward—if you want a share, make yourself available."

Three affirmations followed him as he turned to leave the Grey Room; he almost immediately had to sidestep because the man with the two scimitars on his back appeared in the room.

"Well, well, well, if it *isn't* the pussy!" Meri said loudly.

Elliot stepped through the portal and made his way back to the city, feeling a sense of anxiety build within him the closer he got. He was worried he might find Hannah and Grant still standing where he had left them, ready to shout at him—but they weren't there.

He couldn't shake the feeling even after he had finally stepped through the doors of Aestus's weapon shop. Aestus was once again manning the counter like he had been the last time Elliot had seen him, and he glanced up as the bell above the door jingled.

"Back already?" Aestus wondered, "I haven't found any other spears yet, sorry."

"I've actually come to sell a weapon I found," Elliot said awkwardly.

Elliot opened his inventory for the first time and had a look.

"Yeah?" Aestus said easily, "What have you got for me?"

Elliot slipped through the menu until he found his inventory and found the weapon amidst all of the loot he had found.

Inventory: Legendary Warhammer of Wrath.

He spent a moment checking its worth and stared at the number in shock.

"Legendary Warhammer, value is twelve and a half million," Elliot said, "I'll sell it to you for ten million if you have it on hand."

The man had given him a discount back when he first came here, so he would return the favor—he'd never enjoyed being in other people's debt. Aestus's eyebrows shot up to his receding hairline at the amount.

"Where the hell did you find a Legendary?" Aestus said, alarmed. "Show me, don't hand it over, though."

Elliot removed it from his inventory and immediately sank to the floor under its massive weight—the head of the hammer cracked the stone floor, and he grunted under the weight, forced to put it back in his inventory or be crushed. Aestus started laughing at the sight, and Elliot caught a colored glint streak through the man's eyes as he studied the weapon.

"Twelve-million, five-hundred-thousand, five-hundred, and ninety-one gold," Aestus said, bewildered. "You weren't lying."

Elliot pulled himself back to his feet; this must have been one of the man's abilities to check the value of items somehow because that was the exact amount it was listed as in his inventory.

"Why are you giving me a two-million discount?" Aestus asked strangely, "That's pretty absurd; as long as I made a couple hundred thousand on it, I'd be happy at the profit."

"You gave me a discount already; I'm just returning the favor," Elliot said firmly, "Do you want to buy it?"

Aestus just shook his head in disbelief but pulled his trading stone out.

"Put your hand on it." Aestus said, bemused, "I gave you a *thirty gold* discount kid, it's clearly not the same thing."

Elliot placed his hand on the stone when directed, and Aestus cleared his throat.

"Ten-million-gold," Aestus said clearly, and the stone flashed.

Elliot checked his inventory and nodded.

Inventory: 10,008,968 Gold.

Elliot brought the Warhammer back out of his inventory, he struggled under the weight even after bracing for it, and Aestus reached out, snagging the handle and lifting it off the ground without effort. He studied it for a moment longer before it vanished inside the man's own inventory.

"I think you're my favorite customer," Aestus said honestly, "I'll have to start giving out thirty-gold discounts more often if this is the return I can expect."

Elliot hummed in amusement, but he was already thinking about equipment.

"Have you got an exotic spear in stock?" Elliot wondered, "And a full set of armor that's on that same level?"

Aestus nodded easily, and after a few moments of messing around with his own inventory, he found what he was looking for. A long metal spear appeared in his hand, with a small red braided cord hanging from the base of it; the tip was a triangular blade that glowed orange and tapered sharply to a fine point.

He turned his attention to the bundle Aestus brought out next. A stack of white and silver, segmented armor, with darker colored chain woven beneath the thin plates.

"Spear is one-point-two-million, armor is eight-hundred-thousand for the set." Aestus said easily, "I should be giving it to you for free honestly, you've more than paid for it already."

"Two million for both then?" Elliot said, ignoring the comment.

Aestus moved the trading stone back within range, and he completed the purchase before leaning down to inventory his new equipment.

Inventory: 8,008,968 Gold, Exotic Skypiercer, Rare Segmented Light Armor Set.

"Thank you," Elliot said quietly before taking a moment to equip everything.

The armor seemed to be a perfect fit, which was ludicrous and must have meant that it had reshaped itself to him when he equipped it. It was, however, pretty heavy overall, despite its classification as 'Light Amour.'

"And he thanks *me*." Aestus said, amused, "Thank *you*. Now, are you going to tell me where you found that thing?"

Elliot hesitated for a beat before nodding.

"A man with a really high level attempted to kill everyone in our dungeon; he got most of them." Elliot said quietly, "I helped a couple of level one-hundreds kill him, and I took his weapon during the fight."

Aestus whistled at the story.

"A dungeon killer that was also an outlier?" Aestus said in understanding, "People kill each other pretty often in there, but the combination is pretty rare. Did you find out the guy's name?"

"One of the other people called him Svent," Elliot said, wondering if he should be talking about it out loud.

Aestus blinked at that.

"Svent from The Crushers?" Aestus said seriously, "I've heard of him; there were some rumors going around recently about some fighting in the city between them and the Peacekeepers recently."

"Peacekeepers?" Elliot murmured the name.

"Another faction," Aestus said easily, "They stop fights from breaking out in the city and keep people from murdering each other as best they can. Figure themselves a police force of sorts—there have been several attempts by them to enforce laws on the place, but it never works out well. The other factions always start something up in return."

"Are there any requirements for starting your own faction?" Elliot asked.

"Just the token in the system shop," Aestus said easily, "I'm in the Merchants, so you're aware. You going to start one of your own?"

Elliot noted 'The Merchants' down for future consideration as well but nodded.

"I'm thinking about it," Elliot confirmed. "Thanks for the information, Aestus. I have somewhere to be now; I'll see you next time."

"No worries, Elliot," Aestus said easily before his voice turned more dramatic. "If you find any more Legendaries, feel free to bring them by, and I'll take on the torturous task of buying them for you—seeing as I'm such a nice guy."

Elliot snorted and gave him a wave over his shoulder as he stepped back out onto the street. He made his way back towards where he had seen the badly wrought dragon sign hanging. It was a pretty large building, even compared to the ones around it. It also had quite a lot of people inside; its proximity to the main gates apparently drew people to it like a moth to a flame.

Elliot scanned the room before he spotted Meri's bright red hair; she was sitting with both Arte and Sara, talking amongst themselves. Sara spotted him approaching and raised her eyebrow in surprise, possibly at the change of armor; he wasn't quite sure.

He paused next to their table and frowned, realizing he had a problem.

How was he going to give them their money? Did he just dump it on the table? That seemed rude; he needed one of those trading stones that some people seemed to have.

"How do you get a trading stone?" Elliot said awkwardly as they stared at him.

"You actually came back?" Arte said, shocked, noticing him for the first time. "*Again?*"

Meri started laughing quietly to herself, but Sara was far more helpful.

"You need to buy a House, Shop, or Faction token," Sara said steadily. "It comes as part of the package."

Elliot opened up the shop interface and bought the faction token he was going to buy anyway. Several items were deposited into his inventory, and he switched screens to look at them.

Inventory: 1 Faction Token, 1 Faction Settings Scroll, 1 Trading Stone.

Elliot removed the stone from his inventory and held it out to her. Sara stared at his hand for a long moment before placing her own hand on the trading stone.

"Two-million-gold," Elliot said evenly, and the stone flashed.

Elliot moved the stone over the Arte and held it out. Meri's laughter quickly descended into a coughing fit. Arte just stared at him.

"*Elliot.*" Sara managed, sounding strained.

Elliot shook the stone when Arte didn't immediately move to touch it.

"Two-million-gold," Elliot said before moving on.

Meri didn't even wait; she leaned bodily over the entire table, sending their drinks falling to the floor in her rush, and planted her hand flat on the stone. He repeated the phrase, the stone flashed, and he deposited it back into his inventory.

"Come here, sweetheart!" Meri said happily, "I want to kiss you!"

Elliot immediately stepped back from the table in alarm and waved to the three of them before heading back out of the door. Arte called out for him to wait, but he didn't hang around, already heading back towards the Torii.

There were still three dungeons left to clear before the day was over.

Interlude: Hannah Walker

Nothing ever seemed to go the way Hannah planned; it was like she was cursed. Things she thought were givens and people who were supposed to be there for her—none of it ever worked out.

Hannah had spent so many nights wondering if the problem lay with herself—but she'd put in so much effort, changed *so much*, and everyone else just seemed to be sitting still.

"What's your point?" Marlene said, barely listening.

"They are talking about possibly closing down schools—transitioning everything into online classes and stuff from home," Hannah said, frowning at the complete lack of interest. "What am I supposed to do then? I can't work while Serah's at home with me."

"I'm not sure I'd call what you do 'work' in the first place," Marlene snorted. "I don't know what to tell you, Hannah; figure it out."

Hannah felt her cheeks burn at the comment—why did she always have to say things like this? Would it have killed her to actually show some empathy for once?

"There's nothing wrong with my job, Marlene," Hannah said, pinching her leg hard to stifle her frustration. "Instead of taking potshots at me, can we actually have a discussion for once?"

Marlene scoffed.

"Flashing your tits to a bunch of creeps on the internet isn't a job," Marlene said, brushing her off. "Find a babysitter, or drop her off at daycare—it's not my problem."

Hannah brushed her hair out of her face in frustration, patience wearing thin.

"I didn't say it was your problem—God, you are such a bitch," Hannah said, reaching her limit. "Whenever you come to me for help, I always fucking help you—but as soon as I ask for anything, you act like a total cunt."

Hannah had to stop herself from listing off all the things she'd done for the older woman—all the times she had let her stay when she didn't have a house to go home to, without ever asking for contributions to rent or food—

"A sex worker calling other people cunts," Marlene said snidely, "Now I've seen everything."

Hannah flinched, and for a moment, she didn't know what to say—she felt like she had just reached an epiphany. All these years, all the things she'd done, Marlene had never appreciated any of it. It was all take and never give, all for her own benefit without ever thinking of someone else.

All that time and Hannah hadn't seen it for what it was.

"Fuck you," Hannah snapped, "There's nothing wrong with being a sex worker—and just because nobody wants to look at you naked doesn't mean I'm doing something wrong."

"What the hell is that supposed to mean?" Marlene said, offended. "Why are you getting angry—"

"Figure it out," Hannah hissed, hanging up in frustration. "Fuck!"

Hannah kicked the chair's leg in front of her, sending it spinning across the floor, and then slumped down against the cabinet, burying her head in between her knees. Her fingers dug into her hair, pressing hard against her scalp, and she sat there, breathing shallow breathes.

Hannah didn't move for a long time.

Hannah's Apartment, Saltwall City.
March 3rd, 2020, 5:35 PM

"All three of the grade-seven kids were pushing Joey around, and they were also stuffing the bark-stuff down his shirt," Serah said, frowning. "You know the stuff they put under the platforms, in case you fall off?"

Hannah frowned as well; the same three boys had been picking on him for a while. Serah had reported them to her teacher multiple times, but nothing more than a 'warning' had occurred, and the boys hadn't stopped the bullying.

"I know the bark-stuff—where was Albert?" Hannah asked curiously. "Aren't they usually together?"

Serah nodded, her frown vanishing.

"Albert went to the toilet," Serah said, snickering. "But he came back right in the middle of it—it was so funny, Hannah."

Oh lord.

"What did he do?" Hannah asked, failing to fight down her smile.

"Albert ran straight up behind the big one and kicked him in the nuts!" Serah managed. "You should have heard the noise he made—It—it was like a squeak and a groan—"

Serah descended fully into giggles, and Hannah grinned.

"And—and, he threw up!" Serah wiped at the tears in her eyes, "The other two grade-sevens chased him, but when they finally grabbed Albert, a teacher stopped them."

"Oh my god—Albert is a menace." Hannah giggled, "Did any of them get in trouble?"

Serah nodded, still grinning.

"All three of the grade sevens got written up, and Albert got detention for kicking him." Serah snickered, "But—but! Albert told the teacher that the detention wouldn't break his spirit because he was a tough nut to crack!"

Serah descended into peals of laughter, and Hannah couldn't help but follow.

Apartment, Saltwall City.
March 5th, 2020, 5:35 PM

Hannah leaned back on her hands, arching her back until it let out a satisfying crack. She eyed her phone out of the corner of her eye—they were getting low on just about everything now, and drinking black coffee was a punishment she wouldn't inflict on anyone, not even Marlene—if they were still talking to each other.

She used her toe to depress the mute microphone button beside the laptop and then scooped the phone up. The number was already in her contact list; she'd been getting groceries delivered regularly for years at this point, and they had a regular order in the system for her.

"Good morning, this is SWG; how can we help you?" A man's voice said pleasantly.

It was a new voice, and he sounded young—Hannah pegged him at late teens early twenties.

"Hi!" Hannah said brightly, "I usually get a bunch of stuff delivered every two weeks? My number should be in the system already—you'll probably need my name too."

"Miss," The man said apologetically, "I'm afraid we've had to stop performing deliveries."

"You're not delivering anymore?" Hannah said hesitantly

Nothing was going right this week—Hannah sighed.

"Not at the moment," The man on the phone said, "We have been shut down for a couple of days until we can get the zero-contact procedures perfect; we should be delivering again by the start of next week. If we fulfilled the order then—would it be too late?"

"Yeah," Hannah admitted, "It's fine; I'll just go down and buy the essentials for now. Eggs, milk, that kind of thing. I'll leave everything else to when you guys are delivering again."

"Sorry about that, ma'am," The man said genuinely, "We've had a lot of customers that don't have access to their own transport calling about the same thing. We have plenty of Eggs and Milk, but if you're looking for toilet paper, I'm afraid you're sh—uh. I'm afraid you're out of luck."

The man laughed awkwardly at the almost slipup.

"That's fine," Hannah giggled, "What time do you open tomorrow? Eight?"

"Yes, Ma'am." The man said sheepishly.

"Thanks for helping me," Hannah said, smiling.

"It was my pleasure," The man said, "Enjoy the rest of your day, Ma'am."

Hannah dropped the phone and fell back onto her bed, facing the laptop. It was only another hour before she had to pick Serah up, so she would have to go down to the grocer's tomorrow—if she did it early in the morning, she would only lose an hour of work.

Downtown, Saltwall City.
March 6th, 2020, 8:04 AM

Hannah pushed her trolley out into the car park and eyed her apartment building in the distance.

"Maybe I shouldn't have bought so much?" Hannah sighed.

It would have been fine if she could take the cart with her, but she could vividly remember Marlene telling her about how they set off an alarm if you took them out of the car park. Hannah bent down to check the wheels, and sure enough, there was a small black box attached.

It was possible that the box was a bluff, and it wouldn't actually go off, but if she risked it and it did end up having an alarm—it would be far too embarrassing to deal with that.

Hannah sighed, resigned to her fate, and rifled around in the trolly, hooking her fingers into the handle of each of the bags. Once she'd gotten two bags situated in each hand, she hauled them out with some effort and started off down the path, leaving the trolly to linger behind her.

A tall man walking down the path opposite saw her ditch the trolly in the middle of no man's land and glared at her—Hannah felt a flush climb up her neck and quickened her pace.

The plastic of the handles coiled into a tight thread that immediately started to dig painfully into the grooves in her fingers. One of the bags in her left hand was far heavier than the others, and it wasn't easy to keep it level.

Hannah fought onwards—she was pretty sure she could make it to her building elevator, and then she could have a short rest.

"Way too much," Hannah managed, straining. "Good job, idiot."

The smoke that had been lingering in the air when she first stepped outside was still present, and the distant sounds of sirens made itself known—it wasn't just a single one either; it had to be at least four of five sources.

Hannah wondered what had happened; the smoke had been there for a while now, almost forty-five minutes—it must have been a building fire. Try as she might, she couldn't see which building, but the smoke looked like it was maybe two blocks away.

Hannah stepped out onto the street, still looking high over one of the buildings at the smoke, and then the handle on the heaviest shopping bag snapped. The effort she'd been putting into holding it up made her arm surge upwards at the sudden loss, and she stumbled forwards, the toe of her shoe catching on the tarmac.

Hannah crashed onto the road knees first, failing to catch herself but desperately lifting her hand upwards to break her fall—a searing pain rushed up to her hand as she dragged it knuckle first across the rough, unyielding surface of the road.

"Fuck!" Hannah cried out.

Hannah cradled her bleeding hand, two of her fingernails were missing, and the largest knuckle of her right hand was showing the pristine white of bone beneath. The flesh of her hand was shredded, and blood was already welling up in the gap.

She was sobbing almost before she'd registered the pain and pulled her hand in close against her chest, desperately seeking to muffle the pain.

The rumblings of a large vehicle grew loud in her ears—

The Deep

Elliot watched the timer count down; it was already reaching as low as ten seconds which must have meant he'd entered later than most.

There was a large group of people standing together, with an assortment of equipment and weapons. Notably, each and every person in the group seemed to be wearing an armband with a few different prominent shades seeming to signify something, but he couldn't tell what. They must have been another faction who participated in dungeons as a group, unlike Tsunami and Amber's duo.

"To summarise for those who struggle with complicated directions," The leader explained, "Teams of three, don't engage large groups of monsters, retreat to the main group if your team gets wiped, and for god's sake, be careful."

There was a murmur of agreement from some and a few more ironic cheers from the more boisterous members.

"Remember, target the lone monsters first, pin them down and claim them; if there's two or three, leave one alive and kill the others." The man continued, "Don't try and claim several at once; it tends to end up with someone making a mistake and getting their team killed."

Another round of agreements, as the timer approached single digits.

"Any questions?" The leader offered before hastily clarifying. "If you ask me a personal question *again*, I'm kicking your ass, Lute."

"Damn." Lute said, "Cut down before my time; how could you be so cruel, Karm?"

"Any *serious* questions?" Karm repeated.

"Are we looking for anything in particular?" A cheerful-looking man wearing robes asked.

Karm turned towards the voice and smiled.

"You're the new guy—Stanley, right?" Karm stated and got an affirmative. "We aren't looking for anything specific this time, but if any of you comes across a Midas, a Healer, or a Maker, prioritize them over anything else."

Elliot ran the keywords over in his head for a moment; it sounded like he was talking about a classification rather than a species name.

"Are they common?" Stanley asked. "I've heard of Healers, of course, but not the other two."

"No," Karm said with a shake of his head, "A Midas is an enemy that can turn one substance into another, and a Maker is one who can create things out of nothing."

"Ah," Stanley commented, "I can see why they are considered valuable then. I'll keep an eye out."

Karm just nodded in agreement and turned towards the timer.

"Alright, get in your teams. This will be the last countdown." Karm ordered, "Be fast, be careful, and don't die, ready?"

The group let out another round of half murmurs, half cheers, and broke off into teams of three—with a single unit of four leftovers which might have been the 'main team,' he'd referred to. They formed up behind Karm while the other people in the Grey Room who weren't part of the faction shuffled around awkwardly.

Elliot moved up to stand behind the group; he would have to make sure to keep one of the teams within his range—in case he was chased by another monster while he looked for the chests.

A few members of the faction turned back to look at him curiously, but he paid them no attention, and when the timer finally hit zero, the door appeared. Karm led them out through, and Elliot noted that the temperature was dropping rapidly with each step.

Elliot could see why as he stepped out into the snow and quickly scanned the environment for the movement but found nothing.

The faction spread out in every direction, already moving away from the entrance. He set off on his own course, at an angle away from the furthest team on the left, the one with the man called Stanley and his two teammates.

It wasn't as cold as he thought it should be, and he felt that maybe his new armor had something to do with that, but even so, his breath came out as a mist, and the wind stung his cheeks as it whipped past.

Elliot stared around, wondering at the futility of searching for white light in a sea of white snow; if he found even a single chest this time, he would be pleasantly surprised. Regardless, he continued on his task, keeping Stanley's team at the edge of his range.

Walking was much harder than he had thought possible; he sunk into the snow almost with every step, and the effort of lifting his legs high enough to trudge through was slowly wearing on him already.

Once his legs started to burn, he began swapping forward in small bursts instead.

Something appeared on the edge of his range, on his left side, where none of the teams had gone—the obvious conclusion was that it was a monster of some kind. Elliot brought his spear out of his inventory, trying to search out anything he could about the signatures.

He hadn't intended to fight anything this run, but if he couldn't find any chests and didn't kill anything—he'd essentially put his life at risk for no reason.

The single larger humanoid signature was joined by two others, rounded in the middle with the wrong number of appendages. They quickly approached it from behind, and Elliot turned to squint in the direction he could sense them, but the snow had a varied elevation across the white field, enough that he couldn't see anything from his current position.

He made the decision to investigate and swapped just below the top of a snowy hill. He trudged the last couple of feet and peeked over the top—and for his trouble, he received a front-row seat to a battle between the two other teams.

The humanoid was roughly as tall as a human but thicker, and it had what looked like six arms that all ended in bladed talons. It was cloaked in a thin layer of brown fur, and it moved sluggishly in the snow as it desperately tried to fend off the smaller monsters.

Despite its size, it was nowhere near as physically powerful as the smaller things.

He shivered when one of them stopped moving, long enough for him to get a better visual. They were visually upsetting in a way he had never seen before. Looking at it felt wrong—like it shouldn't exist or that it couldn't possibly have come about naturally.

The closest approximation Elliot could think of to describe the alien creature was some kind of mixture of a squid and a spider with a thick-lipped mouth that covered most of its central body. The arms on the thing were long, thin, and they moved with a fluidity that disturbed him—and they were in the dozens.

They were throwing themselves around the snow with their long thin limbs, and one of them had already managed to get on the larger brown-furred things back, wrapping its many limbs around its head.

The furred monster fell back onto the snow and was desperately trying to tear it away from its head to no avail. The second squid-spider latched onto its legs and started dragging it bodily into its now gaping mouth, looking like it was trying to swallow it whole.

Elliot watched, frozen, as the furred thing was slowly eaten alive, unable to bring himself to move.

The furred creature struggled the entire time, but most of its lower body was somehow *inside* the smaller tentacle thing now despite the fact it shouldn't have fit. Its arms were growing weaker as it continued to fail at removing the other one from its face.

Elliot forced himself to stand up and took his spear in both hands.

There wasn't going to be a better time to attack these things than now, while they were locked down and trying to eat it. Elliot swallowed and steeled himself as he decided on the best order to take them out.

"Kill the one of its head first, then the furred thing." Elliot decided quietly, hoping the words would spur him to action. "The one eating it won't be able to move easily like that; it can be last."

Elliot took another deep breath and then swapped with the snow beside the creature's head, appearing without sound above it. He drove his spear down towards the Spidersquid's center-mass, and it passed through it without resistance, continued through the furred monster's head, and buried itself in the snow.

Loot Gained: 102 EXP, 102 Gold, 5 x Sleek Hide.

Elliot fell forwards, not at all braced for the complete lack of resistance, and found himself laying on top of the now-dying Spidersquid horror. The adrenaline, already trying to tear his heart from his chest, surged higher as his terror grew.

Loot Gained: 145 EXP, 145 Gold, 7 Bladed Claws.

Elliot swapped towards the other side, directly behind the second monster—his fear driving him to ruthless violence. He braced himself before stabbing downwards, the spear tip passing through the center of the second Spidersquid's mess of limbs.

It screeched in pain, having somehow survived the first attack, and Elliot drew the spear back—he'd stabbed it three times before it finally died, and the very second he saw the prompt appear, he removed himself from the battlefield, appearing on top of the hill once more.

Loot Gained: 93 EXP, 102 Gold, 8 Sleek Hide.

Elliot sat in the snow, watching the three bodies for a long time—there was no way he was going to approach them, even after he was sure they were dead. Three minutes passed as he caught his breath, and still, nothing moved.

Elliot left, moving back towards the team he'd been following—already wishing this dungeon was over. He stopped when they came into range, and another pang of fear surged in him.

There were eight signatures instead of the expected three.

Elliot felt so much resistance to the idea of going down there, even knowing they most likely needed help. He forced himself to move closer to the team, and eventually, he had the elevation needed to see what was happening.

Stanley was standing at the back of the team firing a series of fireballs at two of the Spidersquid's, but nothing seemed to hit—they were highly mobile, dragging themselves out of the way of each one with their vastly superior speed.

The heavily armored woman in the group was trying to set up a pincer on one of them, aiming to pin it between Stanely and herself. It never came about, as she had to contend with two more of the creatures as well. The last member of their team was an archer, and he couldn't help Anyone because he was desperately trying to pull his lower body out of another Spidersquid's gaping mouth.

Stanley seemed to evaluate the fight before turning and fleeing—leaving his teammates to their fates, two of the Spidersquid's went after him.

Elliot watched as the man crested the snowy hill and vanished—left without help, the armored woman was quickly overwhelmed by the two she was fighting. One of them had latched onto her upper body, doing its best to pull her head into its mouth as she tried to hold it—the second one was busy organizing her feet.

Elliot buried his fear and acted—appearing next to her and pressing the spear through the creature on her face, carefully killing it without taking her head off. It died from that hit alone, and the woman sobbed, doing her best to get air back into her lungs.

Loot Gained: 147 EXP, 147 Gold, 12 Sleek Hide.

The one trying to eat her legs lashed out at him with its many legs, but he hadn't stopped moving since he'd appeared, once more swapping directly behind the creature. He thrust the spear down through the center mass again, the spear staking the Spidersquid between the woman's ankles.

Loot Gained: 89 EXP, 89 Gold, 6 Sleek Hide.

Elliot turned back to the Archer—by now, the thing had gotten basically the man's entire body in its mouth. He switched out with another patch of snow and carefully used the tip of his spear to cut its face in two to free him.

Loot Gained: 129 EXP, 129 Gold, 7 Sleek Hide.

One of the things had apparently given up on Stanely, returning to prey on something less mobile. The tank woman found herself the target once more, still prone as she was on the snow, and when Elliot moved to kill it, he ended up slicing her upper arm in the process.

Loot Gained: 153 EXP, 153 Gold, 13 Sleek Hide.

The woman crawled away, openly bawling and fumbling to bring out her potions. She drank them as quickly as she could manage. Elliot thought briefly about going after the last one—the one that had gone after Stanely, but he couldn't bring himself to give chase.

He stared down at the Archer. The man's legs—and basically everything below his shoulders was just gone. The snow was growing red now; he'd been wrong. The creatures hadn't just been trying to swallow him whole—it had been eating him as it went or dissolving him in some way.

"Fuck." Elliot cursed, sitting down in the snow beside the remains. "*Fuck* this place."

Killer teammates, disturbing creatures, and death—this place really was hell.

"You have enough health potions?" Elliot managed—he wasn't going to ask her if she was okay. "Do you need help moving?"

"I can move...." The woman sobbed. "This wasn't supposed to happen."

Elliot pushed himself to his feet and stumbled over to her in the snow. He reached down and patted her armored shoulder once—the thick metal plate made the gesture far less intimate and easier for him to manage.

"I know, but you can't stay here." Elliot said quietly, "Come with me; I'll take you back to your group."

The woman sobbed something that might have been an agreement, and Elliot helped her to her feet.

"What's your name?" Elliot said quietly as he led her back towards the entrance.

"Michelle." Michelle managed.

He wanted to ask what the Archer's name had been, but it would only be opening a fresh wound.

"I'm Elliot," Elliot said evenly.

They walked through the snow in silence, with only the sound of rushing wind and the occasional of emotional torment breaking through. The entrance came into view in the distance, and they angled back towards it; all of this snow was making it difficult to orientate himself.

Michelle had begun to pull herself back together by the time they returned, and he took a chance in asking her a question.

"What's the name of your faction?" Elliot asked.

"Menagerie," Michelle mumbled.

Better than anything he would have come up with for a name, Elliot thought. He stopped next to the doorway that was floating in the middle of the snow.

"If I leave you here, will you be alright?" Elliot asked hesitantly.

Michelle actually looked at him for the first time and shook her head.

"I know you aren't in Menagerie, but you shouldn't go off on your own." Michelle mumbled, "Please don't leave me here on my own."

Elliot nodded hesitantly and moved to sit down on a nearby boulder.

"Thank you," Michelle murmured.

"It's fine," Elliot answered.

It *was* fine; Elliot had no interest in running into any more of those creatures—he'd done more than enough for one dungeon. They fell into silence, and Elliot keep a careful watch on the surroundings, but nothing came into his sensory range.

Eventually, to the distant north, the portal appeared, spearing up into the heavens through the snowfall, the light reflecting harshly off the white.

Dungeon Complete: 749/749 Enemies Defeated.

Michelle moved to follow him towards the portal in silence.

"I'm sorry about your friend," Elliot said belatedly. "He was dead before I could get to him."

Michelle ducked her head for a moment.

"He wasn't my friend," Michelle said quietly, wiping any lingering wetness from her cheeks. "I only knew his name—it was Jacob."

Elliot just nodded and decided it was better that he just kept his silence from now on; he'd never been good at this kind of thing. They reached the portal without any more words exchanged between them, and they both left the field of snow behind them.

Loot Gained: 2607 EXP, 2874 Gold.

He noted with some degree of trepidation that the dungeon had only been a C rank difficulty.

The vast majority of Menagerie was already inside the grey room, and three of the other non-members appeared within a minute, but Stanley was nowhere to be seen. Michelle murmured a parting thank you before she slowly made her way over to her faction, eyes locked on the ground.

Elliot watched her go without comment before he turned and made his way to the exit once more; he moved behind the Torii to sit at the edge of the world and think.

This place continued to surprise him with horrifying situations and even more disturbing beings with every additional dungeon. Was it going to be this way forever? Elliot had a feeling that it wouldn't last *quite* that long—eventually, *he* was the one who would end up not coming back.

Jacob the Archer probably hadn't thought this was the dungeon that he wasn't going to live through; Surrounded by the members of his faction and well equipped—it had probably seemed like a normal run for him at this point.

After a thousand clears, Elliot wondered if he would have the same attitude as that man he had spoken to. Would that be *him* in a month? A year if he survived that long? Killing for the fun of it, for the incremental increase to his power, that seemingly continued ever higher.

Would it be wrong if that was how he turned out? No matter how resistant he was to the idea, he would be forced back in after a week, so no matter if he did it willingly or by force, he would have to continue.

Elliot wondered what happened to those who died in the dungeons. Would Jacob be reborn somewhere back on earth? Or would he arrive back in the grey room after a period of unknown time, changed perhaps, and a tale of how he died on his lips? Something else?

Elliot had no way to tell—but what he did know was that he had two more dungeons to go.

It was that much harder to go back into the dungeon this time, the fear and stress weighing him down—He knew that those disturbing creatures would greet him in his dreams.

Four dungeons in one day had been a complete overestimation of his mental fortitude. Still, he'd never broken his pre-commitment before, and he wasn't going to start now. If he did, then it would just become another useless tool in his arsenal.

If it breaks once, it will break the next time again too.

Elliot stepped through the Torii—the very second he was inside the grey room, and the decision had been made permanent, he found himself settling. There was no going back once you were inside; all he could do now was press on.

The removal of options was somehow a comfort to him. To think he would learn something about himself here—he'd have to remember that for the future, the fewer options he had, the more actionable he became.

Elliot found himself in the midst of a small crowd of people, several hundred at least, and most of them looked like they'd done this many times before—with full armor sets and every manner of glowing weapon.

It also made no sense when he actually stopped to think about it; where had all these people come from?

Elliot had been sitting next to the gate for the last half hour, and *nobody* had even approached it, were they all pulled in at once, their individual time limits ran out? Or were there actually other ways to enter the Grey Room beside the Torii?

Were there *other* Torii in the endless plain floating amongst the stars? Elliot realized he had never even considered the idea before.

He'd figured that the other species had their own Grey Rooms, and if that was the case, they must have had their own Torii. What was there to say that there wasn't more of them here? There *must* have been for the number of people who were inside without passing through behind him.

If there were other Torii, were there other *cities* as well? This new world seemed suddenly much larger than he had initially concluded.

The timer was already in the single digits, and Elliot realized that he was one of the latecomers this time, one that had arrived just as the timer was coming to an end. Elliot tried to estimate the total level of the room but found it impossible with so many people moving about.

He found his attention flittering around to the standout members of the crowd.

There was an absolute *giant* of a man only meters from him, bigger than even Svent had been by a head and a half, one of the tallest and most muscular people he had ever seen—in both of his lives. The cheerful smile on the man's face put him at ease; he was practically *radiating* good-natured cheer; the giant had a mop of unruly blonde hair dangling from his round head.

The man met his eye with a smile, and Elliot felt a pang of embarrassment for staring.

"Hello, young warrior!" The man said happily, "I am Jacque!"

Elliot found himself flustered by the suddenness of the greeting and fumbled for the appropriate response.

"Nice to meet you, Jacque," Elliot managed, unable to match the man's energy, "I'm Elliot."

"A fine name, Elliot!" Jacque said boisterously, "Are you prepared for the trials ahead?"

"No," Elliot admitted evenly, "I have no idea what might be waiting this time, but I doubt I'll ever be prepared for it."

"A good answer!" Jacque said thoughtfully, voice loud. "All we can do is push forward! Do not lose that sense of caution, for overconfidence often leads to a man's downfall!"

Elliot just nodded as the timer hit zero and the door opened; they both turned towards it, but the crowd in the tunnel suddenly stopped moving, and the voices were getting louder in a wave back towards them.

Elliot eventually heard the words, 'water,' 'no land,' and 'in the air,' and felt a growing sense of unease in him. Nobody was leaving the room; in fact, they were pushing back inside and talking amongst each other.

"Curious!" Jacque said thoughtfully, "I wonder what the problem is, young Elliot?"

Elliot wanted to know as well; lacking information was an easy way to die.

"I'll be right back, Jacque," Elliot said politely. "I'll find out."

"Very well!" Jacque said cheerfully.

Elliot swapped with someone who was near the end of the tunnel but not too far in and slid around the last few people to get a good view out of the dungeon entrance.

Water.

That was it, the doorway was floating about ten meters above it, and the water just stretched on endlessly; Elliot stared down at it with unease. There was nothing to stand on, no land, no debris, nothing, just water.

Elliot moved back up the tunnel and then swapped with someone who was standing on their own before pushing his way back to where he could see Jacque standing.

"Elliot!" Jacque said, seemingly intrigued, "You suddenly disappeared! How interesting, did you find anything?"

Elliot just nodded, getting used to the man's volume.

"The door to the dungeon is floating above the ocean; there's no land anywhere in sight, just water," Elliot said evenly. "Nothing to stand on. Everyone will have to swim."

"I see," Jacque answered. "Which means we will all need to take off our armor, leaving us defenseless. A daunting task for many, most of all those with low defense attributes."

There was another wave of conversation about several people who had apparently gone into the water. Elliot frowned in thought; he could swap with the water to move around quickly, but if he ever stopped, he'd be taking a swim, and it was likely to be *freezing* given the complete lack of land.

"Oho!" Jacque said suddenly, looking at something across the room that he couldn't see. "Seems like there is a Maker here!"

A Maker, Elliot thought, someone who could create something out of nothing—the question was, what exactly were they making? Elliot struggled to see what the man was looking at but eventually caught sight of something brown.

Wood? Were they trying to make a boat? Or a raft, maybe?

"Let us move closer, Elliot!" Jacque said cheerfully.

Elliot followed in the man's wake as everybody either moved out of his path or was gently moved aside by him. Eventually, the man called something out and stepped up next to the tunnel where the group was working.

"-Platform, if we get enough of these, this guy here says he has an ability to lock the elevation of it above the water." A woman said, smiling as she tied two of the large rectangular pieces of wood together with some wire to make a large square. "It's going to take a little while, though; you want to help me tie these together?"

The woman had a confident smile on her face, shoulder-length brown hair, and a sharp gaze. The man who would be locking the elevation was blonde, with his hair shaved down to almost nothing.

"Of course, miss!" Jacque said happily, "Elliot, let us assist these fine people with their task!"

"My name's Jane," Jane said dryly.

Elliot found himself suddenly inside the circle as the big man gently pushed him inside before he moved in himself. Elliot stared around at all the people watching him for a moment before dropping his gaze to the floor.

There was a small stack of wire in front of her, and a line of wire was emerging from the tip of her index finger—Jane was also a Maker, it would seem.

The gazes of everyone around him felt like a physical pressure weighing down on him—every time he looped the wire around the wood, he felt as if he was being judged a thousand times over for his poor technique, and he felt his anxiety building to a fever point.

"We will need to move them through the tunnel one at a time and then lower them down to the water first," Jane said, looking completely at ease even with all of the attention on her.

"What we really need is to find someone who can get me down there," The blond man said briskly, "Because I'm not getting in the water just to be able to reach it—Names Marcus by the way."

Jacque shouted out another welcome to the man before turning to face the crowd.

"Attention, friends!" Jacque called, "Is there anyone with the powers of object levitation, telekinesis, or the ability to fly?"

Elliot winced at the mans booming voice—busying himself with tying off another one of the panels. A response to Jacque's call washed back, countless voices repeating the question to each other a hundred times over.

"Clear the way!" A woman's voice called from several meters deep in the crowd. "I can move objects remotely!"

The crowd parted to let the young woman through, and she was soon sitting cross-legged in the circle with them. Elliot spent a moment to memorize her feature—cropped black hair styled in a pixie cut, a small button nose, and only about five-foot-tall at best.

One of the most petite adults he'd seen in recent memory—her presence next to Jacque's massive frame only accentuated that fact.

"How big are we going to make the platform?" Pixie-cut asked after they filled her in on the plan.

The stack of panels had already grown to half a hundred as more and more of the crowd joined in on the process. They'd begun focusing on tying the panels together in lots of four, creating a single larger square panel that a person could stand on comfortably.

"More room, the better," The older man who was making the panels said, "Costs nothing to keep making panels except time—suppose we keep going until we have enough room to fight on."

"How big are we talking, old man?" The pixie-cut woman said idly. "Boat? Football field?

The old man snorted at the title.

"Rude little shit—names Steven." Steven reprimanded and got a smirk in return. "The size of a football field sounds like a decent point to aim for. Can you lock that much in place?"

"There is no discernable limit on the number of things I can lock simultaneously, and these are all under the size limit," Marcus explained, frowning. "Even so, unless we stay at this for several hours, we aren't going to make something big enough for *all of us* to fight on."

Jane nodded at that.

"We need to play this smart then—sending a smaller group out to fight the enemies to save on space," Jane said, "Anyone wants to volunteer for the fighting team? The more, the better—if one gets wiped, we are going to have to send another."

Elliot had already decided he was going to go outside—this was the second dungeon in a row where he had no access to the chests. He certainly wasn't going to go swimming to find them—more than anything else; he needed to earn more gold.

Jacque spoke up before he could.

"Young Elliot!" Jacque said cheerfully, "Will you join me in battle?"

"Yes," Elliot answered, nodding at the man.

Jacque reached out with a massive hand and patted him on the shoulder before turning to the crowd again to begin the loudest recruiting drive Elliot had ever heard. A great deal of the crowd was backing away from the massive man.

"Fuck!" Pixie-cut complained, sucking on a bleeding finger. "Stupid wire. Quiet-guy, what level are you?"

"Eleven," Elliot said evenly.

Pixie-cut caught herself mid nod and snapped her gaze up to him.

"Eleven?!" Pixie-cut yelped. "Why the hell do you want to go out there?"

Elliot ignored the question entirely, moving onto the next panel; the stack was growing larger by the moment. They would soon have to start moving them down to the water and locking them in place—to make room if nothing else.

Several people had come forward to stand with Jacque now, all looking like they were exceptionally high level. He couldn't help but compare their glowing weapons and elaborate armors to Jacque's more simple equipment.

His armor was minimal and made from a smooth grey hide rather than the metal most of the others were wearing. Notably, he didn't have any visible weapons on him, which didn't mean much, given he could be storing them in his inventory as many others did.

Elliot wondered what level the man was.

There was two woman wielding glowing bows, while a third woman held a massive greatsword. Beside them was a man with a long wavy sword that ended in a point, and the last man was carrying what had to be the longest Katana he had *ever* seen before, at least twice as long as Jacque was tall.

It looked ludicrous.

"Alright!" Jane called, "Let's get these finished panels to the exit and down to the water—Pixie, that means you're up."

Pixie-cut scoffed at the nickname.

"My name is *Claire*," Claire said, annoyed, as she stood up. "You heard her assholes! Let's go!"

Elliot pushed himself to his feet, retrieving two of the four tiled panels, and made his way through the cleared pathway to the door. He followed the others to the tunnel and placed his panel down onto the stack that was piling up by the edge. He checked outside, but nothing had changed, and there was no movement to be seen.

Claire reached down and touched one of the large panels, and then it lifted up off the ground entirely on its own. It floated away from her hand, vanished over the edge to hover roughly a meter above the still water.

Marcus frowned, pointing out the obvious problem with the idea.

"I need to touch it—I can't do that from up here." The man said, annoyed. "How do I get down? If you think I'm jumping in the water, you can all get fucked—"

Elliot swapped with the top of the water directly next to the floating panel, quickly stepping onto it before he could fall into the water.

"Whoa!" Claire said from above, sounding strained. "Almost went for a swim there, Eleven! Weight is an issue for me, you know—warn me next time!"

Elliot snorted at the nickname before swapping places with Marcus. Claire grunted as the much heavier man send the panel wobbling.

"What the fuck?" Marcus yelped, flailing.

"Just freeze it already!" Claire gritted out.

Claire sighed in relief a moment later, the tension bleeding out of her features.

"Done!" Marcus called, annoyed, "Bring me the next panel!"

Elliot checked; the man was standing squarely on the slightly mis-aligned panel, completely without issue. Claire moved the next panel down for him to take, and Marcus froze it once more. They repeated the system for almost ten minutes.

"Hey, Eleven," Claire said, "Can you get me down there? He's getting too far away."

Elliot took one of the panels off the stack and tossed it out of the tunnel, watching it spin towards the locked platform below. Just before it hit, he switched with it, canceling the momentum and dropping the last foot of distance to the floor.

Elliot swapped with Claire from his new position, depositing her on the platform below.

"Thanks!" Claire called up to him.

"Elliot!" Jacque said cheerfully. "Is there anything we can do to assist you in the meantime?"

The big man's team had been joined by another woman, a mage this time judging by her green robes.

"Jacque, can you each pick up a stack of the panels?" Elliot asked evenly. "We need to start moving them down for Marcus."

"Of course!" Jacque said happily and picked one up.

Elliot tossed another panel off the edge, repeating his swap system, leaving Jacque on the platform below carrying, hands full of panels.

"Thank you, Elliot!" Jacque called from below.

Elliot glanced back to make sure the next of the combat team was ready before moving each of them down one after another. They continued the process over the next hour, the platform slowly growing in size, and still, not a single enemy had shown itself.

Steven must have had some degree of control over the shape of the wood he produced because a rough ladder showed up strung together with tightly wound wire. Marcus returned long enough to lock it into place below the tunnel exit. The addition freed Elliot up from transport duty, allowing him to join them on the platform.

He noted how very strange it felt for such a ramshackle platform to be so perfectly steady in the air—there wasn't any give in it, not even when he jumped. It was like solid ground for all intents and purposes.

Elliot spun in a slow circle and once again felt that sense of unease at the complete lack of any land in sight. Wherever this place was, did it even *have* a landmass? Or was the entire planet just water?

There had to be something surely; how else would the air be breathable if only water existed here? Was this more proof of the dungeon's artificial nature? Biome's that didn't make sense when considered on their own? Or was there some other mechanism at work here?

"This is pretty cool," Claire said from behind him, and he turned to study her. "It would be nice to just fish here or something; relax for a while, you know?"

Elliot almost smiled at the strange direction the woman's thoughts had led her. They were in the middle of a death game, and she was thinking about fishing? It was ludicrous.

"I think the cool thing here is that we all worked together," Elliot said, voicing his own opinion. "It reaffirms how strong humans are and that with a small bit of cooperation, we can solve complicated problems."

"Yeah," Claire wondered, "That *is* pretty cool—what's your name anyway, Eleven?"

"Elliot," Elliot said evenly, "You're Claire, right?"

Claire nodded before a voice called something out—they turned to find the combat group readying themselves. Elliot scanned the skyline and found several dark shapes in the distant sky.

"They're pretty small." Claire said, "It could be birds?"

Elliot turned to look at her in disbelief.

"It *could* be!" Claire argued.

The distant 'birds' grew larger as they approached, and details became easier to see—they were flying humanoids, covered in feathers and equipped with dangerous natural claws. They surged downwards, swiping at the team as they passed, and Elliot readied his spear. There were too many to keep track of easily, but the two of them were lucky that they were so far back.

The others that had been milling around by the ladder fled back to the Grey Room without comment, and—Somewhere below him, deep down in the water, at the furthest edge of his swap range, Elliot felt something move.

Elliot's gaze snapped down to the wooden platform below him with wide eyes, adrenaline surging up inside him. The signature skirting the edge of his range vanished, and then he no longer had any time to think as the feather attackers surged downward again. The combat unit couldn't hold its tight grouping anymore, and they scattered across the platform in running fights against the creatures.

There were so many fights going on that he didn't know where to look—he saw Jacque, and the man fought like a force of nature, leaping impossibly high up into the air; he snatched one of the flying creatures by the face, laughing all the while.

The man's momentum changed somehow as he surged downwards with a jarring speed and pulping the creature's head against the platform in the process—the previously immovable wood panel shattered like glass beneath the force.

The entire platform rolled under the force but managed to hold, sending the stacks of loose panels scattering everywhere.

Elliot couldn't split his attention any longer as one of the closer creatures bodily crashed into a man, tackling him to the ground in a burst of feathers. Elliot swapped with one of the many loose panels littering the platform to appear behind it, spearing it through the chest and dragging it off the shouting man with a grunt of effort.

The bird-person flailed in agony, its winged arm colliding with Elliot's face. He stumbled backward away from it, and the spear slid out of its chest with a sickening sound of wet flesh. It tried to take off but crashed into the platform, unable to gain any lift—it dragged itself away from them, slowed, and then fell still.

Loot Gained: 143 EXP, 143 Gold, 15 Feathers, 2 Talons.

"Thanks." The man croaked as he took out a health pot.

The man's face and chest were a mess of cuts and blood where the bird-person had savaged him with its claws. Elliot didn't reply. Instead, he turned back to where Claire had been, swapping in to assist her against another of the things.

"Die, you feathered fuck!" Claire screamed.

Fire streamed out of the staff she now held, her stat growth now obvious as someone who was magically inclined. The wave of fire washed forward in the air, raising the temperature in an instant.

The bird-person was immolated, but it did nothing to stop its forward momentum—Claire screamed as the now flaming monster crashed into her chest. The two of them were send tumbled in different directions.

One of the creature's legs got trapped between the panels, arresting its momentum in an instant and practically ripping the leg off at the hip. Claire reached the end of the platform, and Elliot swapped out with her before she could skate off into the water.

He swapped back towards the now screaming bird-person and stabbed the burning mass to the platform with his spear.

Loot Gained: 157 EXP, 157 Gold, 22 Feathers, 1 Talon.

"Look out!" Claire shouted, and he could feel the reason why coming at him from behind.

Elliot vanished just before it reached him, swapping places with the still burning corpse—it didn't have anywhere near enough time to abort its attack and crashed bodily into its burning comrade.

The two bodies spun through the air, clipping the platform and bleeding off momentum—then Claire's fireball crashed into them, sending fire and feathers scattering in every direction.

There was a moment of peace in the storm, where they weren't under attack.

Elliot took in the battlefield with wide eyes, barely able to hear anything over the beating of his heart and the blood rushing in his ears. There was so much going on—claws and weapons crashing into each other all across the area.

He spotted Jacque once more, fighting one of the few truly massive bird-people. The man's physical power left the platform broken everywhere he went, even his footfalls alone enough to tear them apart like paper.

The massive winged beast attempted to break away from the man and took off into the air—Jacque sprinted after it without hesitation. Elliot watched the man reach the edge of the platform, not slowing down at all.

"Elliot!" Jacque shouted.

The man's voice and the destruction of the platform as he leaped returned sound to his focus, the cacophony overpowering the beating of his heart.

Elliot reacquired the man high in the air just as he crashed into the massive bird-person, and seconds later, three distinct pieces fell from the air, the wings torn from the torso of the monster, and it tumbled towards the water below, trailing blood and feathers.

Elliot targeted Jacque, depositing the man safely back on the platform, and found himself spinning in the air for a moment. This far away from the platform, he could feel another immense creature in the water. He swapped with one of the corpses at the edge of the platform before returning to where he'd left Jacque.

"Thank you, Elliot!" Jacque laughed.

Elliot couldn't believe the trust the man had just placed in him—when they were almost complete strangers, but it sent a wave of something through him that made his eyes sting.

"Jacque," Elliot managed, "There are monsters in the water, deep down, at least the size of a whale."

Jacque's smile vanished for the first time as he considered the information—without a way to target the creatures, they were screwed.

"There is another group of creatures circling us, far out in that direction." Jacque gestured to the west, and Elliot turned to look but couldn't see anything. "They are running on top of the water with some sort of ice ability; Sirit noticed them before."

Elliot had no idea who Sirit was, but it must have been one of the others on the combat team.

"Let's deal with the rest of the bird-people first," Elliot said, taking in the ongoing attack. "I'll catch you again if you call."

"Thank you, my friend!" Jacque cheered, "Let us do our best!"

Elliot watched the cheerful man tear off across the platform towards the rest of the feathered creatures.

"How is he so happy? We're under attack for fuck's sake," Claire complained, "I'll stick with you—make sure to save me too, man. I don't want to die any time soon."

"I'm on it," Elliot said dryly.

Claire raised her staff, fire flickering into existence at the tip—a fireball erupted from it, it grew larger as it traveled, and crashed into a group of three who were working together again the woman with the greatsword.

They mostly avoided the blast, the distance too great for an easy hit—It served to allow the woman a moment to regain her bearings, and two of the creatures broke off from the trio, coming towards them.

"Aim your fireball at my next location," Elliot ordered, "I'll set you up."

"Uh," Claire said quickly, "Are you sure—"

He swapped away from her, and she turned slightly to target him. He felt the heat on his back and switched places with one of the creatures, depositing it in front of the incoming fireball. He spun in the air, swinging his spear at the second creature and missing—it spun under the attack, aborting its attack run and breaking away from him.

Elliot swapped back to the ground to avoid a rough landing and waited for Claire's next attack to land. The monster banked, barely avoiding the next fireball, and Elliot swapped in front of the fireball's trajectory, waiting for it to reach him, and then switched out with the bird-person.

It screeched as it collided head-on with the same fireball it had already avoided, erupting in flames—the heat threw off the complicated system of wind flowing under its wings and sent it into a violent tumble along with the platform, dead before it had even come to a stop.

"Elliot!" Jacque called.

Elliot snapped his head around and found the man—fifteen meters in the air, just as he was kicking off one of the creatures. The attack sent it tumbling away uncontrollably, right in the direction of the man with the ludicrously long Katana. The man's blade flickered too fast to follow, and it fell in three pieces, blood splattering around him.

Jacque somehow changed direction in mid-air again, grabbing onto the left wing of another passing creature. He kicked off the body, and the wing was torn off, the rest of the creature spiraling to the ground with a twisting trail of blood following it. It left him once more in the open air, with no platform left to catch him, and apparently unable to use his directional movement ability more than once in mid-air.

Elliot swapped him back onto the platform again, without comment, and then moved himself back to Claire. Jacque's thanks were still ringing in his ears as more signatures came into existence on the edge of his range—this time, they were running across the water at high speed.

Jacque had been correct; they were creating platforms of ice with every step, either conjuring it or freezing the water on contact—and they were much, much faster than the feather creatures.

Something round and black was tossed high into the air, and then a black line intersected it, originating from the platform. The orb burst, and in a seemingly unending attack, arrows erupted downwards, showering the approaching creatures in thousands of arrows.

Failing to make landfall on the platform, they circled around, skirting the edges of the attack until they reached the area that Jacque and the rest of the combat team were waiting.

Three of them broke off from the main group, continuing to follow the edge of the platform; one of them went after the bowman, while the other two came straight at Claire and Elliot, the only other group still on the platform.

The closer they got, the more Elliot realized he wouldn't be able to keep up with them. They were moving absurdly fast, and only the distance that separated them was allowing him to track them. If they were going to survive this, they needed to kill one of the creatures right at the start because there was no possible way they could fight two of these creatures for any length of time.

Elliot, mind racing, burst forward from his place on the platform, running straight towards the one on the right and making his target obvious. The thing took it as a challenge, the angle changed, and it stepped on the platform for the first time, freezing the first two panels before the effect vanished.

It had already begun to blur around the edges, and Elliot's vision tunneled in on it, noting its ice-blue skin; all of his attention honed in on the moment trying to *see, and everything began to slow.*

It had something at its waist, a sword of some sort, buried in a white bone sheath. Time crawled along as the blurring creature stopped in front of him on a dime, reached down, and drew the sword out.

It spun it once, held it up to the side, and then cut downwards at an angle, and for the barest instant, Elliot found their eyes locked on each other. His mind groped outwards, grasping the elevation locked panel directly behind the creature, and he willed himself there.

Elliot's position changed during the transition, his spear already placed against the Ice-bringer's head when he arrived, and he pushed—like everything else he'd hit with it so far, the creature's head parted before it without resistance.

Then everything started moving again, as his mind failed to function at that level any longer—the other creature jaunted to the left, slamming into him from the side with obscene speed before the kill had even registered.

Loot Gained: 195 EXP, 195 Gold, 1 Rare Shortsword, 1 Rare Amulet.

Elliot was flung away from the force, and he couldn't feel anything except the pain in his arm and shoulder as he tumbled across the platform. Elliot's mind grasped onto something that was far away from the creature. He swapped away just as it reached him once more, appearing in the air high above, having exchange positions with one of the last remaining bird-people.

Elliot pulled a health potion out of his inventory as he fell through the air, and more of it splashed around his face than in his mouth, but the pain had already begun to fade as he approached the ground.

By the time he'd swapped back to the ground, the Ice-bringer had killed the bird-person and started back towards Claire.

A series of violent but frantic fireballs splashed uselessly around the creature, tearing burning holes in the platform as it evaded everything with absurd ease. Elliot forced himself into action again, swapping with a distant panel and then moving Claire out of the things range.

Elliot swapped with another panel further away, but the creature didn't even bother changing direction, running parallel to them both. Ice started forming in its wake, tearing the platform apart down the middle as it crossed the width of it in a few instants.

The two sections stayed perfectly level above the water but broke away from each other, no longer tethered as a single large mass. The combat group was on the other side of the platform, along with Claire—he was on his own, and the Ice-bringer seemed hyperfocused on him now.

Elliot did the only thing he could—run away.

He swapped with the top of the water, and then as his foot hit the ocean, he immediately swapped with another patch some distance away.

The Ice-bringer gave chase along the water, leaving a solid column of ice trailing behind it.

Elliot kept swapping across the water as best he could, unable to stop lest he falls—the thing kept following him, but his sudden direction changes seem to prevent it from catching him. He felt a monstrously sized creature in the water below, following the two of them.

He was going to die, Elliot realized.

He couldn't outrun the Ice-bringer, and now the thing below the water was surfacing—terror began to build up in him as it came within meters of them. The Ice-bringer must have finally noticed it because it suddenly broke off, heading back towards the platform.

Elliot pushed all of his feelings into that tiny corner in the back of his mind, and as the color fell away from the world, everything became crystal clear—He dropped into the water, sinking beneath the surface from the weight of his armor.

It was freezing and almost black, even this close to the surface—The massive thing just below him surged upwards in a smooth motion that belied its size, he watched the dark shape without feeling, and then there was a wall of bone-white material right in front of his face.

Elliot swapped places with the Ice-bringer.

He tumbled to a stop on the platform, coughing—the air on his wet armor sent a spike of physical pain through him; the paralyzing cold of the ocean hadn't been something he could have prepared for.

The color bled back into the world, and he shivered violently.

The massive creature breached the water, following its trajectory upwards; it looked not unlike a terrifyingly large whale. It was colored a cool white and covered in white spikes that may have been wrought from bone. Elliot had never seen a living creature so large, not even the whales it resembled from back home compared.

The Bone-whale vanished back beneath the waves—Despite its mass, its terrifying appearance, and its location in the water, Elliot could feel it was perfectly within his ability to exchange places with.

It gave him an idea.

"Jacque!" Elliot gasped out.

The man had been fighting off the largest of the ice creature, but even the Ice-bringer's blistering speed wasn't enough to keep up with the man—less than a minute later, he joined Elliot, hands now covered in blood.

"You're freezing!" Jacque said, concerned.

"D—doesn't—matter." Elliot managed.

Jacque nodded with a frown, accepting his statement.

"Those creatures are quite large, indeed—" Jacque asserted. "I cannot see a way to get close with all of those spikes in the way."

The fact that the spikes were the problem and not going into the water after the creature said something about the man—Elliot just wasn't sure what it was.

"I can—switch—places—with them. I just—need—someone to—to—*to toss*—something—into the air." Elliot gritted out through the shivers. "Do—do—*do we have*—anyone—that can—hurt it. R—*range*—preferred."

"Sirit!" Jacque called out.

The other group had finished with the last of the Ice-runners, and one of the women with the bow broke off from the other group at the sound of his voice. Leaping across to the other half of the platform.

"Jacque?" Sirit said, and her voice was sharp. "Have you figured out a strategy to deal with the creatures in the water?"

"Elliot has graciously offered to handle that—he will bring them above the water!" Jacque boomed, "You'll just need to kill them before they fall back out of sight!"

Sirit scowled.

"I only have four scrolls powerful enough to do *anything* to that kind of armor," Sirit said tightly, "This dungeon is *such* a waste of money; I'll be living on the streets after this."

"I'll—reimburse you," Elliot managed, trying and failing to force the shivers away. "I'll need—something—up in the air—in the exact place—where you want—the Bone-whale."

Sirit looked at him for the first time and raised a thin eyebrow.

"You'll reimburse me?" Sirit said sharply, "I'll take you up on that offer—do not even *think* about trying to hide from me afterward. I *will* find you, regardless of which city you reside in."

Elliot ignored the threat. Instead, he made sure there was something close by to switch with. He found a target for his return swap and turned to face the water.

"Ready," Elliot shivered.

"Ready!" Jacque cheered.

"Firing," Sirit said sharply. "Now."

Elliot felt the arrow lance up into the air; it started curving back towards the water as its momentum ran out, and he swapped with it at the peak. Elliot found himself spinning in the air once more, and he drew in a deep breath, trying to brace himself for what was about to happen.

He swapped with one of the massive creatures circling beneath the platform.

There was no light at this depth, and his mind blanked, overwhelmed from the sudden temperature change; he floated listlessly before he managed to grasp at the panel he'd picked out earlier—Elliot appeared back on the platform on his hands and knees, gasping for breath.

Once more, the air on his wet body burned painfully, and he curled up on himself, shivering.

"Elliot!" Jacque called, approaching his position. "Well done!"

He couldn't respond, and forcing himself to get up was perhaps the hardest thing he'd ever done, and turning to face the water once more did nothing to help. The creature wasn't visible, only large foamy ripples forming on the surface; the ocean water had clearly been disturbed by something large.

There was a large dark cloud of something spreading out through the water.

"R—ready." Elliot lied.

Sirit eyed him for a moment before turning back to face the water.

"Firing," Sirit said sharply, "Now."

Elliot traced the arrow back into the air, picking his target in the water ahead of time, and then swapped with the arrow. The wind bit at his skin, somehow worsening the chill—water surrounded him, and now, even when he was prepared for it, it still took a moment to focus his mind.

He managed to stay upright this time as he appeared back on the platform—the series of swaps were fast enough this time for him to see the Bone-whale fall from the sky, a pale blue light fading away. A thick black liquid poured out of the massive hole in its center—and then it smashed into the water, vanishing once more.

"Ready," Elliot whispered.

"How many are left?" Sirit demanded, "I only have two scrolls remaining."

"Three." Elliot shivered, "If you give me more arrows to use, I can try to bring two up at once."

Sirit frowned.

"I'm not at all confident in your ability to pull that off," Sirit rebuffed, voice scathing. "We will figure something else out for the last 'Bone-Whale.'"

"Geez—why are you such a bitch?" Claire spat, a dark look on her face. "He looks like he's about to collapse, and you're shit-talking him? Get a fucking clue, lady."

"Let us not argue, my friends!" Jacque cheered. "Victory approaches!"

Sirit didn't even twitch, eyes locked on Elliot—he turned back to face the water.

"Ready," Elliot forced out.

"Firing," Sirit said sharply, "Now."

The series of swaps that followed left him dizzy and numb to the cold, the temperature playing havoc on his body—Elliot managed to draw a health potion from his inventory, drinking it quickly and barely noticing the bizarre taste.

The dizziness vanished even as the feeling of cold returned.

"Elliot!" Jacque cheered, holding his fist up to accentuated his passion. "Your determination is otherworldly—I only wish that I could assist you in this task!"

"Thanks," Elliot mumbled, without feeling.

He'd never considered himself impressive at anything, and even now, he felt no connection between himself and the man's compliment. It washed over him without effect, almost as if it had been meant for someone else entirely.

"Ready," Elliot said, glancing down at himself.

"Firing," Sirit said sharply, "Now."

The Bone-whales had begun to spread out as they realized they were somehow getting picked off, and Elliot had to string a furious series of swaps together to get the creature close enough, and the falling mass of water was reused to place him back in position.

Once the Bone-Whale was in the air, he traded places a final time, crashing onto the platform, already fighting to get another potion out. He consumed it as quickly as he could, but the cold remained—he sat on the platform in wet misery shivering.

"You alright, Elliot?" Claire said quietly, kneeling down beside him.

"I'm never going swimming again," Elliot murmured.

"Me either—*fuck water*." Claire said honestly, "How are we going to kill the last one?"

The rest of the combat group had eventually joined them, watching quietly as Sirit methodically shot each of the creatures out of the sky, wasting her precious scrolls one by one.

"A good question!" Jacque declared. "Does anyone have something that could kill the last of these creatures?"

"I am now *completely* out of scrolls," Sirit said, glaring at everyone. "Expect no more help from me in that regard, Jacque."

"Of course, Sirit!" Jacque said cheerfully, completely unbothered by the woman's cold demeanor. "Anna! You look like you've had an epiphany!"

"Why don't we drop it on something?" Anna offered, her greatsword already returned to the sheath on her back. "Get the guy that froze these panels to stick something sharp in the air."

Elliot, still shivering, turned to look at the woman with interest—that was a very creative solution to the current problem.

"How about the world's longest samurai over here?" The man with the wavey sword said, amused.

"Idiot," Mr. Long-Katana huffed, annoyed. "It's only a rare; it probably isn't even strong enough to cut through the things skin—let alone the bone."

Anna drew her massive greatsword off her back without effort and with only the use of a single hand—Elliot stared at the feat, reminded once more of how strange this place was.

"Mine will work; where has the guy with the shaved head gone?" Anna offered.

Jacque immediately turned towards the floating doorway and the ladder.

"Marcus! We are in need of your assistance once more, my friend!" Jacque shouted towards the tunnel.

Marcus appeared a few moments later and reluctantly climbed down the ladder they had made and made his way over to them. A minute later, and with Claire's ability to levitate an object, they had the glowing greatsword floating just above the water, blade pointed upwards.

Elliot was wondering how Anna planned to get her sword back when the portal opened up on top of it.

"Elliot, are you ready?" Jacque said cheerfully.

Elliot frowned before shaking his head and preparing himself—she must have had some kind of plan in mind.

"Ready," Elliot managed, drawing purpose from the fact this was the last time he would need to do it.

It took six swaps to find the creature, as it had moved a great distance away from the platform; it took twelve to move it close enough to the sword. Elliot landed on the platform, flat on his back, gasping, looking at Sirit.

"Firing," Sirit said sharply, "Now."

The angle of her shot was much higher this time, directly up, and he lay on the platform, waiting for its vertical axis to align with the sword below. The two intersected, and then he closed his eyes and swapped back into the water. The Bone-whale had almost managed to swim out of his range with its obscene swimming speed, but he managed to catch it before it could vanish.

Dungeon Complete: 317/317 Enemies Defeated.

It took almost five seconds for him to regain his bearing enough to swap back onto the platform. He was immediately blinded by the light of the portal that was only three feet away from him—he rolled over to face away from it and shivered.

Everyone from the combat team and even Marcus were gone, swallowed by the light of the portal, but Elliot could just feel the now missing woman's greatsword, locked in place above the water right on the edge of the portal.

"Fuck." Elliot hissed.

He was going to have to collect the woman's sword first; if she hadn't offered its use in the plan, they would be stuck here—he owed her to at least retrieve the sword for her.

People were already flooding out of the doorway, down the ladder, and towards the exit. Elliot dragged himself up to his feet and circled the platform, moving to the far corner. From his new position, he could just see the handle of the sword sticking out of the light of the portal.

If he swapped with it, he might get taken through to the other side, which meant he was going to have to swap with the water. The sword was about level with his torso when he was standing on the platform, not that far above the water level.

Elliot took a deep breath, braced himself before swapping with the top of the water, right at the edge of the portal. He reached out for the handle of the sword and missed it, sinking knee-deep into the water before he swapped again. This time his fingers brushed the edge of it as he fell out of range.

Elliot gritted his teeth and swapped a third time, adjusting his position before he arrived—his curved fingers hooked onto it, straining to hold himself aloft—he inventoried the greatsword and swapped with a panel on the platform before he could sink much further into the water.

He wasn't sure how long he laid on the platform after that, but eventually, he stumbled through the portal and back into the Grey Room—Three down, one dungeon to go.

The Situation

Elliot was greeted with the dungeon prompt flashing into existence before his eyes.

Loot Gained: 2012 EXP, 695 Gold.

He glanced over the statistic information presented by the prompt and frowned. They'd all been punished by the long time it had taken them to complete the dungeon—194 minutes total, with almost all of that going towards building the platform.

The time taken had resulted in an 'F' rating, and because the dungeons worked by taking the lowest rating across the board and using it as a multiplier—well, there was no multiplier this time.

"What a waste," Elliot murmured.

The difficulty rating of the dungeon had been a 'B' which was interesting and daunting when he considered what they might mean for the higher ratings.

Worse than that, it made him wonder just how lucky they had been to have the right people on hand to create the platform in the first place. If Steven hadn't been there, they wouldn't have access to his wooden panels; if Jane were missing, they wouldn't have had the wire.

If Marcus weren't there, they would have all been swimming because, without the ability to lock the elevation of something, they would have been completely screwed. That was before they even got into dealing with the Bone-whales, the Bird-people, and the Ice-bringers with the exact combat team they'd had.

If even one of those people had been missing.... Elliot shook his head before finally turning his attention to the room. There was nobody else in the room with him, not a single person. He was completely on his own—That was greater evidence towards his theory that there were multiple Torii in this place.

Unfortunately, it also meant that he would need to find Anna to return her sword *and* Sirit to recompensate her for the scrolls his plan had required. Sirit had clearly known this was going to happen, given her choice of words in the dungeon.

Either way, it was a problem for later; right now, he had one more dungeon to complete, and then he could finally stop. Elliot stepped out of the exit before turning and rentering the dungeon for the final time.

So much had happened today that he was having trouble keeping it all straight in his head—everything just seemed to blur together. Elliot had definitely underestimated the mental toll this was going to take on him.

He would have to rework his plan; four dungeons a day were completely unrealistic if this was the level of opposition he was going to be facing. On the other hand, three dungeons per day were far more realistic, or perhaps even two if one of them was particularly taxing, that seemed like something he could maintain for much longer than four.

The Grey Room was occupied when he arrived, although there were far fewer people than before—there was also nobody from the last dungeon, at least none he could recognize anyway. He spent a few moments doing a headcount and placed the room's population at somewhere under thirty people—he began tallying up the estimated levels.

There were three people with glowing weapons, which probably put them somewhere over level two-hundred. There where a group of people—seven strong, without any armor at all, and they were looking at him worriedly—it completely derailed his attempt at tallying the levels.

He watched them, watching him for a long awkward moment—was this how Annette had felt, back when he studied her in that first dungeon?

"Excuse me?" A woman called anxiously, "Can I ask you some questions?"

Elliot turned towards them but didn't make a move to cross the distance, remembering how he had felt when Anette had approached him so suddenly and the flash of panic that had cut through him. It wasn't something he would want to inflict on somebody else.

"Yes," Elliot said, as evenly as he could. "Ask away."

"Thank you," The woman said more confidently, "My name is Mary, by the way."

"Elliot," Elliot offered.

"What *is* this place?" Mary asked helplessly. "What is that timer on the wall for? Why do we all have weapons? Why do *you* have armor?"

Elliot listened to the question carefully and nodded.

"This place is called the Grey Room; you come here when you die in the real world." Elliot said evenly, "Everyone who arrives here is given a starting melee weapon of some kind, although you can purchase armor once you have acquired enough money."

Elliot paused for a moment, trying to keep the information clear and to the point. The group was watching him intently, and he forced himself to keep on talking despite the discomfort.

"Once the timer hits zero, a door will open; beyond that door is an environment that people here call a 'dungeon.'" Elliot said carefully, "There are monsters inside, and we will not be able to leave until they are all killed or captured. The monsters will be attempting to kill or capture you as well."

Mary looked suddenly worried again, but one of the people in the group started laughing.

"You're joking? Monsters?" The man said, disbelieving. "What's next, magic?"

Elliot glanced at the man for a moment before nodding.

"Yes," Elliot said evenly, "Place your hand against your chest, and say 'Status.'"

Elliot demonstrated slowly, and his status appeared in the air before them, indecipherable lettering to them before it vanished a moment later.

"What the hell is that?" The same man said, bewildered.

Mary repeated his directions, and the rest of them followed a moment later with exclamations of surprise and wonder. Elliot needed to warn them about the other threats they were likely to encounter.

"The things inside the room are terrifying, but some of them look like close approximations to humans," Elliot said evenly, drawing their attention once more. "Some move so fast you can't follow them with your eyes; some are strong enough to crush stone to powder; some can use magic."

Elliot was thinking of the Ice-Runners and their strange ability and of the sword he had taken from one of them.

"Some of them have equipment as we do, but most I have encountered so far do not," Elliot said before struggling for a moment.

Elliot had always hated talking to groups of people, and this was no exception. Mary smiled understandingly at him, seemingly realizing that this was hard for him.

"I have some advice for you," Elliot said after a long moment. "Keep your weapons out at all times, do not go off alone, or you will get picked off, work together against enemies to maximize your chances of surviving. Concepts like honor and fair play don't exist here; use anything at your disposal to win because they will do the same."

Elliot wondered if he should tell them they would have to do it all again in a week but decided against it. It would only demoralize them, potentially distracting them from surviving this one—perhaps that was why Anette hadn't mentioned it.

"The last enemy to die will be the location where the exit portal appears; simply step into the light to leave the dungeon," Elliot said evenly. "I wish you all the best of luck, don't die."

"Thank you!" One of the others called out to him as he turned away once more.

Elliot couldn't help but feel like he had forgotten to tell them something important, but he couldn't remember what it was. He shook his head, they had a larger group to work with than Hannah, Grant, and he had, and they looked far more prone to cooperation as well.

Elliot watched the timer until it hit zero and then moved towards the door. He followed the tunnel, incredibly glad that there wasn't any sign of water on the other side—there wasn't any sign of much else because the doorway was blocked by some kind of tall, white grass.

It was clearly higher than the entrance, and once he pushed through it, he realized it was far higher than that.

He hadn't made it three feet into the mess before he felt a large rectangular box appear on the edge of his range—he turned in the direction and spotted the white glow.

"Of course, I find a chest now," Elliot sighed. "It only took two whole dungeons."

The ground was covered in a thick layer of dead grass, so he didn't have to do much to select a lump of it to swap with. Elliot used his spear to scythe a section of the white grass and cleared enough of it to get a better look at the chest.

Secret Found: 1/100.
Loot Gained: 500 Gold, 1 Uncommon Bow, 1 Uncommon Bracer, 1 Uncommon Boots.

Nothing unusual as far as the chests went—something moved into his range to the west, but whatever it was had a goal in mind, angling north-west, seemingly unaware of his presence. Elliot headed back towards the entrance, searching for any more of the chests along the way.

He checked on the group of seven that had spoken to him and found them sticking close to the entrance, cutting through the grass to create a large clearing. He moved further east, swapping with more of the dead grass, rather than attempt to fight through it physically.

Elliot stopped as soon as he felt a new signature in his range—it was standing scant meters away from a chest. It felt like a human to his swap sense, at least in shape—other than the thing that was swinging behind it along the ground—a long tail of some sort tapered to a point.

It was also standing perfectly still, having stopped dead in its tracks a mere second after he had arrived.

Had it heard him in the grass? It might be able to sense temperature or something else. Elliot didn't know how fast this one could move, but he wanted the chest. Given the white glow and the fact that they weren't looking in the right direction, he thought he could safely assume that it didn't know it was there, hidden in the grass as it was.

Elliot took a single experimental step towards the creature, the grass rustling quietly with the movement—the signature turned its head in his direction. Probably sound then, it would most likely hear him if he swapped with the grass next to the chest—the monster suddenly started strafing in a wide circle around him, away from the chest.

He blinked, slowly moving in the opposite direction, matching the wide circle. The monster made no move to come near him, seemingly content with both of them going their separate ways. That was fine by him.

He reached the chest and knelt down as the monster moved further away.

Secret Found: 2/100.
Loot Gained: 500 Gold, 1 Uncommon Claw, 1 Uncommon Dagger, 1 Uncommon Spear.

Elliot felt a small flicker of annoyance at having finally found a spear *long* after he had actually needed it. Unfortunately, it was uncommon and completely paled in comparison next to the weapon he'd bought with Svent's death.

He frowned when the monster stopped moving again, standing perfectly still right at the edge of his range—then it turned around and started sprinting back towards him. Elliot frowned at the sudden change of heart—another signature bloomed, wildly different from the first.

"You want help, huh?" Elliot said quietly.

He wondered if this was how Amber and Tsunami felt when he led that other thing right towards them. Elliot raised his spear, spinning in a circle and scything all of the grass down. The creature heard the noise but continued straight for him, barreling into the clearing and throwing itself to its knees.

Elliot kept the spear pointed at its throat, listening to the rapid-fire series of noises, the language completely indecipherable to him. The much larger creature, still in the grass, slowed to a crawl as it realized there were now two of them in the clearing.

The monster on its knees was strikingly human and completely naked—the pale red skin, the bizarrely elaborate eyebrows, and the long red tail being the exceptions. Elliot was happy to see that the top of its head was firmly in place, and there were no signs of needle teeth _or_ tentacles.

It shuffled forward, keeping its head firmly pressed against the dead grass—a pile of weapons, armor, and other things appeared as the being dumped all of it out onto the grass.

The other, much larger creature started moving again, stealthily rotating around behind the two of them about twenty meters out from the clearing. The pleading creature at his feet stared up at him worriedly before placing its own hand on top of its head.

It was clearly surrendering, seeking to be captured instead of killed by the other creature. Elliot didn't want to capture anything intelligent, but if he didn't, then he'd still have to kill it—or someone else would in order to finish the dungeon.

The large many-limbed thing crept closer to them through the grass.

"Alright, just for now—you're on your own after we leave the dungeon,"

Elliot murmured before reaching out and placing his hand on the monster's head. "Claim."

The sparks of light washed over the creature.

Enemy Captured
Name – Tyralklivi
Species – Ptretian
Sex – Female
Age – 32
Level – 37

Elliot wasn't going to even attempt to pronounce her name, and he doubted she could have understood him either way. He swapped back towards the entrance of the dungeon, then again with Tyralklivi. The large multi-limbed monster crashed through the grass towards them as one of its prey vanished, and then Elliot swapped next to the alien he had just unwillingly enslaved.

Tyralklivi let out another furious barrage of incomprehensible syllables, her tone somewhere between excited and terrified. Elliot didn't even try to understand the words. Instead, he moved to combat the monster before it reached them.

Elliot swapped with the dead grass behind it, and it spun on its massive feet, immediately identifying his new position.

The thing roared so loud that Elliot actually froze for a moment, the noise striking something inside him—the massive creature stomped through the grass. Elliot caught a glimpse of coarse black fur, too many limbs on its torso, and razor-sharp teeth.

Elliot swapped behind it, holding his breath and not moving at all. His spear was clenched in a white-knuckled grip, and the creature grunted at his disappearance. He must have evaded the creatures hearing this time before he made to move to turn around.

Tyralklivi was making her way back towards him now, somehow knowing where he was again—the beast heard her movements through the grass and started towards her again. The tall white grass bent under the creature's weight and size, and Elliot stayed perfectly still as the monster stomped past him.

Then he stabbed it in the side of its torso.

He didn't wait, immediately swapping away, and was thankful before the monster swung outward with all of the limbs on the right side of its body, shredding the grass where he had been standing a moment before.

Elliot listened to the thing's roar of agony, the massive hole he'd left in its side unable to be ignored. He only had a moment's reprieve, however, because it turned and leaped, crushing the ground beneath it as it threw itself in Livi's direction.

Elliot did a swap rotation to more her out of the way again and ended up beside her in the grass— Tyralklivi turned to stare at him in terror, and he quickly lifted his hand, tapping his own ear with one finger, then pointed down at her feet.

His message was clear; the monster was following her by the sound of her moving— Tyralklivi swallowed, nodded, and then sprinted away through the grass.

Elliot stared after her in complete disbelief as she did the exact opposite of what the message suggested. The creature hunting them roared out another challenge that sent another spike of fear through him before sprinting through the grass after its fleeing prey.

Elliot swapped next to it, stepped forward, and staked it through one of its thick legs before swapping away again. The monster screamed, its leg collapsing when its full weight came down on it. It was moving too fast to stop quickly enough, and its upper body hit the ground first.

It dragged itself back up to its many feet with a pained growl and a great deal of effort. It angled off away from them both, dragging itself through the grass and apparently giving up on both of them. Elliot wasn't going to let the clearly violent creature go; it was too dangerous to leave alive.

He followed it as it limped away, and when it turned to growl at him, Elliot swapped to its more damaged side and stabbed it in the hip, directly below the first hole. He vanished before the counterattack could rend him into pieces and continued to follow behind the creature as it grew more and more sluggish.

Elliot stepped forward once it could scarcely move and put his spear through the back of its head.

Loot Gained: 177 EXP, 177 Gold, 13 Claws, 8 Durable Hide, 1 Uncommon Amulet.

Elliot glanced down at the Exotic spear in his hand—if he didn't have this, he would never have been able to kill this thing. He couldn't help but wonder just how many people had found themselves in exactly this situation without having the tools to survive. If he hadn't had the spear, if he couldn't feel where everything around him was, if he couldn't reposition instantly to attack from an unblockable position—he shook his head.

Elliot once again realized how lucky he had been so far.

Tyralklivi was still stumbling around in the grass, attempting to be the distraction that he hadn't even asked for. He sighed, moving towards her position, and she slowed down as he approached, most likely taking his lack of hurry as a good sign.

The red skin reminded him of the Levelheader that had almost killed Amber, and he couldn't help but tense. That tenseness washed away after she started speaking in her alien language at a breakneck pace.

Clearly excited to be alive, she pushed the monster's corpse with her foot, apparently testing to see if it was still alive—then she turned and said something to him, clearly a question.

Elliot stared at her helplessly.

"I have no idea what you are saying," Elliot said hesitantly. "Just—look, I've seen monsters running around in the city; I'll free you when we get out of here, and you can do whatever your people do, okay?"

Tyralklivi looked confused, and if he was reading her correctly, impatient that he was talking so slowly. He sighed, spinning around and heading back to where Tyralklivi had dumped all of her items in the grass. He waved a hand at the mess and then at her.

"Put it back in your inventory," Elliot tried.

Tyralklivi tilted her head at him but eventually leaned down, picking up one of the swords, vanishing it into her inventory, and then waited to see what his reaction was. Elliot nodded and gestured again— Tyralklivi quickly started putting everything back inside her inventory.

This language barrier thing was going to be a problem—he could already tell. Elliot waited for her to finish and then started off towards the south. He wasn't sure how many enemies were left, but he wanted to find some more chests before the portal opened.

Tyralklivi fell in step beside him, saying a bunch of different things that he couldn't understand. Elliot wondered why she was even bothering when neither of them could understand the other. He listened to the strange words anyway, attempting to divine something about the language.

He glanced down at her naked chest for what had to of been the hundredth time—unable to help it, he shook his head and then returned his gaze firmly to the front, promising himself he wouldn't look again.

It took several minutes before he spotted the white glint in the distance and then angled directly towards it. Once they arrived next to it, Tyralklivi looked intrigued at the object he had led them to. Elliot wondered if she had seen one before; they didn't seem to be common knowledge.

Elliot hesitated for a moment, he was already in a decent spot, and she would probably need some money once he freed her in the city—He pointed to the chest on the ground and then waited.

Tyralklivi bent over at the waist and flipped the latch open.

Elliot found it strange to be the one watching someone else open the chest for once. There was no prompt for him to see, to indicate what she had received. From a visual perspective, it was just an empty chest, and her wide-eyed reaction was bizarre when considered without context.

Dungeon Complete: 118/118 Enemies Defeated.

Elliot sighed in relief as the light of the portal seeped through the gaps in the grass, showering them in light. He'd only managed to find two chests this time, and he'd donated one of them—at least he was finished for the day.

That was all four dungeons completed—just like he had set out to do. He'd never felt as tired as he did right now, and he doubts even another health potion would help him. He was just completely mentally exhausted.

Elliot started towards the distant portal, trying to decipher what Tyralklivi was attempting to tell him.

"You seem far too excited to be going into an aliens portal," Elliot murmured, "I would be terrified that it's a race of cannibals, and you are about to step into their cafeteria."

Tyralklivi said something incomprehensible, and he found himself speaking up again in turn, despite the lack of comprehension.

"I suppose cannibals isn't the right word considering that we are both different species." Elliot frowned, "I suppose Omnivore is more appropriate—doesn't exactly carry the same connotation to it, though."

Elliot actually found it somewhat freeing to talk to somebody he knew couldn't understand him. He paused when they reached the portal, and he frowned again. If he took her through the portal now, while people were still inside the Grey Room, they might attack her or something—the rest of Livi's 'team' had to of been killed for the dungeon to open. Which meant that anyone inside could have fought and killed them or had people they know killed by them.

They would absolutely recognize her as a member of that species—Elliot bit his lip in thought; there were monsters running around in the city. He'd seen them, but he really didn't know the protocol here.

Tyralklivi was watching him intently, and he wondered at the look; perhaps standing next to the portal was making an implication of some kind that he hadn't realized.

Did she perhaps think he was reconsidering killing her?

"Livi," Elliot said, shortening the name, "We need to wait a little while, so the people on the other side leave."

Tyralklivi tilted her head at the name.

"Livi?" Tyralklivi laughed suddenly. *"Tyralklivi."*

Elliot sighed.

"Elliot." Elliot pointed at himself and then at her. "Livi."

Tyralklivi looked amused, and he decided to just get this over with and stepped towards the portal; Tyralklivi followed.

Loot Gained: 1995 EXP, 3831 Gold.

Thankfully the Grey Room was empty, so he took his time reading over the information—not even enough exp for two levels this time, but he had some leftover exp to make up the difference. Tyralklivi let out a surprised noise as she stared around at the room before looking towards the exit.

Elliot wondered what she was thinking; if he was right and every team had their own grey room, this would be confirmation for *her* because she would have seen her own, and then this one.

Alternatively, her own 'Grey Room' might be completely different, and she was surprised because this one looked strange in comparison.

Elliot caught himself staring at the alien's chest *again*—Even precommitment failed *sometimes*.

He stepped out of the grey room, with Tyralklivi a step behind him, staying close and looking around with great interest. He started in the direction of the distant city, thinking over the current situation they had found themselves in.

Elliot had already compromised on his promise not to enslave any sentients, and he already intended to fix that situation as soon as he could figure out how to release her. He was well aware that it was the only way in which she could exit that place alive, but it still prickled at him how quickly he had done such a thing.

Tyralklivi was in a worse situation than he was by far; she was now amongst a completely foreign species, one in which she didn't speak the language and most likely didn't understand the cultural differences between the two.

Elliot knew there had to be some big ones—she still hadn't made any move to cover her nakedness, and if she'd considered it a problem, she would have equipped the armor he had seen her dump on the ground earlier.

If the situation wasn't as uncertain as it was, he probably wouldn't have even worried about asking her—but they had no idea how anyone was going to react to seeing her. Doubly so, given the fact that she was both attractive and naked.

"How do I tell you to put something on?" Elliot said, frowning.

They couldn't understand each other; how did people *usually* control the monsters they captured? They seemed to follow them around the city easily enough, but he had yet to see any of them interact further than that, so he didn't know.

Tyralklivi, for her part, watched him curiously, something weary edging into her eyes at his expression—Elliot decided to just mime out the actions.

"Elliot," Elliot said evenly, then pointed at his armor. "Armour."

He tapped the chest piece noisily and then pointed back at her.

"Livi," Elliot continued, waving his hand down to gesture at her body, feeling heat rise to his cheeks from the action. "Naked."

Tyralklivi's elaborate red eyebrows pulled together, seemingly in thought, but made no move to put anything on. Elliot sighed and inventoried his own armor, leaving him in just his shirt and pants.

Tyralklivi grinned at him, and he had no idea what it meant.

"Naked," Elliot said stoically.

He wasn't technically naked, still clothed in fact, but he was hoping she could associate something with the idea of putting something *on.*

"Naked." Tyralklivi agreed, smiling.

Elliot stared at her as she made no move to put anything on—he swapped his armor set back on and took his common clothes out of his inventory, holding them out to her. Tyralklivi looked down at the bundle of clothes curiously before taking and holding them.

"Put them on," Elliot tried again.

Tyralklivi just watched him curiously.

Elliot forced himself to step forward, taking the shirt off the top of the pile, unfolded it, and then tugged it over her head.

Tyralklivi squawked out a complaint—one that he had no idea how to interpret as he pulled it down enough for her head to pop out of the collar and trapping both of her arms beneath the material.

Elliot stepped back, ignoring the upset look on her face as she fumbled around to get one of her arms through the sleeves. The shirt was far too big for her, and she was short, so the shirt fell almost to mid-thigh—Elliot took the pants out of her hand and held them open near her legs.

Tyralklivi huffed and, after a moment of hesitation, put her foot in one of the legs, and in a few moments of struggle, he got the pants high enough to sit at her waist. Once again, they were way too big for her, but his belt was still wrapped through the eyelets of the pants, so he tugged it tight and tied it off before stepping back.

Her tail was stuck down the inside of her left pant leg, the material bunching up against it.

"Tyralklivi," Tyralklivi said sullenly, "Armor?"

She was following the pattern he had tried to tell her earlier—that was a good sign, but he shook his head.

"Tyralklivi," Elliot said, mangling the name, "*Livi*, Clothes."

Tyralklivi smirked at his failure to say her name, and Elliot ignored the look. He tapped on his armor and said the word 'armor' before pointing at the shirt she was wearing and stating 'clothes.'

"Clothes." Tyralklivi agreed, pulling the front of the shirt outwards to look down the collar. "Naked."

Elliot turned to head back towards the city again, not willing to address that one.

This might actually be worse than he had initially thought; if even wearing clothing was somehow a distinct difference in the two species, what else was different? Did they only eat a certain type of plant? Did they only eat meat? Was the opposite considered horrifying to them?

Tyralklivi was going to have an impossible time trying to find a way to live here, and he didn't know how to send her back.

He could try to exchange the claim to another member of her race inside the dungeon if he could find one, but how did they both leave the same dungeon alive when only one side could be the victor? Was there some kind of trick he could use to ferry her back to her own side?

Elliot didn't know, but he would have to find out; he had brought her here, so he held some kind of responsibility for the situation.

Elliot began to notice the lingering stares and disgusted glances as he threaded his way down the main street. They weren't looking at him, he knew, but the attention still felt like an awful pressure bearing down on him.

There was clearly a dislike for non-human species amongst the population here, and for obvious reason. Everything that wasn't a human had tried to kill them inside the dungeon hundreds of times, more for some of the veterans. The vast majority of those times, they'd probably succeeded too—how many of these people had lost friends to them?

Tyralklivi seemed to go out of her way to avoid combat during the dungeon—it could have been that her species as a whole preferred to avoid conflict. It could also just be something more unique to Livi—he had no way to tell.

None of it would matter to the people here, and he could already see the kind of prejudice she would experience just by existing here. It's not like she could hide the red of her skin, the tail in her pants, or the strangely bright red hair.

Elliot ducked his head as he spotted the hotel he had stayed the night in with Grant and Hannah. It had been less than a day since he had seen them, but it felt so much longer. This place did strange things to his perception of time.

Elliot led Tyralklivi past the hotel, unwilling to come into conflict with either of them after he had made such a fool of himself that morning. He just needed somewhere to sit still for a while and just think.

Elliot located another tavern further down the road, and one street back from the main street, stepping inside. The keeper of the bar looked up as they entered and frowned as soon as he saw Tyralklivi behind him.

"Fucking monster." The man spat, loud enough for them both to hear. "What are you looking for here?"

"A room, permanent, I'll pay for a month upfront," Elliot said evenly, ignoring the obvious racism.

"You better keep that thing in the room; if it starts wandering around unattended, you'll be the one buying the health potions." The man said, uncaring. "I'm tacking on a fee as well, four hundred in all for the month."

Elliot stepped up to the bar and paid the man with his trading stone, and received a key in turn.

"Room seven," The man said briskly, "You can pay one of the barmaids to bring your food up to the room because there is no way in hell monsters are eating in my bar."

Elliot just nodded without comment, the man was a total asshole, but Elliot didn't need to like him in order to use the room.

Tyralklivi seemingly understood the tone of the discussion, however, and avoided going anywhere near the man, along with making sure Elliot was in between them at all times. The room was small, which he had already guessed judging by the ten gold a night price tag, had a single bed with a mattress and sheets on it, another thicker blanket folded neatly at the end of the bed.

Elliot almost sighed; he was going to buy a building within the week—sleeping against the wall was going to get old, real fast.

Tyralklivi was already investigating everything in the small room with great interest, studying it all with the same focus she'd had at the exterior of the building. The food stalls along the main road had also caught her attention, but the looks they'd received had stopped that in its tracks.

Elliot slipped down the wall to sit against it and closed his eyes.

He wondered how the dungeon interacted with those who had been captured and then freed on this side. Did Tyralklivi have to continue entering the dungeon now? If she did, would Tyralklivi appear in this

Grey Room, surrounded by humans who would probably kill her at the first opportunity?

All of those situations were varying levels of danger. People would most likely target her outside of the dungeon, and her own allies would target her inside the dungeon. The only way she would ever get home was if she came up against her own species in the dungeon. Tyralklivi would need to kill everyone on her team and then let someone from her race claim her.

Elliot shook his head; that was her problem to deal with—his problem was figuring out how to break the claim connection and setting her free. Once she was free, she could do whatever she chose to. Then he needed to find a permanent residence, one that wasn't reliant on the whims of an angry racist.

Elliot glanced up as Tyralklivi came to stand beside him, having completed her inspection of everything inside the room. He realized he'd forgotten a step along the way; Step zero would be to establish some rough form of communication between them; at least a system of yes or no would be a start.

How would he do that? Symbols? *Drawings* were the answer, he had quit practicing several years ago, but he should be able to design a rough strip of images that explained what he wanted to convey; he would just need some paper and a pen.

He hadn't seen any stores that sold anything like that yet, but he hadn't been looking. Sirit had apparently had a series of 'scrolls' which he hadn't seen personally but implied the use of some kind of paper or at least bark. Worst case scenario, he would find an empty field somewhere and sketch it in the dirt with his spear.

The obvious solution that he had been avoiding thinking about was taking her to see Grant because he could easily understand the monsters.

Still, he had already burned that bridge; he doubted the man would want to talk to him again.

Tyralklivi noised out a series of strange words when he zoned out in thought, dragging him back to the present once more.

"Tyralklivi," Elliot tried, but it sounded as bad as before. "We are going to play a game."

Tyralklivi looked amused, Elliot tapped the ground in front of him, and Tyralklivi slid down to the floor to sit in front of him, tugging at the belt that was digging into her waist.

Elliot took a single stone from his inventory and held out both of his palms up, one of which held the stone. Tyralklivi had managed to un-clip the belt; the pants drooped dangerously low on her hips.

Elliot kept his gaze firmly on the stone in his right hand.

"Stone," Elliot said clearly, holding it up for her to see.

"Stone," Tyralklivi repeated easily.

Elliot closed both his hands and inventoried the stone before moving it to his left hand. Elliot held his empty hand out towards her.

"Stone?" Elliot asked evenly.

Tyralklivi reached out and tapped the hand it had been in—Elliot opened the hand to reveal nothing.

"No," Elliot said clearly, before asking the question again. "Stone?"

Tyralklivi tapped the other hand, and he opened it to reveal the stone.

"Yes," Elliot said evenly.

Elliot reshuffled them before restarting the game, and Tyralklivi looked interested; before reaching out to touch the one on the right, he opened it to reveal the stone.

"Yes," Tyralklivi said, pleased.

Elliot fought down a smile, she'd gotten the idea almost immediately, but he ran her through the exercise several times before he thought they'd ironed out any problems. Now he just needed to see if she could apply the concept to something else.

"Hungry?" Elliot asked evenly while retrieving one the many apples from his inventory before miming taking a bite of it and then holding it out to her. "Yes? No?"

Tyralklivi scrunched her eyebrows together.

"No," Tyralklivi said curiously.

Elliot pulled the apple back, and Tyralklivi grinned in understanding.

"Yes," Tyralklivi said firmly.

Elliot held the apple out, and she took it from him before taking a big bite out of it, pleased with herself for figuring out what he was trying to explain. Elliot sat back against the wall, feeling satisfied that it had actually worked.

Unfortunately for her, it was a tip of the iceberg situation; having a simple understanding of yes, and no was a good thing. On the other hand, if that was the *only* thing she knew in this strange place, then she was screwed.

Tyralklivi said something after a moment that he couldn't understand.

"Sorry," Elliot said, lost, "I don't know what you want."

Tyralklivi tugged on the front of her shirt—He nodded in understanding.

"Shirt," Elliot named it for her.

Tyralklivi tugged on the pants.

"Pants," Elliot explained.

"Shirt, Pants." Tyralklivi said clearly, "No."

He should have known.

"Yes." Elliot sighed, turning to face the door and opening his inventory.

Tyralklivi immediately divested herself of the clothing, and Elliot returned to thinking about his next step. There were several things he hadn't had the time to address yet, or that he had put off until later. One of them was the Faction item he had received when he purchased the token.

Inventory: Faction Token, Faction Settings Scroll, Trading Stone.

Elliot selected the 'Setting Scroll' and removed it from his inventory. He wrapped his fingers around the scroll, and another interface appeared in front of him, looking much the same as most of the others, but with only two options available to him.

Create Faction, Discard Scroll.

Elliot selected the top one and was immediately prompted to enter a name, to which there appeared to be very few restrictions. Elliot mulled over a name for a long moment, trying to find something that fit with both his goal and seemed appropriate.

Elliot wanted to become as strong as he could; he wanted to protect the people he could and become *something*—more than any of that though, he could never, ever fail, he had to keep pushing forward because if he made a mistake—even *once*, there wouldn't be any second chances. Failure here meant death, and he had already done that once.

Elliot needed to grow; in strength, in mind, and in character. He needed to drag himself as *high* as he possibly could go, and then maybe this time, he wouldn't jump.

Elliot made his choice.

Excelsior
Faction Rank
[N/A]
Faction Level
[1]

Members
Elliot Archer – Founder
[Invite to Faction]
[Kick from Faction]
[Create Group]

Communication
[Send Global Faction Message]
[Send Private Message]

Community
[Faction Bank]
[Faction Bonus]
[Faction Statistics]

Settings
[Set Alias]
[Set Faction Join Requirements]
[Set Faction Rules]
[Set Faction Tribute]
[Set Faction Punishment]
[Set Faction Goal]
[Set Member Ranks]
[Set Faction Benefits]
[Purchase Faction Building]

Elliot spent almost an hour going over everything and fiddling with settings until he had something that fit with his idea of what his Faction should accomplish. He restricted access to the faction bank by rank and dumped all of his money into it. He set the Faction Benefits to pay each member a minimum of one hundred gold per week, enough to pay for food and a room at least.

There was nothing inside the 'Faction Bonus' menu yet, which he assumed would change when he either reached some invisible threshold or increased the rank or faction level. Likewise, 'Faction Statistics' was also completely empty, probably because he had yet to do anything.

The requirements to join the Faction were set to human-only by default, but you could change it to 'Allow-All,' which was interesting. The 'Faction Goal' seemingly allowed you to set a goal that the members of the Faction were required to work towards within a set period, and a brief look showed a massive amount of different options there—gold, kills, materials, recruitment, and plenty of others.

The 'Faction Rules' allowed you to create a series of rules that, if broken, automatically incurred the associated punishment. The 'Faction Punishment' menu allowed you to dock benefits, impose several different penalties on the members, including forbidding them to enter the dungeon for a certain duration, at the cost of the offender, which seemed to line up pretty closely with the Skip Token price.

'Faction Tribute' seemed to be a payment from the members to remain in the Faction; it had a minimum cost that he couldn't go below, set at 100 gold, which forced him to raise the benefits to 200 gold to allow for the Benefits to supply whoever joined with enough money for the week.

'Member Rank' seemed pretty straightforward, allowing him to create and assign ranks to members, essentially gate-keeping them out of certain things based on rank.

Elliot sat back against the wall and pressed the last button he had avoided touching. 'Invite to Faction' popped up with an empty panel surrounded by a white outline, and he frowned at it for a moment.

Elliot tried pressing it to open some kind of typing panel, but nothing appeared.

Tyralklivi crossed in front of him, once more investigating the room, and he glanced up at the movement. Then, he quickly dragged his gaze back up to her face after another monumental struggle.

Flustered at the grin she was beaming him with, he returned his gaze to the prompt and found that it had activated. He read the text, the prompt asking if he was sure he wanted to invite Tyralklivi to Excelsior, to which he selected yes.

Tyralklivi yelped as a panel flickered into existence in front of her, the writing completely alien to Elliot's eyes. Tyralklivi seemingly read through it in barely a moment before turning to look at him, surprised.

Tyralklivi said something excitedly, and he glanced back down at the faction menu.

Members: Elliot Archer, Founder. Tyralklivi, Servant.

Tyralklivi suddenly sat down in front of him again with a grin, the translucent prompt not doing much to block his view of her—he was starting to think she was doing this on purpose.

Elliot needed to figure out how to free her, and he had a choice to make.

He could ask for assistance from Kara, the dangerous woman in the Servant shop, or he could attempt to figure it out himself while stuck in this room with a naked alien who was grinning at him like *he* was the one out of his depth.

Which was the safer option here?

The Platform

The decision was one that had no decisive answer, so instead, he com-promised—firstly, he would attempt to free her on his own, and when that inevitably failed, he would go and ask the owner of the Servant shop, Kara, for assistance.

"Tyralklivi," Elliot said. "I am going to free you now—or at least try to anyway."

Tyralklivi smirked at his continued failure to say her name, and Elliot held his hand out to the side, away from her and palm facing down—the deliberate nature of the gesture caught her eye.

"Unclaim," Elliot said.

He stared at his hand for a long moment, waiting for something to hap-pen.

"Damn." Elliot sighed before listing off every word he thought might work in its place. "Release. Unlock. Free. Open. Abandon. Disclaim?"

Elliot frowned at his hand.

Was Disclaim the opposite of Claim? Actually, was it even a word at all? He wasn't sure, and he had no easy way to check without access to the internet or a dictionary.

Tyralklivi watched him intently, probably wondering what the strange being was doing. It made him uncomfortable, like he was attempting to perform a magic trick but forgot to bring the cards.

Did she think him stupid? Bizarre or even incompetent? Here he was sitting on the floor, saying random things with his hand stuck out, trying to pretend he knew what he was doing.

He ducked his head to avoid acknowledging the look–Tyralklivi said something with the lilting quality that *almost* sounded like a question, and he lifted his head quickly, realizing that he was once more staring at her naked chest.

Elliot turned to look at the door as the echo of embarrassment he'd been feeling swelled into something he couldn't easily ignore. He couldn't begin to wonder what her question had actually been, so instead, he began running over each of the words that he already knew existed as command phrases.

Status, Inventory, Faction, Shop, Claim.

Singular words with strong meanings, and most of which would ring familiar for those who had to play any sort of video game before.

Status represented the state of something, while Inventory was less explanatory but referred to the available items in any given location. Faction denoted allegiance to a group, and Shop was the most obvious of all of them.

The meaning of the word Claim was to take ownership of something—Ownership. Ownership. Ownership.

"Disown," Elliot decided.

A series of red sparks—not unlike the color of her skin, burst forth from his hand, scattering across the floor between them. Elliot was entirely surprised that he'd actually manage to discover it without help—it spoke to the intuitiveness of the system he'd found himself within.

Tyralklivi made a noise of interest and then attempted to repeat the word he'd said in what was clearly a pale imitation of English. Elliot couldn't help but smile at the obvious disappointment as nothing emerged from her own hand.

She noticed his amusement and then quickly muttered something in her own language, summoning the blue sparks of the original 'Claim' command to make her own light show in response. Then she proceeded to stick her tongue out at him, apparently seeing it as some kind of competition between them.

Elliot just shook his head before leaning forward and slowly stretching his hand out towards her head—Tyralklivi's eyes snapped up to track his hand, looking wary, but she didn't move away.

His hand settled down onto her messy hair, just enough to make contact.

"Disown," Elliot said firmly.

The flash of red sparks washed over her head, almost lost in the brighter red of her hair, and a transparent panel appeared between them. Elliot glanced down at it, reading the text, and she stared at it in return, unable to read the unfamiliar language.

Are you sure you want to disown Tyralklivi?

Elliot accepted, pressing his finger against the panel, and it vanished.

He slumped back against the wall and opened up the Faction menu, searching out the list of members. Seeing as there were still only two names, it wasn't exactly hard to find. Tyralklivi's role within Excelsior had updated from 'Servant' to 'Basic Member,' which was the default name for the first available rank.

"Looks like I don't have to go find Kara after all," Elliot said, relieved.

He'd spent far too much time these last couple of days in the company of others, and I was draining him quickly. Worse than that, he would have felt extremely awkward turning up at the woman's Shop with a monster and then *not* selling it to her, considering the discounted sale he'd agreed to.

Tyralklivi started speaking, her already rapid language coming out at twice the speed he'd grow used to, and Elliot wondered at how much easier this would be if he could pull himself together enough to apologize to Grant.

"I still don't know how to get you back to your side," Elliot said in the tiny gap she might have left for him to respond. "I'll try to figure something out; there might be some kind of trick to it."

Elliot fell silent, listening to her excited chatter and feeling awkward every time she left an obvious pause for him to reply; lucky for him, Tyralklivi didn't seem to be bothered by his failure to hold up his side of the conversation.

He turned his thoughts inward once more—he'd completed one of his short-term goals here in freeing her, now he needed to start working on the others. He needed a safe place of his own, away from the thousands of strangers that roamed the streets with massive weapons.

Elliot opened the Faction Menu and scrolled through the options to once more familiarise himself with them. He found the 'Purchase Building' option once more; pressing his finger against it opened up a small panel adorned with a detailed map of the area.

Elliot studied it with interest.

The city he was in wasn't exactly neat and organized; he could see that from the Torii up on the edge of the world. It certainly had streets and buildings in loose columns or even blocks, but it couldn't have been planned by a committee of city builders. It looked more like people had just started putting down building foundations wherever they pleased, cramming different-sized buildings in where they could find the space.

It seemed to be locked to his position, showing several blocks in each direction, but it was cut off long before it reached the edge of the city. He'd need to leave the inn and walk around if he wanted to see the rest—something he wasn't planning on doing, as walking around with proof that he had enough money to buy a faction was just asking for trouble.

The map was made of a series of squares, rectangles, and even circles in some cases. There were two primary colors represented that he could see—blue and red. He spent a while just trying to figure out where the building he was currently in was to confirm his suspicions.

The inn he was currently renting was blue, as was the one where Hannah, Grant, and himself had been staying. Aestus weapon shop was blue, and Kara's Servant shop was blue—it was more than clear that shops, inns, and potentially houses were represented by the color blue.

The red buildings were overwhelmingly larger than their blue counterparts, with the smallest one he could see being twice as long as the weapon shop. The largest red building he could see stretched back from the street, between several blue buildings. It was long, at least eight weapons shops long, and two wide with its shorter side facing the road.

Elliot pressed on the inn that Grant and Hannah were in, hoping to see some kind of panel appear, but it just flashed a darker blue color for a moment before returning to its normal shade—nothing happened. He frowned at the map, pressing down on one of the smaller red buildings, but once again, it flashed a darker red shade before returning to normal with no explanation.

"What am I doing wrong here?" Elliot mumbled.

Was there a third color that he couldn't see because he was in a popular part of the city? He might need to head to the outskirts if that was the case—The largest building he'd found earlier flashed grey, the only rectangular outline on the entire section of his map without color. Elliot pressed his finger against it to test whether or not he could actually interact with anything at all—the building turned bright green before growing slightly darker.

Then the map disappeared.

Faction Building Purchased
Loot Gained: 1 x Faction Key.
Loot Lost: 1 x Faction Token.

Elliot stared at where the panel had been a second before and wondered if he'd just made a terrible mistake, he had assumed that it would give him some information about the building first, or another prompt would appear.

He didn't even have a chance to go see what it looked like—what if it was a hollowed-out husk of a building? Or if it had been an empty plot of land? Or the previous owner had burnt it down for the insurance money?

"Fuck." Elliot said quietly.

He might have just wasted *one-hundred-thousand gold* because he tapped a button on a screen.

"Fuck?" Tyralklivi wondered.

Elliot sighed, feeling worse than he had all day—hard to believe considering some of the things he had seen. He should have slept first and approached this with a refreshed mind instead of trying to grind out everything in a single day.

He needed to sleep.

Elliot eyed Tyralklivi for a long moment—if she'd had any plans to dispose of him, it would most likely occur when he was asleep. He considered going back down to the innkeeper and buying a second room for the night.

The idea of having to deal with the man downstairs was enough for him to decide otherwise—if he woke up, he'd deal with it tomorrow if Tyralklivi killed him in his sleep—at least he wouldn't have to deal with any of this insanity anymore.

"I need sleep," Elliot mumbled, watching her for a moment. "I'd appreciate it if you didn't kill me."

Tyralklivi tilted her head at him, and instead of playing charades again, he rolled over and faced the wall. He listened to her speak in rapid bursts and ruminated on his mystery purchase for several long minutes before he finally fell asleep.

Elliot rubbed at his eyes, somehow feeling worse than before—the room was empty now, Tyralklivi missing, and the bed unoccupied. It made sense, and he wasn't at all offended—in her place, he wouldn't have trusted him either.

Something red caught his eye under the crack in the door, and he stared at it. It pressed forward against the crack, and with a sick pop, the tip of a finger stretched out from under the door, followed by the rest of a hand.

Elliot felt his heart thudding in his chest as more red began to pool under the door. A second hand joined the first, and then a third, and a fourth—a white hand with long spindly fingers joined the others.

He felt frozen as a mouth filled with flat white teeth pushed its way under the gap, dragging itself further into the light. Elliot reached for his spear, but it wasn't in the room—the top half of the creature's head was missing, a flat expanse of red skin.

Elliot backed up away from the door, and the long-fingered white hand begun to stretch upwards towards the door handle. More hands joined it, clawing at the seams of the door and tearing grooves in the wood.

He spoke, verbally reaching for his Inventory, but nothing came out of his mouth. A wash of warm air passed over his face from above, and he couldn't bring himself to look up. He pressed his back flat against the wall as the long white arm finally reached the door handle—

Elliot slowly opened his eyes as something breathed on his face, and he found himself staring straight into the eyes of Tyralklivi, laying parallel to him, her nose almost touching his own. The red woman was watching him quietly, and it took a long, long while for his heart to stop trying to tear its way free of his chest.

He didn't know why she was on the floor with him, but it was the most terrifying way he had ever woken up in his life.

Tyralklivi said something quiet, three short unfamiliar words, and it sounded like a question.

"I don't know," Elliot said, just as quiet.

He very carefully moved his arm, which was trapped between them, and used it to push himself into a sitting position against the wall. Tyralklivi made no motion to move from where she was lying, cheek resting against her palm.

Elliot checked the crack under the door, but it was far smaller than it had been in the moments before he'd woken.

"I need to go find out about the building I just paid for," Elliot said, trying to put the nightmare behind him. "Do you want to come with me, or would you like to stay here?"

Elliot pointed to himself and then the door, making the gesture obvious, before repeating the motion with Tyralklivi.

"Yes. No?" Elliot asked.

"Yes?" Tyralklivi said.

Elliot pushed himself to his feet and felt a flash of pain arc up his back; sleeping on the floor truly sucked in a way few things did. Tyralklivi bounced up to her feet in a few quick motions, and he had to tear his gaze away from her again.

"Shirt," Elliot said.

"No," Tyralklivi declared.

They were going outside, and not wearing clothing was a really, really bad idea.

"Yes," Elliot said, staring her down.

Tyralklivi eyed him for a long moment before spinning around to the bed and taking hold of the clothing she'd thrown there. He waited as she took her time putting it on, either through unfamiliarity with the process or because she was sulking.

Elliot stepped out into the hallway once she had finished, and together they moved down the stairs. Almost as soon as they stepped out of the staircase, she moved to his other side, furthest away from the counter.

Lucky for them both, the unpleasant man wasn't at the front desk.

They stepped out into the light and turned towards the entrance to the city—the street was littered with people, most of which were investigating the food stalls that had appeared. Fruit, vegetables, and skewers with unknown meat threaded on them—Elliot purchased some of everything, inventorying it all and keeping a few skewers in his hand.

The stall owners watched them warily, Tyralklivi's presence dissuading them from speaking more than needed, but none of them approached outright hostility.

"Here," Elliot said.

He handed her several of the skewers, more of a test than anything—if she didn't eat meat, it was best that they found that out now. Tyralklivi took them quickly, biting a big chunk of meat off the end of one of the skewers without pause—she was an omnivore then. Both apples and these meat skewers seemed to be in good supply, so it wouldn't be much of an issue for either of them.

Elliot continued in the direction of the gates; the building he had accidentally purchased had been on what he'd been calling the 'Main street' in his head. Its size made it easy to pick out, sitting between two squat single-story shops and whose signage proclaimed them an 'Apothecary' and a 'General Store.'

He could see over the roof of the apothecary enough to see that the building he'd purchased went pretty deep into the mess of buildings surrounding it. It was also two stories tall and made from smooth stone blocks.

It had a worn but solid-looking wooden door and three stone steps that preceded it. Four windows adorned the front of the building, two on either side of the front door, and a small wooden balcony hung overhead with two more windows on either side.

"It's way better than I thought it would be," Elliot said.

He moved up the steps, and Tyralklivi was quick to follow.

Elliot removed the 'Faction Key' and unlocked the door. they stepped through into the front of the building, and then he turned to shut the door—

"Hey, asshole!" A woman called from out on the street.

Elliot opened the door slightly and studied the angry woman who was standing on the road by the steps; She was tall, perhaps an inch taller than he was, with blonde hair and brown eyes; a rounded mace sat against her hip. Another two people stood behind her, a red-haired man with a bo-staff strapped to his back and a brown-haired woman with a pair of knives at her waist, both looking displeased.

He had never seen any of them before, but it wasn't hard to guess what this might have been about—Up until last night, this had been someone else's building.

"You fucking *rat*!" The woman said angrily. "How long were you hovering over our building for?"

Elliot didn't particularly like being accused of something before they'd even established what the hell was going on.

"I wasn't hovering over anything," Elliot said, frowning. "I opened the map last night and pressed on the first grey building that appeared."

"Fuck *off*!" The woman hissed, genuinely upset. "What's your name?"

"Elliot." Elliot said, "Who are you?"

"Koren," Koren spat, "I'd keep an eye on the bounty boards if I were you—I'm going to be coming for you personally."

Elliot looked over her shoulder at the other two, but they didn't say anything in response. Was she threatening to kill him over something that was clearly an accident? It was an incredibly immature reaction to something that might have been solved by Koren offering him a Faction Token in exchange for the building.

"So you're a group of bounty hunters then?" Elliot said.

"As if you don't know who we are," Koren snapped, "What's your Faction called—how many members?"

Elliot wasn't sure if the protocol here was to keep it to himself or not, but this 'Koren' was actually managing to get under his skin, which hadn't happened in a long, long time. She was also threatening to come after him—he wasn't going to be telling her anything.

"Sorry, Koren," Elliot said, eyeing her down. "I'm not looking to recruit anyone to my faction—maybe try somewhere else?"

Koren's fiery anger turned to a colder fury.

"Are you fucking kidding me?" Koren hissed, "Everhunt has been around for *years*, and you think you can just take our building?"

Everhunt—it certainly seemed like the name of a group of bounty hunters would use.

"I'm pretty sure it's my building now, seeing as I paid a hundred thousand gold for it," Elliot said. "Why was the building available if you didn't want to sell it?"

"Why do you think, you little fuck!" Koren raged, "Our fucking leader died!"

An unfortunate event, but Koren had come into this interaction swinging, and he'd never had much sympathy for people who couldn't hold their tempers.

It *was* interesting information, though—the building would become available if he ever died. Would the Faction dissolve as well, or did it get passed down to the next highest-ranking member?

"Did Everhunt get passed on to you?" Elliot asked.

"*Yes,* I'm the leader of Everhunt now." Koren snapped, stepping closer. "Listen to me; you're a fucking vulture, but I'll give you *one* chance to make things right; Return the building to me, and you get to live."

Koren wasn't offering an exchange to compensate him for the building; she was expecting him to hand it over to her in exchange for his life. It had cost one-hundred-thousand gold to buy the Faction Token in the first place, and it was consumed during the building purchase.

That was a hell of a lot of gold, and this was gold that he had risked his life to obtain.

Given what he knew of this system so far—he very much doubted that Everhunt got any of that money back when their Leader died, most likely leaving them to come up with a hundred thousand gold to purchase another building.

Most likely one of the driving forces for why Koren was coming at him so hard.

"I get it now," Elliot said, watching her. "You can't afford to buy a building."

Koren looked stunned.

"You should probably work on that, Koren," Elliot said, eyeing the three of them. "Nobody is going to respect a faction when they don't even own a building."

Elliot shut the door in her face.

"Oh, you *little* fuck—" Koren shouted from the other side of the door.

He had made an enemy of the woman and most likely the rest of Everhunt, but that didn't bother him, not really. He'd died once already, and he spent most of yesterday on the edge of meeting that same fate. If the best Koren could come up with was to threaten his life—in a place like *this*—well, she was lacking in creativity.

Elliot turned to find Tyralklivi was watching him, looking worried.

"Don't worry," Elliot said quietly, looking around for the first time. "It will work out."

The bottom floor of the building was a single large room with a high ceiling and a stone floor. Tables, benches, shelves, and empty bookcases lined it. A massive stone fireplace sat near the center of the building, flat against the left wall.

There was a staircase on the right side of the room that led to an elevated balcony that looked over the rest of the bottom floor. There was another larger staircase on the left side of the room that must have led up to the second floor proper.

A long wooden countertop crossed most of the back wall, a bunch of stools on one side and shelving behind it—a bar. To the right of it, against the back wall and underneath the balcony, was a closed wooden door leading to an unknown room.

There were zero personal effects in the building, no rugs, no wall hangings, no paintings, nothing stocked the shelves behind the bar, no wood in the fireplace, just naked stone and wood. Either all of their personal effects had been placed in their Faction Bank when Everhunt had lost ownership of the building, or it had vanished.

"Home sweet home, huh?" Elliot muttered quietly.

He dropped down onto the nearest bench and just studied the room for a while. Tyralklivi was already investigating seemingly everything in sight, opening doors and vanishing into rooms and up stairwells.

He had a base of operations now; he wouldn't have to worry about having somewhere to stay in the future even if he ran out of money. All he needed to do now was make sure he kept a large supply of food handy and make sure he didn't die in the dungeon.

That was the real problem with this place; it wasn't just that the dungeon dragged you back in and put you in danger. It was that it did it while all these other pressures existed as well—making decisions while under copious amounts of stress was flirting with death.

The chances of someone living past their second dungeon would increase if they had somewhere to go afterward. Suppose they had a safe place to retreat to, filled with people who understood—they might even be able to break fears grip and move forward.

No place to stay, no food to eat, no warmth, no safety.

Solving those problems would alleviate most of that early stress, and a person could focus their mind entirely on protecting themselves in the dungeon if they had access to proper starting gear If they didn't have to choose in the first week between eating and getting eaten in the dungeon because they couldn't afford armor.

Elliot had an idea—what if he could help fix those problems?

What if he started bringing in more people, finding those who were lost, scared, and without hope. He could give them a place to live, a place where they didn't need to worry about equipment, or food, or warmth.

What if he stockpiled all the amour, health potions, and weapons he could find, allowed them the chance to actually go into the dungeon prepared? Once they'd outgrown that equipment or bought their own, they could donate it back for new members.

He could give them the information they needed to live here; in this strange place, they could work together to lift everyone up.

Elliot knew that he wouldn't have survived if Anette hadn't told him what she had or If that man with the impressive beard hadn't advised them to make goals, or if the armored man, who'd told them he hunted monsters for fun, hadn't helped them kill the bark-goblins.

If Amber and Tsunami hadn't fought the half-header for him, saving his life—if Aestus hadn't shown him the goodwill he had, or if Kara hadn't shared with him the information on how to save Tyralklivi from being slaughtered.

Tyralklivi herself had distracted that monster and assisted him in taking it down, even if she had misinterpreted his plan at the time. Arte, Meri, and Sara had all worked together with him to deal with Svent when he had tried to kill everyone.

Jacques had looked past his low-level and quiet demeanor and fought beside him against the monsters in the dungeon. Sirit had used up her expensive resources to help *everyone* in the ocean dungeon, despite her complaints.

Claire had fought with him as well, and hundreds of people had worked together to build the platform. Anna had sacrificed her Exotic greatsword, worth *millions* of gold, to get them all out of that dungeon.

There were others, people who had died fighting the monsters, unseen in each of the dungeons he'd participated in. Jacob the archer had died fighting, and even if Stanely had left his comrades to die, he had initially fought them as well.

Michelle had fought to save them both and ended up being the only one left alive.

Grant and Hannah had stood with him at the beginning, against a nightmare, and although they had been strangers... the three of them had worked together to survive. They'd told him not to go back in alone, and despite barely knowing him, had been willing to risk their own lives.

All of those people had helped him in one way or another, and without a single one of them, he wasn't sure he would still be alive.

He remembered having a conversation with Grant and Hannah about what this place might really be, about what it got from their participation in a death game. A farm for souls, energy, or something else entirely—it didn't matter what it was really; It only mattered that it needed *something*.

What happened when each new person to wake up in this place was met with a mentor in the Grey Room, provided with a set of armor, and protected until they could stand on their own two feet?

What happened when nobody else died?

Elliot couldn't wait to find out.

He had spotted the communication menu earlier when he was looking through the Faction settings, but he hadn't had the presence of mind to check it out further. Now he had that time, and he navigated to it once more.

Communication:
Send Global Faction Message.
Send Private Message.

The prompt that Tyralklivi had received when he had originally sent her the invitation to join the Faction had clearly been in a language that he couldn't read, but she could read it without issue, which meant that any prompts or menus that belonged to her were in her own language.

Private Message:
Hello, my name is Elliot. I'm sorry I didn't think of using this to communicate before. I also apologize for not being able to pronounce your name. Please send me a response when you receive this.

Elliot pressed confirm and leaned back in his seat, thinking, only to be immediately distracted when Tyralklivi called something out from up the stairs. He watched as she hopped off the bottom of the step and headed straight towards him.

Tyralklivi stopped in front of him, grinning, and rattled off a series of things he had no chance of deciphering. At his lost expression, she frowned before calling a menu up in front of her in that strange language; she knelt down beside him so he could see the transparent screen.

There was a small panel with the same type of layout as his own sent message, and as a test, he sent a second message to see how it updated on her own panel. It bumped upwards as the next message took its place—it was clearly working, so why wasn't she using it to reply?

He blinked as he realized there was something missing on her panel, and after a moment of comparing it to his own, he realized what it was. Where he had a prompt to enter a message, there was nothing on hers.

Private Message;
You can read this, but you cannot respond?

"Yes," Tyralkivi said, grinning over her shoulder at him.

Elliot gripped his neck in annoyance—it was one thing after another. He could still use it to make sure their already existing form of communication was understood.

Private Message;
The word 'Yes' means that you agree to something. For example; Are you hungry? 'Yes' would mean that you are hungry, 'No' would mean you are not hungry. If I asked you; Do you want to go back into the dungeon, 'Yes' would mean you would, 'No' would mean you do not. Do you understand?

"Yes," Tylraklivi said barely a second after he had sent it.

For a second, he wasn't sure she had even read the message—her reading speed was leagues above his own. The translation was actually really useful, even if she couldn't send a message in return. He spent several minutes composing a new message that hit all the points he wanted to address.

Private Message;
Tyralklivi, I am sorry you were brought away from your world. I do not currently know of a way to send you back without getting myself killed in the attempt. I will endeavor to find a way to send you back, but in the meantime, you are welcome to stay here; I have set faction benefits to give out enough gold for weekly food supplies. In the event that the shops will not sell it to you, I will purchase it for you. Is this acceptable?

Tyralklivi spent three seconds reading through the message, and he couldn't help but notice that her own panel's translation of his message was far more verbose and had many more words than his own had.

"Yes," Tyralklivi said, beaming at him. "Elliot."

Elliot glanced away at the sound of his name—feeling a bit strange.

Private Message;
I understand that you do not like to wear clothing, but it is a normal
custom here to do so when you go outside. If you do not wish to cover
yourself, other people may attack you or worse.

He sent the message, and she immediately frowned at him. Elliot sighed and typed out a shorter message.

Private Message;
You can do whatever you wish. Sorry.

Elliot pushed himself to his feet, heading for the stairs.

"Elliot!" Tyralklivi squawked.

He didn't reply, already feeling awkward, and instead moved towards the second floor. The building looked more empty the further he moved; the stone was also not the best for heating, so he'd need to buy floor lining of some kind.

The bottom floor did have the basic furniture, so he was optimistic that the top floor would have some kind of sleeping quarters with beds; otherwise, he was going to have to buy several. That meant finding someone who worked with wood and then looking for another person who knew how to sow.

The second floor was, in fact, a series of doors that led to small individual rooms, five in total, with the front end of the building being a common room of sorts with several large windows and the door that led to the balcony.

Elliot checked the first room and was relieved to find a relatively large bed, along with a small table, a cupboard, and a mirror.

"No more floor," Elliot said, relieved.

Elliot checked the other rooms and found them pretty much identical except for the last one, which was twice as big as the others. The fact that the closest bathroom was downstairs and the bedrooms were up here was pretty annoying. If, at any point, someone needed to use the bathroom, they would need to climb down the stairs and cross the bottom floor.

Tyralklivi stepped in beside him to look curiously around the room, and he stepped back out to let her look around unobstructed.

Elliot opened the door to the balcony and glanced out before shutting it. There were far too many people walking around outside, and he also noted that the three bounty hunters were sitting at the tavern across the street watching the building.

That was going to be a problem—but one he would deal with later.

He had already dumped half of his food supplies, all of his uncommon and rare equipment, into the common part of the guild bank for anybody to use.

Tyralklivi would be able to open it, and she would have enough food to last her for several weeks in the event of his demise. Since she was the only other member of the Faction, she would likely be promoted to Leader then as well, which would allow her to use the money in the guild bank.

Elliot sat at the table by the upstairs windows and opened his Status. He had a bunch of unspent exp sitting there, and by the time he'd finished, it had jumped from Level 11 to Level 15.

Status
Level 11 > 15
Speed 66 > 90
Strength 11 > 15
Magic 11 > 15
Defense 11 > 15

The attribute spread he possessed was starting to look more and more lopsided with every level. He couldn't do anything about it, though, because the points were automatically assigned.

Elliot wondered how fast a '90' made him relative to a normal unaltered human, but there was no way of checking, at least not without asking a level one for a footrace, which wasn't something he would ever bring himself to do.

Elliot shook his head, focusing on more important things.

He had a base of operations now, and he had two million gold sitting in the guild bank to help support anyone that joined. He wasn't going to do the math, but two million gold, distributed at 200 gold a week, was going to last a long while. When more people were recruited, the drain would grow, but if he could find more like-minded people to help him, then keeping it funded should be possible.

It fed well into his primary goal—to get stronger. The stronger he was, the more dungeons he could clear and the more money he could make—which would satisfy the secondary goal of keeping the bank full.

Elliot had to make a decision on the recruitment process; his initial plan had been to simply invite every new level one he encountered. That was still viable, but they would need to find accommodation elsewhere because the faction hall itself had limited rooms.

Elliot wondered if he should start buying up other buildings and letting people live in them for free— that would end up making the cost needed to keep everyone fed and housed static.

Tyralklivi came to sit near him at the small table, and deep in thought as he was, it took almost ten seconds before he realized he was staring straight at her naked chest—she'd dumped her clothes again.

Tyralklivi started speaking, a string of words so fast that he could barely follow the syllables—Elliot didn't respond, busy weighing the benefit of buying another building now or once they ran out of room.

Seeing as most of the larger buildings he'd seen on the map had been factions, he likely wasn't going to be picking any of those up any time soon—not in this section of the city at least. It was probably better to conserve funds until he knew more about what he needed, then spend it appropriately towards that end.

Tyralklivi was frowning at him again.

Private Message;
Sorry, I was working out what I'm going to do from now on. Would you like me to tell you?

"Yes," Tyralklivi said, beaming.

Elliot spent the next half an hour sending carefully worded messages explaining his general goal and how he intended to accomplish it. Tyralklivi seemed interested by the idea, from what he could gather anyway.

Private Message;
Want to help me save everyone?

"Yes," Tyralklivi grinned up at him.

Private Message;
I really need to teach you some new words.

"Yes," Tyralklivi said, tone smug.

Elliot spent the rest of the day 'sending messages to Tylraklivi and trying to expand her ability to communicate. He hadn't gone into the dungeon yet, but he was already feeling tired—and going into there now would be stupid.

He'd sleep first, then go.

Elliot headed into the bedroom closest to the stairs; none of the beds had sheets on the mattress, which was something he would have to deal with tomorrow as well. There was, however, a single pillow on each, albeit without a cover. He lay on the bed clutching the pillow, listening as Tyralklivi's voice floated up the stairwell, singing some strange song downstairs.

Elliot wasn't sure if he just couldn't appreciate the song or if Tyralklivi was just bad at singing.

Elliot sat up in his bed on high alert as the door clicked open, his heart furiously beating in his chest.

"Elliot?" Tyralklivi said quietly.

His hand, already wrapped around his spear, clenched into a fist as it vanished back into his Inventory—and once he was certain that hands weren't reaching out at him from the shadows, he finally managed to speak.

"Tyralklivi," Elliot sighed.

Tyralklivi took her name as permission to enter, slipping into the room and leaving the door wide open, much to his annoyance. He watched her cross the room and sit down next to his bed with her back to the wall.

Elliot had been consistently having nightmares now, and he could hazard a guess that she might be experiencing the same thing—that or she just wanted some company.

Private Message;
Can't sleep?

"Yes," Tyralklivi said softly.

Private Message;
Bad dreams?

"Yes," Tyralklivi said quietly, tucking her head into her knees.

Private Message;
I have them as well, every time I sleep.

Tyralklivi watched his face for a moment before reaching out and holding his wrist through the sheet. It was such an empathetic motion, so humanlike that he paused for several seconds before he managed to type his next message.

Private Message;
I can't imagine what it must be like for you here, in this alien place.
Are you scared?

Tyralklivi shook her head in the negative, something he had managed to teach her earlier in the day. Elliot noted she was smiling at him again.

Private Message;
You are braver than I am; I would be scared, I think.

Tyralklivi snickered to herself, apparently finding his cowardice amusing, but laughing at him meant she wasn't thinking about whatever terrors chased her awake. Tyralklivi said several things, clearly amused, before grinning up at him again.

Private Message;
I have no idea what you just said, but I'm almost certain you are mak-
ing fun of me.

"Yes," Tyralklivi said, smug.

Elliot wondered how smugness could be so universally clear, but he imagined sarcasm couldn't be far behind it. Tyralklivi suddenly yawned, and he found himself turning his face into his pillow to cover his own.

Private Message;
I know the dreams are bad, but you should try to sleep.

"No," Tyralklivi mumbled, still gripping his arm.

Elliot just watched her quietly.

Private Message;
Tomorrow, when I wake up, I will be returning to the dungeon twice.
What will you do?

Tyralklivi bit her lip at the message; no doubt distressed with the idea of willingly going back into the dungeon. Elliot realized that his message might have come off in a way he hadn't intended.

Private Message;
I'm not asking you to come with me; I will go alone. I'm asking if you
will be okay here on your own?

Tyralklivi turned, meeting his eyes in the dark room. She opened her mouth as if to say something, before stopping, and letting out a clear noise of frustration.

Private Message;
Not being able to understand you sucks, sorry.

"Yes," Tyralklivi said, aggrieved.

The was a lull in the one-sided conversation, and he found himself drifting back to sleep despite his best efforts.

A substantial amount of time must have passed while he was asleep, because the next time Elliot woke up, he found that he was no longer alone in the bed. Elliot swallowed at the feeling of her arms encircling him.

He quietly used his free hand to tip his pillow off the edge of the bed, and onto the ground before switching places with it. The freezing cold floor chased away the panic and he quickly made his way to the door.

Elliot looked back only once, to see if Tyralklivi had woken up during his escape—she hadn't, but it would be almost an hour before he had managed to shake the sight of her naked body curled around his pillow from his mind.

The Kings

With speed born of embarrassment, Elliot prepared himself before stepping out of the faction building. Sure enough, one of the three bounty hunters—the man—was sitting at a table across the road, watching.

As soon as their eyes met, the man stood up, and Elliot switched with a discarded strip of leather several buildings away. He switched twice more, moving closer to the gates each time, and once he'd gained enough distance that he was certain the man wouldn't have known where he'd gone, he returned to a normal walking speed.

The Torii stood where it always did, golden adornments as shiny as the first time he'd seen them. There were two groups milling by the gate, waiting for something, but they didn't bother him when he approached.

Elliot stepped through the gate and into the Grey Room. It was already filled with people, and Elliot immediately noted that—like usual—they all looked to be at a much higher level than him. Or at least they had the equipment of someone possessing a high level; Elliot himself was proof that if you were exceptionally lucky, you could stumble upon equipment far above your level and profit from it.

For all of the glowing weapons and elaborate armors that were visible within the grey room, there was something far more attention-grabbing. In the far corner, towering over everyone near him, was a familiar face, and Elliot immediately moved in his direction.

Elliot had only managed to cross half the distance between them his presence was noticed.

"Elliot!" Jacques boomed in surprise. "It is good to see you again—and so soon!"

The behemoth of a man stepped forward to clap him on the shoulder with a gentle impact, completely at odds with the size of the man's massive hands.

"It's good to see you to Jacques—I didn't think I would meet you again for a while either." Elliot said, faintly embarrassed, "I hope there's less water this time."

Jacques laughed at the comment, looking like he was in complete agreement. Elliot turned his attention to the other familiar face at his side.

"Anna?" Elliot tried hesitantly, hoping he'd heard her name correctly.

The woman managed a smile for him, and he took it to mean he had the right of it—she looked tired and sullen.

"That's me," Anna said, injecting some levity into her words. "You were in ocean dungeon the other day—Thanks for going into the water; I'm not sure I could have done the same."

Elliot just nodded at the thanks and moved to angle slightly away from them both, making sure he had enough room. Then he lifted his hand out and pulled her greatsword out of his inventory—Elliot stumbled under the unexpected weight of it, having never actually picked it up; the sheer mass the thick slab of metal had was even worse than Svent's Hammer.

The blade of the sword crashed into the floor of the grey room with a noise of tortured metal, and he grunted as the weight almost crushed his leg—Jacque's hand flashed out and caught the edge of the blade before lifting it up without difficulty.

"Thanks," Elliot managed, flushing. "Anna, I managed to get to your weapon before I left; I was hoping to run into you so I could give it back."

Anna's eyes were wide, and she seemed genuinely stumped.

"Sorry I dropped it," Elliot said, feeling uncomfortable at the silence.

This low strength score was becoming an issue—

"Elliot!" Jacques boomed but failed to follow it up with anything.

He held the massive blade out to Anna, handle first still effortlessly holding it—Elliot found himself wondering about the man's level once more. Anna took her weapon back, showing a similar lack of effort as she hefted the blade with ease.

"I can't believe you managed to get it back at all—it should have been right in the middle of the portal," Anna said, staring at him. "I'm even more surprised that you are just giving it back to me."

"The handle was just sticking out the back of the portal," Elliot admitted, remembering the searing cold of the water. "You were willing to sacrifice it to get us all out of that dungeon—I wanted to make sure it got back to you."

"Such diligence!" Jacque declared, clenching his fist. "It was most fortunate that we could meet with you so soon, my friend."

"I didn't even know your name until Jacques just shouted it at the top of his lungs," Anna said, flustered. "Not that I wouldn't have remembered it—I just hadn't heard it before."

"I wasn't completely sure what your name was either," Elliot admitted, not at all offended. "It doesn't really matter, though; we're even now."

"Are we?" Anna mumbled to herself.

"Elliot!" Jacques said, "Why are you back so soon—It hasn't yet been a week since you were last inside?"

"I've got a routine I stick to," Elliot said, "Two dungeons a day—it was originally four, but after last time I'm not sure I could keep to that."

"Indeed, the Ocean Dungeon was most unusual." Jacques agreed. "Returning to the dungeon so frequently—your will is strong, my friend."

"Why are you two back already?" Elliot asked. "Are you in one of the hunting factions?"

Jacques grinned, but it was Anna who spoke.

"Um—well, I was complaining about losing my weapon," Anna said, still off-balance. "Jacques decided he was going to help me make enough for another one."

"Indeed!" Jacques cheered. "I, too, owe the heroic Anna a great debt for providing us with a way out of that dungeon!"

Elliot smiled at the two.

"Jacques," Anna mumbled, elbowing the man. "Stop saying it so loud; it's embarrassing!"

"Ahaha!" Jacques laughed. "I apologize, Anna!"

"It is strange that you found yourself in another high-level dungeon,"

Jacques said thoughtfully, voice dropping to a reasonable volume. "I do not know if it is a bad omen to have it happen more than once or a good one because you have shown yourself quite able to overcome them."

Elliot had thought the same thing when he had seen the equipment of every nearby.

"I'm not sure why it keeps happening," Elliot said, admitted, "Most of the dungeons I've been in have been higher leveled ones—at least I think so."

Anna was frowning at both of them now.

"That is very abnormal," Jacques said, eyebrows raised high. "So much is unknown about the dungeon, but it is usually the case that most are kept within a range somewhat appropriate for your level, with a few rare exceptions."

"Outliers," Elliot frowned, "I had a level three-hundred try to kill me and everyone else in one of my first dungeons—I might be cursed after all."

"Truly?" Jacques said, concerned.

"Hold on," Anna said, finding a gap. "I'm missing some context here—what level are you?"

"Sorry," Elliot said, realizing that they had been talking past her. "I'm level fifteen."

"Fifteen!?" Anna said incredulously. "What the hell are you doing here?"

"Elliot is quite resourceful!" Jacque decided, smiling at her shock. "Did you not witness his skill in the Ocean Dungeon?"

"I witnessed him move things around with his ability!" Anna snapped, "This is completely different, Jacques!"

Elliot took a small step back from the woman as she stomped up to Jacques—the massive man simply angled his head down to better meet her gaze.

"There's usually a couple of level ones in every dungeon," Anna said firmly, "But after that first one, they are almost always graded down to within a hundred levels; level fifteen means he's been in at least a dozen or more dungeons—he shouldn't be here."

Elliot wasn't sure that Anna was correct about that because he'd seen multiple dungeons with people ranging anywhere from level one to level twenty-five mixed in with people approaching level two hundred or even higher than that.

Perhaps it was a case of their individual experiences being different simply by how broad a system this seemed to be. If both Anna and himself both had such different experiences, it was likely that one or even both of them weren't entirely correct, which could be a result of a shared misunderstanding of the hidden rules.

It was like that in life sometimes.

People always had personal anecdotes that they built their worldviews around; even the person who lived next door to you could have a series of experiences that were utterly unlike anything you could even have imagined.

In most cases, your experiences were dictated by societal factors; where you live, who your parents are, your access to education, your race, ethnicity, or gender—all of those things collated to create a unique experience.

It wasn't a perfect analogy, but there was some overlap; starting with a conclusion and then only looking for facts that supported it *always* ended with a lopsided view of the subject.

Anna, in her journey through this system, had only experienced dungeons where the level gap wasn't noticeably large. As she pieced it together and gained more information from others who had their own rationale, she likely began to unconsciously rationalize anything that had been slightly out of place with her theory.

In exchange for that rationalization, she had gained a *useful* understanding of the system. Even if it wasn't perfect, it had brought her a sense of stability and control over her own life within this place.

Elliot knew that his own conclusions were likely just as flawed.

His understanding grew with every Dungeon he entered, but he was only seeing a sliver of the entire picture each time, and the variations would no doubt continue to throw off any theory he built. Elliot had his own unconscious rationalizations, his own built-in biases, and as much as he wanted to say that he was aiming for objectivity...

Aiming for something didn't mean you would hit the target.

"What level are you both?" Elliot asked.

"Four-hundred-and-sixty-five," Jacque said proudly, without a hint of hesitation.

Elliot blinked at the ridiculous number—no wonder he was so strong, his attributes must have been monstrous.

"I didn't think you were *that* high," Anna said, sounding a bit caught off guard. "I'm only three-hundred-and-four; wait, this doesn't make any sense—"

"I suppose that means all three of us are out of the hundred level range," Elliot said, frowning.

Anna looked worried that her mental model of this place had been disturbed, but the proof was right in front of her, and she couldn't help but look at it. Their attention was brought around to the timer as it began to reach the high single digits.

"Do not worry!" Jacques declared, "We will fight together—what enemy could hope to stand before the three of us?"

Three enemy combatants with higher levels, he thought. Elliot shook his head; he had no intention of dying again, not when he'd finally found a way to do something real—he had a goal now, one that might end up actually helping people in this awful place.

"That's not the issue here," Anna sighed before dropping the subject. "Fine—what's our plan, Jacque?"

"I will handle the offense!" Jacques declared.

Anna shouldered her massive blade, and the weight of it seemed to bring out some of the energy he'd seen back in the Ocean Dungeon.

"Then, I'll be the defense," Anna said, a confident smile now in place. "I'll make sure to keep an eye on you, Elliot—so stay close to me, okay?"

Elliot glanced away from the look and gripped the back of his neck with his hand.

"You should both handle the offense," Elliot said, keeping his eyes on the timer. "If I see an opportunity—I'll set you up for an easy kill, and if you need repositioning, just call."

The timer hit zero, and the door appeared.

"Onwards, my friends!" Jacques cheered, striding forward.

Elliot and Anna fell in step behind the man as he clear a path to the door.

The first thing he noticed was that the Dungeon was beautiful—healthy, grassy plains stretched out into the distance on gently rolling hills, and the wind revealed its presence by gently brushing through the greenery.

There was some thick forestry to his left, and to his right was a largely mountainous region where the grass quickly turned to cracked and dried crags, colored a rusty brown. The mountains themselves looked like they would take several days to travel to by foot at least. The changes in elevation blocked his vision in much the same way the dunes had back in that Desert Dungeon, which meant there could be enemies over any of the distant ridges.

"It's beautiful," Anna said. "It's been a while since I've seen a Dungeon like this."

A startled shout drew their attention, and when he turned to face the noise, he spotted a man to his left staring past the entrance to the Grey Room, in the opposite direction. Elliot stepped past the doorway, and the second his vision was unobstructed by the tunnel—

"What?" Elliot whispered, stopping dead in his track.

"Oh, god," Anna said quietly.

Jacques remained uncharacteristically quiet.

"T7!" The man shouted, "It's fucking T7!"

A familiar door sat perfectly still in the distance, exactly like the one that acted as the entrance to their grey room—only it was thousands of meters tall, more massive than even the mountains that dotted the horizon.

The thick, misshapen fingers of an impossibly large hand slowly curled around the door, and a creature ponderously dragged itself out of the tunnel. Elliot had never seen something so vast in motion before—It was like one of the mountains had suddenly decided to stand up and move.

The creature's skin was a dark grey, rough and textured, not unlike an elephant. It had two disproportionately large arms, almost like a gorilla. Its face was non-existent; only a wrinkled mass of rough grey skin sat on its uneven shoulders.

Its legs were thick and stumpy, with massive flat soles on the bottom like that of a horse, and its first titanic steps out of the door sent a carpet of debris washing across the ground at its feet. The shockwave hit them a moment later, washing over them all like a sudden gust of wind that tossed Elliot's hair around.

"How are we supposed to kill something that?" Someone shouted, terrified.

"Is this a boss?" Elliot said quietly.

"No," Jacques said seriously. "This is a monster from the world known as T7."

"T7?" Elliot repeated, watching the thing slowly scan the horizon.

"I suppose you are still pretty new," Anna said quietly, "T7 is just a name, a designation given to homeworld of those creatures; it's one of the Death Worlds that have been reported by Archive."

Death Worlds—the implication was obvious; worlds whose inhabitants were absurdly dangerous in some way. But for that information to have gotten back in the first place, someone must have *survived*, which had to mean that it could be defeated.

"Archive is a faction that collects information about the Dungeons and verifies its authenticity," Anna said quietly. "They have a master list of Death Worlds and the categories they fall under."

Now that was the kind of invaluable information that Elliot wished he had known about days ago. He would be making a note to track down Archive in the near future.

"What is the category that a T7 falls under?" Elliot said quietly.

The colossal creature was now staring blindly at something with its back to them.

"Five Kings," Jacque said seriously.

Elliot frowned.

"Why is it called—" Elliot said before trailing off.

Another hand appeared on the edge of the door, even larger than the first one, and it slowly pushed itself out of the tunnel and knocked the first creature stumbling to the side. The ground shook dangerously as the creature fell to its knee beside the door, setting off another burst of wind and dust that washed over them.

"There's five of these things?" Elliot murmured. "What level are they?"

"Five hundred is the lowest one on record," Annan said quietly.

Elliot tried to wrap his head around it; Five creatures with a minimum level of five hundred each was a total level of two-thousand-five-hundred.

No, he could do better than that—there had been easily over a hundred people in the Grey Room.

A hundred people at an average level of two hundred meant that there was a minimum total level of twenty thousand for this Dungeon. That meant that each of these Five Kings could be anywhere from *level five-hundred* up to *level ten-thousand*, depending on the overall level distribution.

"Even the weakest one would be stronger than even Jacques," Elliot said quietly. "Can we even deal damage to something at that level?"

"Exotic, Legendary, and Unique Weapons hurt just about anything," Anna said quietly. "Anything rare or below would struggle or outright fail unless it had a special effect that let it hit above its level."

Elliot would likely be able to damage it because he was lucky enough to have ended up with an Exotic Skypiercer. The problem was, how did he actually go about killing something like this? They were vaguely humanoid in shape, as in they had a torso, arms, and legs, but they had no discernable head, which must have meant that whatever functioned as the creature's brain must have been somewhere in its torso.

The creature's legs were seemingly far more armored than the rest of its body. That could have been some kind of strange trick of evolution, though; for such large creatures, anything smaller than them would have only been able to attack its legs, which might have grown more armored in return.

They were ponderously slow, but because of their sheer size, a single stride carried them a massive distance. Each movement almost seemed to be like watching something move at half-speed, but even then, the terrifying forces that were sent everywhere from such simple actions would probably be enough to toss them around like ants in a gale if they got close.

"We need to stop them from moving around." Elliot said quietly, "The legs are the thickest closest to the feet, but the back of its thighs would be the easiest place to cut through."

'Easy' was relative here because there was no way that killing something like this was going to be easy.

"It won't be able to support its weight on a single leg, so we should attempt to sever one of them," Elliot continued, "Once it's no longer moving forward, we can move onto its back; its arms shouldn't be able to reach behind it with how thick they are. We can start on the arms next or attempt to cut through its back into the torso."

"I was thinking along the same lines." Jacques agreed without hesitation, "The issue will be keeping them from assisting each other."

"Five of them in total," Elliot said quietly, "Six teams; Five of them need a weapon capable of hurting it, so we need to choose the teams carefully. Each team needs to lead one of the Kings away from the other. The sixth team needs to actively hunt down and kill each of the other enemy teams."

"Just like that, huh?" Anna said, swallowing. "Neither of you are even considering that we might lose?"

"Lose?" Jacque said, taken aback. "Absolutely not!"

Elliot nodded in agreement—he had a goal to make real.

"I refuse to lose," Elliot said.

"Boys," Anna said, seemingly baffled. "Too stupid to be scared."

Elliot felt a flash of annoyance at being called stupid, and Anna caught the narrow-eyed look he sent her way.

"Jacques," Elliot said, "You're going to have to take the lead again; we are in your hands."

"Leave it to me!" Jacques boomed.

Jacques turned and headed towards the largest mass of people, shouting for attention at the top of his lungs and explaining the plan to everyone. Elliot watched the man effortlessly take charge—he felt a strange mix of awe at the man's commanding presence and envy that he could never do something like it.

The idea of standing up in front of all those people and trying to get them to listen to him scared him more than the colossal beings they were planning to kill. He noticed that Anna was still watching him, no doubt realizing that she'd managed to ruffle his feathers.

"You've got a strange look on your face, Elliot," Anna said, amused.

"I was just thinking that Jacques is an amazing person," Elliot said quietly.

"Jacques is something else alright," Anna smiled at him. "You're something special as well, you know? I was frozen in terror, and neither of you even blinked."

Elliot had never heard something more wrong.

"I'm not special," Elliot said with certainty, watching as the third titanic creature dragged itself out of the door. "If anything, I'm the opposite; I spent my entire life hiding away, too scared to do anything for fear of failing—and the one thing I did manage to muster up the courage to do? Well, that's why I'm here in the first place."

Anna watched him with an expression that he couldn't decipher entirely—either pity or sympathy, he wasn't sure it mattered. Elliot felt his fingers digging into the palm of his hand, grip painfully tight.

"I've finally found something I want to do, something I'm not allowed to fail at." Elliot admitted, "So I'm directing every strand of my attention into accomplishing it."

Elliot could almost feel her attention weighing down on him, and he felt that immediate pang of regret he always had after accidentally revealing something too personal. Anna's hand came to rest on his shoulder, and he felt a warmth rise to his face at the unexpected touch.

"Self-actualisation," Anna said in understanding.

"I suppose it is, in a way," Elliot said quietly, attention entirely focused on where her hand met his shoulder. "I just had to die before I could reach it."

The arguing from the rest of the group had been steadily growing louder as four of the massive creatures begun to move; the fifth, and easily the largest, was still in the process of extricating itself from its Grey Room.

"None of that matters!" Jacques boomed, disregarding one of the naysayers. "We must come together to defeat the Five Kings!"

"You don't even know if we can!" A man said, "For fucks sake, Jacques—*look at them!*"

There was a general rumble of agreement from a small portion of the crowd, but the rest were silent.

"They are a daunting sight; I will acknowledge," Jacques said passionately, "However, we can not give up the battle before it has even begun!"

The man standing across from Jacque had the expression of someone who was realizing they were arguing against a stonewall.

"Jacque is right," One woman said. "We should at least attempt this task before deciding we are outmatched—Zachary, if you have nothing to contribute, then stop interrupting."

"Fuck off, Amelia," Zachary grunted but fell silent once more.

"Jacques, please continue." Amelia said, "How do you plan on constructing these teams?"

Elliot found his eyes drawn to the woman. Tall, blonde hair and a sharp intelligence shone from behind her eyes.

"Thank you, Amelia!" Jacques said, pleased before projecting his voice. "Elliot—if you could explain your plan once more!"

Elliot almost flinched when he realized what the man was asking, and when Anna's hand landed on his back, he found himself steered towards the head of the group. Jacques pulled him closer and smiled down at him in expectation.

Elliot silently cursed the man as everyone in the field turned to look at him.

"Six teams total," Elliot managed, "Five teams of twenty-five, with at least ten people with Exotic or better weapons per team. Those without weapons capable of hurting these things are on protective detail for the rest of their team; each team also needs at least one person to function as a lookout."

Elliot swallowed, feeling the pressure build as they continued to watch him.

"The sixth team's job is to actively hunt the other enemy teams that are stuck in here with us." Elliot spoke, "The makeup of that team should include at least one person capable of tracking, but other than that, it's up to you."

The pressure bearing down on him felt like gravity had suddenly increased tenfold, and he pushed everything he was feeling deep down inside of him, as he always did when things grew too much. A cold indifference filled him, leaving no space for anything like worry or care.

"The plan is simple," Elliot said, "Each team will attack one of the King's while also ensuring they cannot assist each other. Focus all damage on a single leg, the upper part of the thigh, where the hide looks thinnest—our goal is to ground them first."

There were some mutters at the idea, as each of them considered the massive undertaking they were discussing.

"Simply put, cut through the back of the thigh." Elliot said, "Once your target is downed, move on to the next limb. Once it's incapable of moving, either wait for it to die or begin focusing the damage near the center mass—that's the most reasonable place for its central nervous system to be located."

"What if it's somewhere else?" Someone called quietly.

"If the central nervous system isn't in the obvious spot, it's unlikely that we will stumble upon it blindly." Elliot said clinically, "We will need to start destroying as much surface area as we can and let the thing bleed out while it's unable to move."

"Its arms are far too thick at the shoulders for it to be able to reach behind itself—if you are injured or unable to continue fighting, move to its back." Amelia spoke up, "Be wary; we do not know what type of ability these five Kings possess."

"To summarise," Elliot said, watching them. "Take out one of its legs; Once it falls, start removing the other limbs. Finally, move on to destroying its torso—if all of that fails, begin cutting pieces off until it stops fighting back."

Elliot paused for a moment as he tried to simulate what he would do if something tiny managed to cut his leg off, and he was on the ground.

"The most likely response to being downed is that the creature might roll over in an attempt to crush us." Elliot added belatedly, "Be ready to move quickly if it begins taking any large movements."

Jacques patted him on the shoulder in support, and Elliot stared out at the group passively, feeling nothing at all.

"I'll leave the teams to you," Elliot said, stepping away from the front of the group.

Elliot stopped near the Grey Room to watch as the colossal fifth king—almost an entire third bigger than the next largest. It was rounding the door now, turning away from them almost in the complete opposite direction.

They had been very lucky to be situated right in-between two of the shorter King's paths. If they had begun moving straight towards the group, they wouldn't have had the time needed for Jacques and Amelia to sort everyone into their respective teams.

Jacques was built to lead; he commanded the attention of everyone around him, and his physical size only accentuated the man's presence. The group in large had fallen in line with the man's directions, and hope had begun to once more.

But not for Elliot—he likened it to watching the world through a sheet of glass, in that he could see everything perfectly clearly, but the emotion that should have been there never made it to the other side.

It was an old habit, one he'd retreated to when he was feeling overwhelmed—he would just shut down and float through the situation, detached and indifferent. He'd heard several people comment on it back in the old world; Dimitri and May certainly more than most. Now here he was again, falling back into old habits; the fact that it had gotten him through so much trouble in the past only made it more difficult to stop.

Elliot stared down at his hand, feeling almost as if it wasn't even his.

"Elliot!" Jacques called, "You're on team three!"

Elliot just nodded and traced the man's massives finger to where team three was situated. Anna was standing over there already, along with a bunch of unknown people. He made his way over, joining them without comment. Most of his attention was focused on the King closest to their position—at its current angle, it would soon pass them by completely.

The ground rumbled warningly with its every step, the very land protesting its existence.

"Are you alright, Elliot?" Anna asked.

Elliot just nodded.

"Anna, are you one of the DPS?" Elliot said in return.

"DPS?" Anna said strangely, still frowning.

"Damage dealers," Elliot corrected, "It's a term from the old world."

"Ah, I see," Anna said, smiling again. "Yeah, now that I have my weapon back, I'm going to be one of the ones attacking—thanks again for that, by the way."

"It's fine—" Elliot said.

A spark of light cut across the sky, and Elliot traced its path with his eye before it connected with the upper body of the Second-King—A massive wave of fire burst into existence, expanding over and behind the creature's shoulders as it strode through the conflagration, entirely unaffected.

One of the other enemy teams had decided to begin their own attack.

"We have to kill these things?" A woman with a glowing katana murmured.

The Second-King lumbered onwards, smoke trailing it and Jacques's voice rang out once more.

"The team numbers are matched to the size of the King." Jacques boomed, "Team one will be going after the First-King."

"Of course, you would give us the biggest one," A man from team five said, a massive glowing Warhammer resting on his shoulder, not unlike the one that Svent had used. "Thanks a lot, man. Which team are you on anyway?"

"I will also be joining team five, Dante!" Jacques boomed.

"Nice," The man said, giving a lopsided smile.

Elliot recognized that their previous plan for Jacque, Anna, and himself to stick together wasn't viable anymore. He sought out the Third-King, it was covered in grey outcroppings of jagged hide, and its two arms were widely disproportionate in size, the left barely half as long as the right. The left side, from shoulder to hip, was covered in a massive strip of some kind of dark moss that looked completely out of place on its otherwise grey body.

It was also the one closest King to the group staging ground—at least he wouldn't have to travel too far to attack it.

"This is it, my friends—you all have your teams and your targets!" Jacques boomed, "Fight well and do not die!"

There was a rousing cheer from some of the more energetic members of the Dungeon before everyone began to move. Elliot took off towards the Third-King, sensing the surrounding area with his swap sense in case he needed to use it.

Anna caught up to him, her absurdly high attributes easily matching and surpassing his own speed. The rest of the team followed along with them, everybody keeping together as a single large group.

"That big crater on its right thigh is our target." Elliot said, "It's smaller arm is on the left side; it should have more difficulty holding itself up with the weaker arm, further unbalancing it."

A man with short red hair overheard the comment and repeated it loud enough for the rest of the group to hear. Elliot stayed focused on the Third-King—it had been absurdly large at a distance, but it was only growing bigger the closer they got to it.

The vibrations that followed each of its massive footsteps shook the ground angrily, and the bursts of dust and air were getting stronger. The woman who had been assigned the lookout position on their team pulled up next to them, somehow flying above the ground.

"Captain! I'm going up to see if there are any enemy teams nearby." The woman said brightly. "Is that cool?"

Elliot had no idea why she was calling *him* Captain; he was one most likely the weakest person in the entire Dungeon.

"Do what you want," Elliot said, thinking about the situation. "Try not to stay stationary in mid-air for more than a moment—anyone with a ranged attack from the other enemy teams could take a shot at you."

"Aye, aye, Captain!" The woman chirped before zipping straight up into the air at high speed.

"You sound different than earlier," Anna said, frowning as they ran. "Something happened when you told everyone the plan—"

"Don't worry about it," Elliot said quietly.

They fell silent for several minutes, just the sound of twenty-five pairs of feet hitting the dirt and the Third-King shattering the landscape.

"Which city are you in?" Anna said suddenly, breaking the silence.

Elliot glanced over at her—the hint of more information about this place drawing his attention.

"The one directly next to the edge of the world," Elliot said.

"Hell? The first one?" Anna wondered, "It's been a long time since I've been there; I'm at Vice."

"I wasn't aware the city even *had* a name," Elliot said. "Is Vice substantially different from Hell?"

"Absolutely, and it's *exactly* what your thinking," Anna said, smirking. "A city-sized red light district, more or less—It's great."

Before he had the chance to further investigate, the flying woman reappeared by his side. The Third-King's foot crashed down again, and a burst of dust assailed them.

"No teams nearby unless they are using a power to stay out of sight." The flying woman said, arm up in front of her face to brace against the wind.

"What's your name?" Anna asked, raising her voice over the wind. "I'm Anna!"

"Lili!" Lili chirped. "Have you guys ever seen something like this before? I know I haven't."

"No," Elliot said.

"I've seen some big monsters before," Anna admitted, "But nothing even close to this scale."

"What about you, Charles?" Lili called to the red-haired man from earlier.

"Nope!" Charles laughed, "There was this one world with these massive walking tree monsters, but they weren't even half as tall as this guy's shins."

Elliot tried picturing a giant walking tree; how strange.

The Third-King continued to stride away from them, completely un-aware of their presence—it had gained enough ground that they were now approaching it from the back of its left leg. In a few minutes, it would be moving directly away from them, and it would become a much harder task to chase it down.

There was an ear-splitting crack that came from somewhere far away, and then a wave of force hit them from behind, only slightly less than the shockwaves they were already fighting against. Elliot looked back to see a massive earthen spear angling out of the ground directly in front of the Forth-King.

"That's its ability?" Lili said, alarmed, "How is this fair—it's the size of a fucking mountain!"

The massive spire of the earth was facing the opposite direction that team four had been approaching from, so it must have been aimed at something else—likely another enemy team. The attack began to crum-ble into millions of boulders, each raining down on the ground in an unending bombardment.

Elliot turned his attention back to the Third King, studying the land-scape and trying to find the best place to start the attack. There was a large outcropping of rocky ridges in the distance, and they would need to engage it before it reached them—the fewer things the creature could grab onto, the better.

"What do you think this one's ability is?" Charles called out.

Elliot had been trying to work it out since he first saw the creatures. Each of them was visibly different, and their target was covered in dark moss on its left side. The others all had a more cracked and dry look to them, but this one had an overall smoother appearance than the others.

"Something to do with water?" Elliot said. "Unless it spends a lot more of its time near water than the others."

"Maybe its power is to grow moss!" Lili said, voice hopeful.

"I don't think we're that lucky, Lili!" Charles laughed.

"How are we getting up to the crater?" Anna called.

Elliot eyed the right leg—the folds in its skin coalescing into tracks, trails, and rocky landings more reminiscent of mountainous trails than anything you would expect to find on a living creature.

There was all manner of debris caught amongst the gaps, and in some places, he was sure he could actually see plant life growing. There was plenty of things he could use to trade places with, and he'd be able to switch between the different elevations, moving from one platform to the next.

"Can everyone make the jumps between those levels?" Elliot asked.

He glanced at Charles, hoping the man would take up the mantle of spreading the question to the others. Thankfully he did, repeating it much, much louder—there was a series of responses, almost as loud and mostly positive. Out of the twenty-five people on Team Three, five of them weren't sure they could make the jump.

"Lili, can you carry someone while flying?" Elliot asked.

"Yeah!" Lili said, "I won't be able to do them all at once, though, maybe two at a time?"

"That will have to do—I'll get the rest," Elliot said.

"Yes, Captain!" Lili said in response.

"I'm not the captain," Elliot said, a flicker of something cracking his indifference. "My name is Elliot."

"Sorry, Captain!" Lili laughed.

Elliot sighed.

"See near the right side of the ankle?" Elliot spoke, "There is plenty of places to stand, prioritize safety over speed, and once we are actually on the thing, we should be able to pick our way up the protrusions easily enough."

Charles relayed the words, and he waited for him to finish before speaking again.

"We don't want to get too split up," Elliot added, "Keep all of the damage dealers focused on a single area; we can spread out once it's downed."

Once more, Charles called it out, and they received a wave of acknowledgments.

They were almost behind the Third-King now, and they couldn't move much further right without running into the craters it left behind. The shaking of the ground was far, far worse here, and every step it took sent them stumbling as they fought to get closer.

One of the waves of force that rushed past knocked Lili out of her flight, and she tumbled towards the ground in front of them—Charles lept forward at an absurd speed, snatching her out of mid-air before she could crash.

Elliot was reminded that they were following his pace, and now he was slowing them down.

"Thanks!" Lili yelped.

The Third-King's foot entered the range of his swap-sense, and Elliot was startled to find that he was actually able to swap with it. He'd assumed there would be some kind of upper size limit, but it didn't seem to be the case. Unfortunately, he couldn't capitalize on that because if he switched with it, it would suddenly appear on top of all of his allies, killing them instantly and putting himself on its path forward.

The debris that he had seen from afar fell into his range, rocks and dirt clumps sticking tenaciously in the gaps between the crags. Even the tangled clumps of dark moss registered to his swap-sense. He would be able to use his ability somewhat freely, but he was more than glad that he had restocked his supply of rocks.

Elliot took a deep breath before steeling himself—there was nowhere to go but up.

"Go!" Elliot called.

He swapped with a piece of loose debris on the creature's right leg and lost his balance as the leg lifted up for the next step, and he gripped the stone-like skin of the creature to keep his footing. The wind rushed past his hair, sending it fluttering everywhere as he watched the rest of Team Three give chase.

Elliot could see the five that weren't sure whether they could keep up, already lagging behind the rest of the group and likely with speed scores even less than his own. He braced himself as the creature's foot touched down once more.

The instant that everything finally stopped shaking, he swapped places with the person who was the furthest behind, depositing them in his place on the ledge. The next few seconds were filled with a furious series of exchanges that dropped three more of the group on the platform. Lili carried the last member with her, dropping the man off beside the others.

"Thanks!" A man said nervously, clinging desperately to the leg. "I wasn't sure I could even get up here!"

Elliot didn't stick around to chat.

He found the next area that was large enough for them to all move to. There were three platforms in range; two of them were too far between the things massive legs for it to be safe. The third was too close to the inside of its leg to be safe from the wind.

The stronger members of Team Three had already begun scaling the Third-King with blistering speed, sprinting, leaping, and ascending the platforms with an agility that far surpassed the rest of them.

"Brace yourselves!" Elliot called as his group fell behind the bulk. "We are going up again!"

"Ready!" A blonde woman called, which led to a whole round of affirmatives from the others.

Elliot swapped up onto the platform and scattered a bunch of rocks to give himself more objects to swap with. The creature lifted its leg again, and he held onto the thick grass that was growing out of the crack. He waited for the foot to descend again and then performed another series of swaps to move them up to the new tier, leaving them as close to the grass as he could.

Something appeared in his range above him, and he snapped his gaze up to see a man tumbling downwards, too far away from the leg to catch himself. The leg lifted off the ground in preparation for a step, and the distance abruptly increased, leaving the man free falling.

Elliot tossed a rock out in the direction of the man and then swapped with it; he came out of the swap spinning before launching a second rock as hard as he could. The man came into his range, and Elliot swapped with him, canceling the man's downward momentum.

The two of them began falling again as their descent began to speed up once more. When they were only meters off the ground, he switched a final time, canceling the momentum again and leaving them both to drop to the floor unharmed.

"Holy fuck!" The man managed. "Thank you—man, I thought I was done."

Elliot turned to watch the Third-King continue its stride away from them and began running once more—the other man caught up to him within seconds but slowed to match his pace.

"Can you get back up?" Elliot called.

"Yeah!" The man said firmly, "Do you want me to wait for you?"

"No—I can get back faster on my own." Elliot called, "Be more careful this time!"

"See you up there!" The man called before bursting forward at a blurring speed.

Elliot swapped at his max range and then four more times after that before he was once more within range of the Third King. He swapped back up to the same platform as before and then up to the grass-covered crack he'd landed next to the first time.

He ignored the response to his sudden reappearance, searching for the next spot above them—there were two platforms that were big enough for several people on each.

"Three on that one!" Elliot called, pointing it out, "Two on that one!"

"Ready!" The same blonde woman said in response.

Elliot moved them all up again, splitting them between the two platforms, and then moved them a second time to a larger, safer platform above.

"Kleo! Are you alright?" One of the men called.

Elliot checked—the blonde woman, apparently named Kleo, was look-ing distinctly unwell, and her face was visibly pale.

"This is way too high—" Kleo said weakly, cradling her stomach. "I think I'm going to be—"

Elliot wanted no part of that, so he quickly swapped everyone else up to the next platform, and once he returned for her, he found Kleo vomit-ing—most of which went over herself as the wind picked it all back up again.

"You alright?" Elliot called, hesitant.

"No," Kleo groaned. "Take me up!"

He'd never been afraid of height, so he couldn't quite understand her reaction—the view from even this far up the creature was breathtaking, and it gave him a clear view of the other four Kings in the distance.

The Second-King was still steadily bombarded with flickering sparks and absurd amounts of fire, but it was having just as much effect as it had originally—which is to say none at all.

The Forth-King was actually down to one knee already, a massive gap-ing wound gouged out of the inside of its thigh and visibly even from this distance. The Fifth-King and largest of them was still striding away, seemingly unharmed.

They were almost at the crater he had spotted from the ground now, and with two move series of swaps, the rest of the less mobile members were able to start helping. The other members that had already made it up were already making progress with cutting into the creature's hide.

Anna was at least three meters deep in a tunnel she had carved with her greatsword, and thick black blood already shin-deep was pouring out of the hole. Another man's hammer crashed into an unbroken spot of his own, and a large, perfectly round circle was compressed inwards—blood exploded outwards over him and everyone around him.

Elliot gagged—the smell of the blood was rank, and his throat constricted for a moment as if he might throw up. He gritted his teeth and removed his spear from the inventory, catching it around the handle and moving forward.

It passed through the hide almost without resistance, and he began carving out thick layers of the hide and working his way inwards. He tried his best to ignore the disgusting blood that was pouring out at his feet, but it was almost impossible.

Kleo strode up beside him, nose wrinkled up in disgust and face even more pale than before. Elliot watched her set both of her hands against the hide—a massive spiral of force tore its way through the leg, circling inwards.

It burrowed in further than anything anyone else had managed but the wound brought with it a flood of thick black fluid taller than she was. It washed over her from above, and she was submerged in the substance before being dragged off the edge of the platform by the force of it.

Elliot swapped with her before he'd even register what he was putting himself into and found himself surrounded by the rancid liquid. He was unable to move from the weight of it and desperately switched places with a rock on a lower platform.

He landed on his knees, covered in filth and vomiting. The stench of the King's blood was the worst thing he'd ever smelt, and as much as he managed to scoop off himself, the smell remained.

More of the disgusting blood flooded over the side of the crater, splashing down the King's leg as the wound grew in size. Elliot swapped back up to the crater, the floor of which was now knee-deep across the entire thing.

He found Kleo on her hands and knees again, covered in the vile stuff and once again throwing up.

Elliot coughed as he made his way over to her and pulled out one of the many containers of water he had purchased during his food runs. He upended one of them over her head in an effort to wash the blood off, and she turned her face up into the water. He placed the second one in her hands and then pulled a third out for himself, drenching his face in the water.

"Thank you." Kleo managed. "Did I go off the edge—I thought I was falling."

Kleo began dry heaving again, and he placed another container in her hand before standing up.

"You went off the ledge," Elliot mumbled, spitting to remove the taste of vomit and blood.

Elliot forced himself to move back towards the gaping hole in the Third-King's thigh, unable to understand how it hadn't noticed what they were doing to it yet—did these things not feel pain? It was the only explanation for it, otherwise, it would have done *something*.

The more they injured the thing, the more it bled, and the worse the disgusting smell became. Most of Team Three was throwing up at this point as they struggled to injure the King.

Elliot started widening the wound once more, cutting his way towards the inner thigh. Anna and the man with the hammer had made some significant progress in their own hole and were now thigh-deep in the blood.

Kleo stepped up to the wall again determinedly and placed her hands against the wall, facing the same direction as he was. Elliot took two steps backward, and when the massive spiral dug a trench in its thigh, he swapped Kleo away from the wave of blood.

"Thanks." Kleo said gratefully, "My throat feels like it's on fire."

Elliot took out another container of water and passed it to her—Kleo greedily drank it before trying to wash her mouth out.

"Your power is the fastest method available from what I can see," Elliot said. "Keep your attacks to three-second bursts, and I'll move you out afterward."

"Okay, Captain!" Kleo croaked.

Elliot scrunched his face up at the title and stepped back as Kleo moved forwards again, slopping through the blood. Kleo looked over her shoulder at him, making sure he was ready before she drilled another massive trench out of the side of its thigh.

Elliot swapped her out again before avoiding the wave himself—the blood was getting too high up to his hips now.

"Drill a hole downwards and on an angle there!" Elliot instructed, "So the blood that's pooling can escape out down its leg!"

"Yes, Captain!" Kleo called.

"Stop calling me that!" Elliot snapped. "My name is Elliot!"

Kleo ignored him entirely as she followed his instructions, and the level of the blood immediately started to lessen as it drained out of the tunnel and down the side of the King's thigh.

"Another one there!" Elliot called.

"Here?" Kleo called.

"Yes!" Elliot confirmed.

The blood level steadily lowered as they made more drainage holes, and soon they were moving back to the original task.

"Thanks!" Someone shouted from in the main tunnel. "I thought I was going to have to swim in this fucking shit!"

They continued the pattern of drilling and swapping and then made more drainage holes as they went. After almost half an hour of work, they encountered a problem—a wall of hardened white bone.

"Is this bone?!" Kleo called "Captain!"

Elliot stabbed at it with his spear, and it cut through with a very noticeable amount of resistance, but it did cut. Kleo stepped forward and knocked on it with her knuckle to test its hardness.

"It's bone," Elliot agreed, "Do you think your attack will work on it—"

The wall shattered into millions of inch-long shards of bone, as Kleo attempted to do exactly that. Elliot had started moving as fast as he could, but while he managed to switch them both out, he still ended up with shards embedding the entire left side of his body.

The pain was overwhelming, and he struggled to draw a health potion from his inventory—he didn't even get it to his mouth before he realized he'd need to remove the fucking shards before it would heal.

He drank it anyway.

"Captain!" Kleo said, horrified.

Kleo got out relatively unscathed, mostly because by the time the shards had reached them, he was the only thing left in the area. Elliot gritted his teeth and pulled one of the shards out of his shoulder.

"Help me pull them out," Elliot gasped, yanking the next one out.

Kleo stepped forward and started yanking them out as fast as she could—the process was painfully slow, and by the time most of them had been removed, he'd gone through four health potions. He realized at some point that he'd been silently crying almost the entire time.

The now-familiar pattern of the Third-King's steps changed, the platform beneath them slanted, and the blood that was washing off the edge through the drains began to pool in the tunnels they'd dug. Elliot hit the point where the angle was too steep and, along with Kleo, began sliding down into one of the tunnels.

He swapped with a patch of blood that was still in the air and saw beneath him the Third-King's knee crash into the ground below, shattering the ground for miles and sending everything into the air. Elliot swapped twice more before landing on the side of the platform they'd been digging into.

The Third-King attempted to catch itself with its hands, but the smaller arm failed to hold its weight, and the colossal being crashed into the ground, now laying prone. The leg he was in slide out from under it, and he held on as it too crashed flat against the ground. The instant it stopped moving, he took a deep breath, closed his eyes, and then started swapping everyone out of the blood-filled crater in its thigh.

He'd already lost everything in his stomach already, but it didn't stop him from heaving the entire time.

"Is everyone okay?" Anna managed.

Most of Team Three was too busy following his example to respond, and Elliot struggled to his feet. He stumbled a few feet along the edge of the crater and managed to catch his breath.

"Move to its back!" Elliot called weakly. "We aren't done yet."

Elliot made his way up the Third-King's thigh, moving all the way up to its back, making liberal use of Swap to do so. The King was moving beneath them, trying to leverage itself upwards with its stronger arm but mostly failing, its useless right leg entirely failing to alleviate the weight.

It took him several long minutes to make it to the center of its back, and he stopped washing his face again with the last of his water and waiting for the others to catch up.

"Elliot!" Anna greeted tiredly.

"Anna." Elliot returned, "We need to de-limb it—Head for the right arm, I'll send more people your way."

Anna vanished in a burst of speed, leaving him to wait for the others.

"Captain!" Lili said weakly, the next to arrive. "What are we doing?"

Elliot immediately delegated the task to her.

"I need you to tell half of the group to head to the right arm," Elliot said, "The other half to the left arm—that's where I'm going."

"I'm on it, Captain!" Lili agreed, lifting off again and speeding back down the King's back.

Elliot started moving towards the left arm, and before he'd even made it halfway, he was joined by both Kleo and Charles.

"Captain!" Charles said in greeting. "Thanks for the save back there."

"Not you too," Elliot mumbled.

The left arm was only half the size of the right one, and with Kleo's ability to gouge out large areas quickly, they made significantly faster progress in tearing through to the bone. Even then, the right arm was still the first to break under their assault as Anna's portion of the team managed to cut their way through.

The Third-King crashed back down onto his torso, shoulder now flat against the ground, and its left arm was caught beneath the bulk of its weight—they'd won.

Hours later, the Third-King rumbled beneath them, unable to maneuver with all of its limbs removed.

The left leg had taken just as long as the first had, despite the lack of movement helping things along—everyone in Team Three was tired, and it had slowed them down. The King was getting progressively quieter as the black fluid that served as its blood leaking out in rivers that would leave the already ruined land tainted.

Elliot, for his part, lay on his back staring up at the sky, utterly exhausted.

"We fucking did it!" Charles howled from further down the leg. "Were unstoppable!"

There was a surge of approval from the rest of Team Three as they sat upon the slowly weakening body of their enemy. None of the other Kings were in sight any longer, not even the largest of them.

"Captain," Kleo groaned beside him. "I feel sick again."

"I'm not the captain, Kleo." Elliot said arms spread out at his sides, "I already told you my name."

"I forgot it," Kleo admitted, entirely without shame.

"It's Elliot," Elliot offered.

"I'll remember this time," Kleo said, "How'd you know my name?"

"I heard someone say it earlier," Elliot said. "Are you another one from Vice?"

"Yeah!" Kleo said, "Are you here as well?"

"I'm in hell," Elliot decided, "Funnily enough, I'm told that's also the name of the first town."

Kleo snorted at the weak attempt at levity.

"Hell sucks," Kleo said, rolling over onto her side. "Why are you still there?"

"I woke up in the Grey Room less than a week ago," Elliot said, "I haven't exactly had time to look around—I didn't even know there *were* other places you could go to."

He had suspected it, but the actual confirmation had come from Anna and Jacques earlier.

"What?" Kleo said, confused, "You have an Exotic spear, and your armor looks super expensive."

"I'm level fifteen," Elliot refuted, "A high-level guy tried to kill me, and I stole his weapon."

Elliot could already tell she didn't believe him, but there was no prize for arguing here.

"That's absurd," Kleo said.

"What level are you?" Elliot asked instead.

"Don't you know to never ask a woman her level?" Kleo said.

"I'm almost positive that's age," Elliot denied, "Levels have nothing to do with it."

"Oh," Kleo said, with feigned surprise, "In that case, I'm level two-seven-four."

"Why were you struggling to climb if you're such a high level?" Elliot wondered.

"I'm lopsided towards defense and magic," Kleo admitted, groaning. "I also have *terrible* motion sickness—I still can't believe that followed me to the afterlife."

"That explains all of the vomit," Anna said as she stopped beside them.

"Shut up!" Kleo said in dismay, "That was a group hallucination brought on by the smell."

"The smell of your vomit, maybe." Anna laughed, sitting down beside them. "Your plan worked."

"It was Jacques's plan," Elliot murmured, watching the clouds. "You heard him, he was thinking the exact same thing, and he organized everybody."

"What are you, allergic to taking credit or something?" Kleo said, bemused, "Imposter syndrome? Shy? Ate too much humble pie? What's the deal, huh?"

Rather than answer such an annoying series of questions, Elliot rolled over to face away from them both.

"Captain!" Kleo said in fake anguish. "I am your loyal attendant; don't turn your back on me!"

Elliot ignored her—he should have joined Jacque's team.

"Now what?" Kleo said, apparently unable to tolerate silence. "Should we go find the other teams?"

"Elliot?" Anna prompted, passing the responsibility onto him again.

"Why does everyone keep expecting me to tell them what to do?" Elliot said, frustrated, "Look; we wait for the Third-King to die, then we move back towards Team Four, see if they need any help finishing up then rotate to each team until the portal appears."

"Sounds good to me," Anna said wryly, pausing a beat. "Captain."

Eliot groaned.

The Reunion

By the time they'd finally managed to open the portal, most of the day had passed them by—it was easily the longest Dungeon he'd ever been in, longer even than the Ocean World had been. The Grey Room was, surprisingly enough, still filled with people.

Usually, they left almost as soon as they arrived, no doubt looking to maximize how much time they could spend outside and free before they were forcibly brought back inside. Every single person he could see was covered in black blood.

Loot Gained: 4589 EXP, 100 Gold.

After everything they had just accomplished in there, this was the reward—Elliot shook his head in disgust. Regardless of strength and size, the reward revealed that each of those King's had been worth only as much as each of the humans in the room would have.

Everyone in this system was worth the same amount in death—It was punishingly fair.

The time they'd taken to clear the Dungeon was over ten hours in total, and that score alone had brought all of the other scores down to basically nothing. The difficulty ranking was listed as an A-rank, and his personal contribution proudly declared that he hadn't killed a single enemy.

"Elliot!" Jacques called.

Elliot turned towards the man to find him much like everyone else—that was to say that he was covered head to toe in the disgusting remnants of the Fifth King.

"Jacques," Elliot said, relieved that the man was still alive. "We really need to stop getting these ridiculous dungeons."

The man's good nature seemed as unwavering as ever.

"Indeed, my friend," Jacques smiled, "I must apologize for not fighting by your side as we had planned."

"There's always next time," Elliot said before hesitating for a moment. "Hey, Jacques. You're in Vice with Anna, aren't you?"

"I am indeed within Vice, but that will not be true for much longer," Jacques cautioned, "The return of Anna's weapons means that my business here is now at its conclusion—I seek a greater challenge, so further north I will go, to Valhalla."

"Valhalla?" Elliot said, not even surprised. "Of course somebody would name a place that."

"Indeed!" Jacques laughed, catching sight of Anna in her approach. "When I first heard of it, I decided that I must see it for myself."

"I see you made it out alive again," Anna said, stopping beside them. "Not that I had any doubts."

"Anna!" Jacque said in greeting.

Jacque reached out with two massive hands, catching hold of both of their shoulders, and Elliot almost sagged at the enthusiasm.

"My friends," Jacques said brightly. "We have conquered our opposition once more; we make for a mighty team!"

"We didn't even fight together," Anna said, but she was smiling, "Valhalla, huh? You'll be a small fry again if you go all the way there; you sure you wanna leave already?"

"I must," Jacques said firmly, "More challenges await me, and it would be a shame not to conquer them!"

"The stronger you are, the further north you move?" Elliot wondered, "Is that how it works?"

"It's almost tradition from what I've seen," Anna admitted before giving them a crooked smile. "Screw that, though; I'm never leaving Vice!"

"Then I shall always know where to find you!" Jacque decided.

"I don't suppose they have a bathhouse in Hell?" Elliot asked, glancing down at himself. "Or at least a shower? My building only has a toilet and a sink."

Anna looked down at herself at the comment and wrinkled her nose at the sight.

"Hmm." Jacques hummed. "It has been a long time since I was last there; I do believe there was a bathhouse near the front gates?"

"Yeah—it's right at the entrance, the first street to the right," Anna directed before smiling. "The guy that owns it is a character."

"The owner was a woman back when I first arrived," Jacques said, a bit sadly. "But before I left the city, she had been replaced twice over."

"Thank you for the information and for handling everything back in the dungeon," Elliot said genuinely before hesitating. "I hope I see you both again."

"I will make sure of it, Elliot!" Jacques promised, clapping them both on the shoulder once more. "Should you wish to seek me out, you need only look north!"

"Good luck, Jacque," Anna said, hugging the man. "Don't die."

"Of course!" Jacque agreed, already striding towards the exit. "Farewell, my friends!"

"Bye, Jacque," Elliot smiled.

Anna's arm fell around his shoulder before he found himself pulled into a hug as well—Elliot flushed, unable to defeat her greater strength.

"Aww—you've gone all red." Anna cooed, "Hey, Elliot—thanks for bringing me back my weapon."

"You already said thanks," Elliot murmured, finally managed to break free.

"I wanted to say it again," Anna said, preparing to leave. "Hey, you better come visit me in Vice. I spend most of my time at the Sundog Tavern—make sure you check it out when you get here, okay?"

"I'll make sure to visit," Elliot promised. "Bye, Anna."

Anna waved before heading through the exit and leaving him alone in the Grey Room. He stepped outside and didn't even consider going back in today—two per day or not. The path to Hell was peaceful, and he was sure he would have enjoyed it much more if he hadn't been covered in the black sticky mess.

People heading towards the Torii made sure to give him a wide berth and wrinkled their noses in disgust as he passed them. By the time he stepped through the front gate, his eyes were firmly planted on the path to avoid meeting any more of the dismal looks. He turned onto the first street on the right, seeking out the bathhouse that Jacque and Anna had spoken of.

Elliot had only made it about five steps down the street before he was interrupted.

"Elliot?" Hannah said, surprised.

Elliot flinched, utterly unprepared for the sudden reunion, and he slowly turned around, struggling to lift his gaze.

"Hannah." Elliot managed before his eyes widened. "Wait—"

Hannah scrunched up her face at the smell, but her arms remained tightly around his neck. What was it with people touching him today?

"Oh my god," Hannah burst out, voice halfway between angry and upset. "Why didn't you come back to the hotel—we thought you died!"

"I didn't think you would want me to," Elliot murmured.

Grant was making a valiant effort not to acknowledge the smell but managed to smile at him.

"Idiot," Hannah managed, squeezing tighter. "You said we would stick together; you can't just ditch us because we argued!"

Elliot dropped his gaze to the floor again.

"We've only known each other for a couple of days, Hannah," Elliot mumbled weakly. "Why are you so attached?"

"Why shouldn't we be?" Grant said plainly, "It's more than anyone else we know in this place—We trusted each other back in the dungeon, didn't we?"

"You said we would figure out a way to go see my sister too!" Hannah said, frowning. "Stop going off on your own all the time—We already said we were going to come in with you."

"Okay—I'm sorry for leaving you both behind," Elliot mumbled, face flushed. "Can you let me go now? I need to wash this off."

Hannah stepped back with a huff and then looked down at the mess that had gotten onto her clothing.

"What is this stuff anyway?" Hannah wrinkled her nose, "It smells disgusting."

"Maybe you shouldn't have hugged him then," Grant said, bemused.

Elliot turned, starting back down the street, and they fell in step beside him.

"Its blood," Elliot admitted.

Hannah looked like she'd rather have left that mystery unsolved.

"Blood?" Grant said, frowning. "That's a lot of blood; you look like you went swimming in it."

"That's because I did go swimming in it," Elliot sighed, "Several times, and so did everyone else in the Dungeon. There's supposed to be a bathhouse on this road somewhere."

"There are baths here?" Hannah said, relieved. "Did you know the hotel doesn't even have a toilet? I had to pee in an alleyway—I haven't done that since college."

"So did I," Grant admitted.

Elliot didn't know what to say to the confession, so instead, he stayed silent, leading them towards what was very obviously the bathhouse.

The second he'd stepped inside, the man behind the counter started speaking.

"No way in hell," The man said dryly, "You're going to need to go wash yourself off first—go out that door, there's a small courtyard and a runoff pipe. Come back inside when you're not covered in shit or whatever that is."

Elliot shuffled out the door, keeping his eyes on the floor—there was a pipe hanging out of the side of the building with water rushing out of it into the drainage system below. He stepped under it and started scrubbing the muck off him as best he could.

Hannah joined him a second later while Grant leaned against the door frame, watching.

"Did you learn anything new while in the dungeon?" Grant asked.

"So much has happened in the last two days, Grant," Elliot admitted, scrubbing off his arms. "I honestly don't even know how to start."

"How many times have you been back in?" Grant changed tracks, asking a more specific answer.

"Half a dozen," Elliot said, "I'm level fifteen now."

"Really?" Grant said, raising an eyebrow.

Elliot stood back up, soaked but far cleaner than he had been before—he'd need to clean his armor later, but he still had his old clothing to wear for now.

"You can tell us when we're in the bath," Hannah chirped, steering them both back into the room. "Move it!"

He used his trading stone to pay the one gold per person, and they were directed to a room with shelves lined with towels. There was a single open doorway at the other side of the room, and he could see the water from his position.

Elliot stared at the mixed bath area with unease. Hannah didn't seem to care, snatching one of the towels and moving towards the door. All of her clothing vanished before she'd even left the room, returned to her inventory.

The two of them watched her walk the rest of the way inside, completely unhurried.

"You guys coming?" Hannah called back.

"You're joking." Grant sighed, picking up his towel. "There better not be other people in there."

Grant wrapped his towel around his waist, inventoried his clothing, and then tucked the towel around his hips. Elliot stayed where he was, wondering if he shouldn't go back out to the runoff pipe outside.

"Come on, Elliot," Grant said, turning to face him. "Might as well get it over with."

Elliot picked up a towel of his own and wrapped it around his clothing—he followed their example and inventoried everything on him except the towel. He felt his face heat up, but Grant did not comment on his shirtless form.

A large stone pool sat in the room, perhaps twice as wide as a swimming pool but nowhere near as deep. There was also quite a bit of lingering steam in the room, coming from the heated water, and Elliot wondered how they had managed it. Was this building already here before someone bought it? Or had someone designed it and figured out a heating system?

His thoughts were quickly derailed when he noticed Hannah standing waist-deep in the water, smirking at them and her towel discarded by the edge.

Elliot stopped at the water's edge and faced away from them both; After a moment of indecision, he stepped down into the pool as quick as he dared and left the towel on the stone in front of him. The water was amazing, and he almost thought it was worth the embarrassment.

"This water is nice," Grant admitted, echoing his thoughts. "At least there's something good in this place."

"Well, it would be weird if Hell didn't have any hot water," Hannah laughed, swimming closer to them both.

"Yeah," Grant hummed, amused.

Elliot sunk until only his nose was above the waterline as Hannah reached them, and when her path continued closer, he turned to face the edge of the pool—it was safer that way.

"Why are you so red?" Hannah teased. "You look like a strawberry."

"I'm not," Elliot denied, changing the subject entirely. "I brought a monster back with me from one of the dungeons I went into; her name is Tyralklivi."

"Really?" Hannah said. "What does she look like?"

"I hope it isn't one of the pale things," Grant said, watching him.

"It's not; she looks like a human, only her skin is red, and her eyebrows are this elaborate tattoo." Elliot said, "She's friendly, but she doesn't speak any English—I started using the faction's private messages to communicate with her, but it's not a perfect solution."

"You joined a faction?" Hannah murmured. "I thought you didn't want to?"

"A lot of stuff has happened." Elliot admitted, "I created one yesterday."

"Could she confirm that there was another Grey Room on her side?" Grant asked.

Elliot was reminded once more of how sharp the man was.

"Yes," Elliot said, "It seems to be commonly accepted that there is a minimum of at least five Grey Rooms and five enemy teams in each dungeon."

"So it is a death game after all," Grant said before trailing off.

"How did you make enough for a faction token in two days?" Hannah asked.

Elliot sighed; he couldn't see their reactions with his back to them; he turned around and immediately regretted it because Hannah had moved directly behind him, and he turned his head to the side to look between them.

"I've met several people who believe that the dungeons have a level range, that in each one, the highest level person is usually within one-hundred levels of the lowest level person." Elliot said, "They also said that all of the teams generally have the same amount of total levels as each other."

"Total levels," Grant repeated, "As in; each of the individual levels of a team combined?"

Elliot nodded in answer and hurried to continue when he felt Hannah's toe drag against his shin.

"Anette, an older lady from our first dungeon—she had a full set of armor, at least rare or higher." Elliot said, "I'm certain that she was at level two-hundred."

"That breaks the rule you just told us about—we were all level one at that point," Hannah said, frowning. "There was that guy who helped us kill all those bark-goblins in the other one as well."

"Exactly, the rule is very obviously untrue, but everyone seems to be using it as a guideline," Elliot said, glad they were keeping up so well. "I've been in multiple dungeons with people who were two-hundred levels above me or more, and as Hannah said, it doesn't account for the brand new level one's appearing in dungeons way above their levels."

Hannah's foot continued to 'accidentally' brush against his leg.

"They have a name for it when a high-level person is present in a dungeon that is clearly outside of the level range—an Outlier." Elliot said, "People who appear in the dungeons with a much higher portion of the total levels. There was a level three-hundred in the Dungeon I went into after our argument...."

"What happened?" Hannah murmured.

"He tried to kill everyone in the dungeon," Elliot said admitted.

"What?" Hannah said in alarm.

"Wasn't he on your side?" Grant said, "Why would he try to kill his own team?"

Elliot wasn't exactly sure what to do about Hannah slowly encroaching into his personal space or if he even wanted her to stop in the first place, but his back was against the stone now.

"He wanted the equipment of all the players in the dungeon; at least that's what we assumed." Elliot mumbled, "He killed something like half of the people on our team before we managed to kill him—I managed to steal his weapon in the middle of the fight."

"We?" Hannah asked.

"Others were fighting as well, and a group of high-level people did most of the work," Elliot said, "I sold the weapon afterward and split the money between everyone who helped fight him off."

"What was it worth?" Grant asked.

"Twelve-million, but I sold it for ten." Elliot admitted, "I used the money to buy a faction building—it's on the main street."

"That's an absurd amount of money," Grant said, stumped. "Do you have a plan on how to use it?"

"I bought some gear, then put the rest of it into the faction bank," Elliot said, "There's a system to pay members of the faction weekly, so I set it up to support anyone who joins. I—I thought I could start recruiting level ones and help them when they first get here."

"That's a great idea, Elliot," Grant said, sounding genuinely interested in the idea. "I hope you don't mind if I put my name in for consideration—I'd like to help you do it."

Elliot smiled at the man and silently opened the faction menu.

"I want to be on Welfare too!" Hannah insisted. "I can join too, right?"

"Hannah," Grant said exasperated, "You can't say it like that."

Elliot found it impossible to ignore how her knee was now pressing against the inside of his leg, but he managed to send a faction invite to both of them.

"Thanks," Hannah said, accepting the invite.

"Excelsior?" Grant said curiously, "Nice name."

Faction Members:
Elliot Archer, Founder. Grant Baker, Member. Hannah Walker, Member. Tyralklivi, Member.

"Ty-ralk-livi?" Hannah tried, "Is that how you say it?"

"I don't know," Elliot mumbled, "It's what I've been calling her, but she laughs every time I say it."

Hannah sidled up to him, not even trying to be subtle anymore.

"You should have brought her here," Hannah said, smirking. "Then, there would be two red people in the water."

Grant splashed them both with water.

"Leave him alone, you menace," Grant said wryly. "I've seen some of those monsters walking around—the bark-goblins mostly, but there was one of the tall green people as well."

Elliot nodded in understanding.

"I couldn't even walk around with her without getting awful looks," Elliot admitted, "The hotel I moved to didn't want her there either."

"That's awful," Hannah said, frowning.

"It's just how people are," Grant sighed before sinking lower into the water. "They don't like things they don't understand or people that are different."

"Yeah," Hannah mumbled, sagging slightly against him.

Elliot watched them both quietly; it seemed like the two of them had some personal experience with the issue of being treated differently.

"Where's Tyralklivi now?" Grant wondered, "In a hotel somewhere?"

"I left her at the faction building this morning," Elliot said.

"This morning?" Grant blinked, "How many dungeons did you go into today?"

Elliots opened his mouth to answer before snapping his head around to stare at Hannah, his face bright red—but she just kept on smiling at him.

"Um—" Elliot squeaked. "Just one dungeon—it was kind of long."

"Want to talk about it?" Hannah said coyly, studying his expression.

Elliot just shook his head, completely unwilling to speak.

"Hannah," Grant said, amused, "Get your hand out of his lap before his face explodes."

Hannah just smirked, and Elliot slowly sunk below the water level, wondering how quickly he could drown himself to escape from the embarrassment.

Almost an hour later, Elliot led them up the stairs to the Faction Building—he scanned the Tavern across the road, but none of the three bounty hunters he recognized were there. He unlocked the door, and the three of them went inside.

"This is really cool," Hannah said, stepping forward to look around.

"It's deceptively big," Grant identified, "Are there any bedrooms upstairs?"

"Yeah," Elliot said, "Five of them."

"Hmm," Grant hummed, "They are going to fill up quickly when we start recruiting people."

Elliot nodded; he'd had the same thought earlier.

"I was considering buying one of the hotels," Elliot admitted, "We could get several of them even, keep them free for anyone who joins."

"Buying up half the city only to give it away?" Grant said, bemused, "Are you actually a saint in disguise?"

"Of course not," Elliot mumbled, "It just seems like a better long-term plan than raising the benefit high enough to cover rent as well."

"It probably is," Grant admitted, turning as a voice echoed down the staircase. "Is that your friend?"

"Yes," Elliot said, raising his voice so that Hannah could hear as well. "Tyralklivi is coming down, don't freak out."

Hannah leaned over the balcony to look down at them before turning her eyes to the stairs.

"Elliot?" Tyralklivi said, leaning out just enough to see.

Tyralkivi spotted him, paused as she spotted Grant, and then hesitated.

"Wow, she really does walk around naked," Hannah said and started down the stairs. "That's awesome."

Tyralklivi watched Hannah descend the opposite staircase and then cross the room. Elliot and Grant moved to meet the others, and each of them reached the stairs at roughly the same time.

"Hi," Hannah said smiling, flailing one hand over at the two of them. "Grant, tell her my name."

"What?" Grant said, startled, "I can understand her, not speak her language."

Hannah looked surprised for a moment before scratching her cheek.

"Oh," Hannah said awkwardly.

"Give me a second," Elliot mumbled, pulling up the Faction menu.

Private Message: Member Tyralklivi.
The one standing next to you is called 'Hannah,' the one standing next to me is called 'Grant.' Grant can understand you, but he cannot speak your language. He is going to attempt to translate what you say for us.

Tyralklivi read the message before smiling; she spoke a rapid string of words to Grant, and he blinked. The words kept coming, and eventually, Grant had to raise a hand, looking overwhelmed.

"Wow, she talks really fast," Grant said hesitantly, "There were like three or four different things there, uh."

"We can always ask her to repeat it," Hannah said curiously.

"No, it's fine; So, in order, Where did you go? You were gone for a very long time," Grant said, "There's nothing to do here; it was really boring. Who are Hannah and Grant?"

Private Message: Member Tyralklivi.
I went into the Dungeon; it took a really long time. I didn't think you would want to come with me, so I didn't wake you up. I met these two when I first arrived in this place; we helped each other survive several dungeons.

Tyralklivi rattled off another string of words and then paused to make sure Grant was keeping up.

"The Dungeon sucks; she doesn't want to go back in. It was really, really boring here." Grant said, amused at the repeated point. "She is also up-set that you ran away this morning before she woke up."

Elliot wasn't touching that comment with a ten-foot pole.

"Tyralklivi knows what 'Yes' and 'No' means," Elliot said, "So you should be able to mime things out."

Hannah began attempted to do so immediately, much to Tyralklivi's amusement, and Grant turned his attention to Elliot.

"You look tired, man," Grant said, lowering his voice. "Are you alright?"

"Yeah," Elliot said quietly, "The dungeon today really sucked; I just need to not think about anything for a while."

"I'll distract them both," Grant insisted, patting him on the shoulder, "You should go get some sleep."

"Thanks, Grant," Elliot mumbled.

He made his way upstairs, with Grant playing interference on his be-half. He picked the same room he had the night before and locked the door behind him.

Elliot was tired enough that he fell asleep, almost before his head hit the pillow.

Elliot woke to the sounds of his doorknob rattling, and before he'd even registered what he was doing, he was on his feet. His eyes were locked on the crack in the bottom of the door, and he reached for his spear—the inventory deposited it in his hand in an instant.

"Elliot?" Hannah called.

His heart thundered in his chest, but he forced himself to return the spear to where he'd drawn it from.

"I'm awake," Elliot said quietly, moving towards the door.

"Why'd you lock the door?" Hannah complained through the door.

"It's an old habit," Elliot sighed, moving towards the door. "You scared me, Hannah; I almost had a heart attack."

Elliot unlocked the latch with a moment's effort before pulling the door open. Hannah stood on the other side, hair messy and looking like she'd only just woken up herself.

"Not exactly the kind of surprise I was going for, honestly," Hannah admitted, looking sheepish. "Are you okay? You look pale."

"I'm always pale," Elliot mumbled, "I'll be fine. Are the others awake?"

"Yeah," Hannah noised, "Livi and Grant are talking downstairs, well, Livi is talking, Grant is just trying to keep up."

Hannah hooked her arm around his own and pulled him towards the stairs, and Elliot didn't fight her. Being around somebody who made a lot of physical contact with him was something he still wasn't used to.

Elliot noted her use of the shortened version of the name.

"Did you give up on saying her name as well?" Elliot wondered.

"She told Grant that's what you've been calling her," Hannah smiled, "It's cute, so I stole it."

They soon reached the main hall of the building, and Hannah angled them towards where the others were sitting at one of the many tables.

"Elliot." Tyralklivi grinned.

"Morning, Elliot," Grant smiled.

Grant raised an amused eyebrow before glancing at Hannah, but she just turned her head and avoided the look, and Elliot wondered what exactly it had been about.

"Morning," Elliot said belatedly.

"What's the idea for today, then?" Grant asked.

Elliot sat down at the bench and began typing out a message to Tyralk-liviv.

"That depends on how long it's been since you and Hannah have been in the dungeon," Elliot murmured. "You said yesterday that it was two days?"

"Right; we haven't been back in since we went with you," Grant said. "So I guess that was three days ago now?"

Hannah bit hit a lip in thought before nodding.

"I think so," Hannah confirmed. "There isn't any real way to tell the time since the lighting doesn't change, but three days feels right."

Elliot finished his message and sent it off.

Private Message: Member Tyralklivi.
We are discussing the Dungeon; how long until you will be pulled back in automatically?

Tyralklivi said something, and Grant turned to listen, nodding along after each burst of speech.

"Livi spent all of her money on a skip token," Grant explained. "She was going to use it in four days to skip the next one."

Elliot nodded in understanding.

"There's more than enough money in the faction bank for three tokens,"

Grant said thoughtfully, watching his reaction. "We could skip this one as well."

Surprisingly it was Hannah who spoke up.

"That's probably not a good idea," Hannah said quietly, pulling her knees up to her chest. "If we spend all of Elliot's money on skip tokens, as soon as we run out, we will be in the same position we are now."

"That sounds a lot like Elliot's reasoning for going back in on the first day," Grant said thoughtfully. "You aren't wrong, though; besides, we are planning on taking in more people as well."

Hannah just hummed.

"Anyone we recruit will want to do the same," Elliot said, having already thought about it. "Denying them would create resentment because of the unequal use of resources, but agreeing would drain the funds very quickly, exponentially as we brought in more people."

"There are better uses for the money," Hannah mumbled, "Grant told me about your idea to buy up the hotels."

Elliot just nodded.

"I think we're all on the same page here," Grant said easily, "So where does that leave us? In four days, Hannah and I will be dragged back into the Dungeon, whether we want to go or not, and the exact time is unknown."

"Yeah.." Hannah murmured.

"It's starting to feel more daunting the longer I put it off," Grant admitted quietly.

"It gets easier," Elliot promised quietly, "I've met a lot of good people in the last couple of days."

"Some bad ones as well," Hannah snorted, "What about that guy that tried to kill everyone?"

"Svent sucked," Elliot agreed easily, "I kind of wish you got to meet Jacques, though."

"Maybe we will." Hannah murmured, "We are stuck here; we are bound to run into him eventually, right?"

If the man was going further North, to Valhalla, and considering what Anna had said about him being a small fry if he went there, the average level range must be far different than here.

"Yeah," Elliot said, "Maybe we'll see him again."

"Elliot?" Tyralklivi said curiously, and he sat upon the bench. "Grant? Hannah?"

Elliot opened the faction menu and sent off a quick message to her.

Private Message: Member Tyralklivi.
They went to buy some things; they shouldn't be too much longer. Hannah wanted new sheets for the beds. Apparently, they found a place that sold that kind of thing when they explored the city yesterday. We also needed firewood for the fire here, and Grant said he would have a look around.

"Mm," Tyralklivi said happily, sitting beside him.

Elliot listened to her chatter away for a while, wondering if he would understand what she was saying one day. It seemed like a shame for someone who was so obviously extroverted to be struggling to communicate with others.

Elliot tried to put himself in her place and empathized with her situation. Everything here was different, and she couldn't even hold a proper conversation with anyone around her on top of the rest of it.

He spent a long while typing out a small message and almost didn't send it.

Private Message: Member Tyralklivi.
Hey, Tyralklivi? Can you tell me about what your home was like? I can't promise I'll understand any of it, but I can promise you I'll listen.

Elliot watched her expression out of the corner of his eye as she read through the message. For a moment, he expected her to laugh at him, but her face lit up, and she gave him a bright smile. He was startled when she scooted up onto the bench and plopped her head in his lap.

Livi started talking, much slower than her normal pace, and he did his best to listen to foreign words. He still couldn't understand any of it, but her tone had changed, and her expression was much softer.

Elliot studied her expression, wondering what her homeworld had been like and what kind of culture it might have had. Tyralklivi's language might not have been universally understood, but the small smile on her face certainly was.

Almost half an hour later, the others returned.

"The heroes have arrived!" Hannah said cheerfully. "And we come bearing gifts!"

Considering that anything they'd bought had been stashed away in their inventories, he couldn't see any hint of these gifts.

"Success on all fronts, huh?" Elliot said evenly. "Did you see any sign of the three I told you about?"

"There was a woman with brown hair sitting in the tavern and watching the road," Grant frowned, "She watched us leave, but she didn't try to follow."

"Yeah, she looked kind of bored as well," Hannah admitted before she clapped her hands together. "We found plenty of firewood, and that shop with the needle and thread sign had some okay blankets."

"Good work," Elliot said, nodding.

"Now we just need to get this fire started," Grant hummed.

"It's almost like we're going camping," Hannah said, smiling.

Hannah took a spot on the bench and patted her leg; Tyralklivi moved closer, curious.

"I always hated camping," Elliot admitted.

Hannah got the red-woman to turn around and started pulling lengths of her hair up, separating them from the rest.

"Same." Grant agreed immediately, "My idea of a vacation has a lot more luxuries involved and a spa."

"No way," Hannah denied, "Camping with friends is always fun, as long as there are drinks anyway. I can't remember the last time I went; it must have been before mum died, five years? Six?"

"The last time I went was when I was sixteen." Grant sighed, "It was with my parents, and it was the last time I ever let my dad talk me into it."

Hannah laughed at his tone before tilting her head a bit.

"My dad—" Hannah cut herself off, hesitating. "My Dad was totally in-sane. He tried to kill mum and me when I was little; I haven't seen him in over a decade now."

Grant fell silent, unable to find a response to the sudden information, and Tyralklivi looked up at the sudden break in the conversation, disrupting Hannah's hold on her hair and forcing her to start over.

"Some people are like that," Elliot said quietly. "My dad was pretty cold, but nothing quite that bad; my mum died when I was seven."

"My parents were great," Grant said uncomfortably, "They are still alive; well, they were before I died anyway; who knows what's going on back there at this point. Your dad tried to kill you?"

Hannah just nodded, starting to braid several long pieces of Tyralklivi's bright red hair together.

"I never really got the full story, and I was really young at the time," Hannah said honestly, "I just remember police cars, sirens, and shouting."

"Wow," Grant said quietly. "That's intense; Nothing on that level ever happened to me; I had a lot of trouble in school, people picking on me and stuff, you know."

Elliot had always had Dimitri by his side at school, and nobody had even tried anything with the larger boy around, so he didn't have any similar stories.

"Because you like men?" Hannah asked curiously.

"Yeah," Grant said easily, "My school had a lot of problem kids, so fights were pretty common."

"So was mine," Hannah admitted before smirking. "A boy tried to bully me at school once, and I broke his nose."

Elliot let out a quiet laugh, not really expecting something so violent from her.

"You laughed!" Hannah grinned, "How about you, Elliot? Got anything to share?"

Elliot tilted his head in thought, trying to find something that might fit, given what they had shared.

"I had a friend growing up; his name was Dimitri." Elliot smiled. "I had a crush on his older sister May when I was younger. The three of us were into the same stuff, so we would often hang out, and I always used to embarrass myself around her."

Elliot paused for a moment, surprised at himself for opening up about it.

"You can't just stop there, man," Grant said, curious. "What did you do?"

"It wasn't what I did," Elliot said cagily. "Dimitri invited me over to swim in their pool one day, something we had done hundreds of times before, and he stole my clothes when I was showering afterward. I had to creep through the house to find them."

Elliot winced in embarrassment as Hannah started outright laughing.

"Oh no," Grant snickered, "May was the one who caught you sneaking around the house naked?"

"Yeah," Elliot confessed. "May thought it was funny, but it took me weeks before I could even bring myself to speak to her again."

"A story of unrequited love?" Hannah said, giggled.

"I suppose it was," Elliot said, "She got married this year actually, in January."

Hannah suddenly looked like something occurred to her; Grant had gone quiet as well. Even Tyralklivi had noticed the change in atmosphere, turning once more to look up at them. Elliot couldn't have missed the reaction if he had wanted to, and it only took him a moment of thought to understand.

"That wasn't why I jumped," Elliot sighed.

"It's not?" Hannah asked quietly.

"No, Hannah; Dimitri was my best friend," Elliot said, staring at his hands. "We did pretty much everything together, he was always the one who would push us into things, and when things got hard, I could always count on him to come through. I followed him around like a duckling, really, but he never seemed to mind."

Elliot studied Hannah's expression for a moment.

"He got into an accident six months back," Elliot said, dropping his gaze to the floor, "He hit his head badly in the accident, and he couldn't remember anyone, but then it started to get worse."

Hannah reached out and placed her hand on his leg, a gesture of comfort that drew his gaze for a moment.

"He died a few weeks after the accident," Elliot said quietly, rubbing at his eyes, "I kind of fell apart afterward, and there was a massive hole left behind. Everything in my life was somehow tied to him, and I can't do anything without constantly being reminded."

Grant reached out and clapped a hand on his shoulder.

"That's why I'm here," Elliot said, laughing quietly. "Chasing after my friend like a duckling, I haven't changed at all."

"Maybe he's here somewhere?" Grant said, patting his shoulder again before sitting back. "We are all here after all; why couldn't he?"

"It's a nice thought, Grant," Elliot said, "But there is another possibility, and it's much more likely."

"He could have died in the dungeon," Hannah murmured, squeezing his leg.

"Yeah," Elliot said before taking a deep breath to settle himself. "So, Instead of chasing after him again, I'm changing my strategy this time. I'm going to do what Dimitri did for me and do my best to help people."

"That's something I can get behind," Grant said firmly.

"Me too," Hannah said, smiling.

Elliot smiled; it wasn't going to be easy, but it probably wasn't supposed to be. If they could help the people who needed it the most, then whatever effort they put into it would be worth it in the end.

"It's a bit ironic that we're trying to create a support network for people in Hell of all places," Grant said, amused.

"Is this place really called Hell?" Hannah said, frowning.

"Yeah, that's what it's called," Elliot said, "I don't think this is that Hell though; this city was probably created and named by people."

"Not really enough fire for it to be Hell," Hannah said before she tilted her head. "Wait—If this landmass is just floating in space, and space is freezing cold—"

"No, Hannah," Grant said, amused, "Hell hasn't frozen over."

"You ruined it!" Hannah said, huffing.

Elliot laughed quietly at the byplay.

"You said that there were other places?" Grant said, wondering. "What are the other settlements called?"

"There's probably way more that I don't know about," Elliot said, "But the ones I heard from Jacque and Anna were; Hell, Vice, and Valhalla."

"It's almost like a theme," Hannah said thoughtfully. "I wonder if there are other places, like the nine circles of hell, or even just the seven deadly sins?"

"What are the nine circles of hell?" Grant said curiously.

Hannah closed her eyes for a moment, clearly trying to remember.

"Ugh—I know a couple of them are the same as the sins," Hannah frowned, "Violence was one of them? Treachery too!"

"I think I'd stay away from any city called Treachery," Grant said dryly. "Violence doesn't sound much better either."

"Lust could be a fun city to visit," Hannah said slyly, "Elliot, maybe we should move?"

"Um," Elliot managed.

Hannah smirked, but Grant saved him from having to answer.

"Down, girl." Grant rolled his eyes. "What if these places are the real ones, and the ones we've heard about back home come from this place?"

"We know that Reincarnation Tokens exist if they allow the person to keep their memories of this place when they return," Elliot said, "It's possible that someone saw the name 'Hell' and took it back with them to our world."

"Wouldn't that mean that it would have been someone from thousands of years ago?" Hannah frowned, "Hell's a pretty old concept."

Elliot thought of how different Jacque acted to those around him and wondered if he could have come from a different time and place.

"It's a chicken and egg situation," Grant sighed, "It could work either way, really, but I've never read anything in the old world about a place like this."

"I can see some things that fit with old myths," Hannah admitted. "A landmass floating amongst the stars where people live when they die? That's got to be heaven, right?"

"This doesn't exactly feel like heaven to me," Grant said wryly. "I get your point, though, vague descriptions aside, there was nothing that explicitly that mentioned this place—actually, now that I'm thinking about it, the Torii is suspicious."

Elliot blinked, and his mind immediately started attacking the concept.

"The Torii must have existed before the people in order for someone to even arrive here," Elliot said in understanding, "It was here before people started coming through."

"Yeah," Grant said. "So depending on how old this place is, someone might have taken the idea of the Torii back to earth."

"So is the Torii the chicken and the egg?" Hannah said, clapping a hand onto her fist.

Tyralklivi leaned back at the noise, staring up at her.

"I don't think it works like that," Grant said, amused. "But it's more evidence towards the names of the places here being taken back to earth."

"It's weak evidence," Elliot disagreed quietly, "The Torii could be the only concept that was taken back, and nothing would change; Hell, Vice, or Valhalla could have still been brought here from earth."

Grant nodded, chewing on his thumb in thought.

"I want to name a city," Hannah decided out of nowhere.

Elliot blinked at the sudden derailment.

"What would you name it?" Grant wondered.

"Hannahsburg," Hannah smirked.

"That is a terrible name," Grant said, astonished.

"Hannahsville?" Elliot offered, smiling.

Hannah started laughing.

"Elliot," Grant said dryly, "You sure you want to encourage her?"

Some hours later, Grant, Hannah, and Elliot left the Faction building, keeping a wary eye on the Tavern across the street, but neither of the three bounty hunters was present this time. Seeing the Torii only brought his mind back around to thinking about what Grant had said.

Were all the myths about monsters, demigods, and horrible places designed to punish those who didn't follow the rules all influenced by this place? Was Hell as a concept twisted from someone's experiences with this city?

The demons of Hell could be a role filled by the monstrous beings that they would have faced inside the Dungeon. The plains of Elysium could be accounted for by the endless land that stretched away from the edge of the world. Valhalla could have been a place for the warriors of the world, like Jacque, who sought to hone their skills even after death.

Elliot bent down and began to pick up loose stones along the path, stashing them away in his inventory and ignoring the strange looks from the others.

Or were they overthinking it?

Perhaps it really was just a factory, built to farm their deaths for some unknown purpose, and the poor souls who had found themselves here had named these places after the familiar. Elliot wasn't sure it was possible to know such a thing; however long this had been going on, he doubted there was anyone still around that had access to that kind of knowledge.

They stopped in front of the Torii, and the conversation slowly came to a halt once more.

"Well, this is it," Grant said. "It's not quite as bad standing here again, well not as bad as I thought it would be anyway."

Elliot opened his interface for a moment, finding the shop and refilling on potions. He hovered over another item for a moment before buying two, just in case.

"Yeah," Hannah admitted, reaching out and running her finger across the pane of white energy. "It's weird though, I know there are monsters in there and that I should be terrified, but I'm not."

"I wonder why it's so different now," Grant murmured. "Standing here doesn't feel like there's anything to worry about, even though it's one step from danger."

"I think it's because whatever is inside the dungeon can't pass through the gate," Elliot said, "The tunnel wouldn't even be open right now; it would just be an empty grey room."

"You might be right," Grant said before steeling himself. "We can't wait around here all day; let's get this done. Are you two ready?"

Hannah drew in a long breathe before nodding.

"Yes," Hannah decided.

"Ready," Elliot said quietly.

They stepped through the portal, and Elliot immediately realized that something was wrong.

There were too many people present.

The Ocean Dungeon had been strange, and the T7 Dungeon had been truly absurd, but this was something else entirely; there were easily thousands of people present. A sea of heads stretching away from him, the sound of hundreds of conversations overlapping just made it worse.

It was like he was standing amongst the crowd at a concert, or considering the sheer amount of armor sets and weapons he could see, an army.

"Whoa!" Hannah said from just behind him. "This is crazy; why are there so many people?"

"This can't be normal," Grant said, frowning, "Elliot, have you seen anything like this yet?"

"I haven't been in one with this many people before." Elliot answered immediately, "The most I've seen was a couple of hundred participants."

Grant swept his gaze over the crowd for a moment as best he could before shaking his head.

"I don't think we can estimate the levels here," Grant said, frowning. "Other than we probably have a minimum total of several thousand at least, and that's if everyone was only level one or two."

He was right; if even half the people here were level fifty, the Total Level counter must have been in the tens of thousands.

"Look at that guy's sword," Hannah said, "It's bigger than I am; how is he even carrying it?"

Elliot glanced in the direction she was pointing; the sword in question was twice as tall as Hannah, but the man, five-foot-tall at best, was forced to carry it diagonally on his back. It made for a bizarre sight, but he'd seen Anna do something similar already, even if she wasn't quite that short.

"It's glowing, which means it's probably at least an exotic," Elliot frowned, "That means there are people here who are at least level two-hundred."

That made the Total Level even higher.

"Even if there are only a hundred people at that level," Grant said, frowning. "What does that mean for our opposition?"

"I don't know," Elliot said quietly. "That Dungeon where I came out covered in blood? One of the enemy teams only had five members, each level five hundred or higher."

"You're joking?" Grant said, staring at him. "You didn't tell us anything about that."

"I didn't want to think about it," Elliot said uneasily. "The point there is it could be a few really strong enemies."

"I guess we won't know until it opens," Hannah said, swallowing. "We will figure it out."

The timer was starting to dip into the high teens now, which meant they likely had a couple of minutes left before being let inside. That was enough time to come up with some basic strategy.

"Alright," Elliot said, "For most of the dungeons I've been in, the safest place is to stay near the entrance. You two should stick with the group and try not to stray too far unless they move—we should have brought you some better equipment first."

"It's alright, man; there's more than enough people here to do the fighting," Grant said easily, "You're more experienced at this; we can stay near the entrance, is there anything you want us to do?"

Hannah was starting to look a bit concerned.

"There are a lot of people here; if you two could talk to some of them," Elliot said hesitantly, "We could try and recruit someone? Keep it to less than five people, for now; our bed situation is still pretty bad."

"You can count on us," Grant nodded, "What are you going to do?"

Elliot made sure his armor was on properly and took a moment to test whether he could still freely move his arms and legs.

"I'm able to move pretty fast, and I can get around obstacles by switching with something in most dungeons, so it's easy for me to scout out the area first." Elliot said, "My main goal for this one is to locate as many chests as possible before the dungeon is cleared."

"You're not going to fight anything, are you?" Hannah said hesitantly. "Elliot?"

Elliot shook his head.

"No, I have no intention of fighting anything; the higher-level people can take care of that," Elliot said, "I'll be coming back as soon as I feel anything living come into my range."

"The counter is down to ten seconds," Hannah said. "I think I'm starting to panic now."

Elliot reached out and patted her on the shoulder, hoping she might draw some measure of comfort from the gesture. Instead, she spun and dragged him into a hug that brought a flush creeping up his neck.

"Don't die, okay?" Hannah whispered. "You're not allowed to."

Elliot glanced over her shoulder to Grant, hoping for assistance. Grant just smiled at him, leaving him to his fate.

"I won't die," Elliot murmured. "Stay with Grant and stay near the entrance. Don't fight anything, just run—that goes for both of you."

"I'll look after her," Grant promised. "Five seconds now; I think this is it."

The timer ticked down to nothing, and the door opened.

Interlude: Grant Baker

Grant slipped into the flow of traffic unhindered, and his phone edged closer to the side of the passenger seat, the turning motion enough to shunt it a few inches to the left.

"Matt, I don't know what to tell you," Grant sighed, "They told us it was an 'unlikely' possibility a couple of weeks ago, and apparently that counts as 'advanced notice.'"

Matt's voice was distorted as it was boosted through the phone's speakers.

"That's what I'm saying—It doesn't count because it's not written notice," Matt said, annoyed, "An offhand comment isn't enough to satisfy the requirement there—"

Grant felt his frustrations building—Matt had always been the more solution-minded of them, and that's what he was doing right now, solving the problem. Only Grant didn't want a solution—at least not one where he'd have to get into an argument with his boss.

All he wanted was for Matt to listen to him.

"I'm not going to start a big fight over it," Grant said, annoyed. "I might not even be one of the ones who get let go anyway—there's no point in worrying about it until it happens."

"You can't just let them do what they want—" Matt hissed.

"It's not like anything I can say to Clark will change anything!" Grant snapped, "He's not the one making the decisions—he's just our fucking manager."

The sound of a deep breath being taken was barely audible over the car speakers.

"I'm just saying," Matt said, with forced calm. "That if they do end up letting you all go, you have something of a—Shit, I have another work call; I'll have to call you back."

Grant sighed.

"Besides, I told you to stop calling me when you're driving," Matt said pointedly. "We can talk about it later when we're both at home, okay? Love you."

"Love you too, Matt," Grant sighed.

Golden Salt Hotel, Saltwall City.
March 4th, 2020, 9:29 AM.

Grant leaned against the back wall, waiting for the meeting to start. There was a tense atmosphere amongst everyone present, and when Clark finally left his office to join them, the tension grew taunt.

"Well, the word is in," Clark said, striding into the room. "We're definitely getting shut down."

The man had never been one to sugarcoat things but damned if he couldn't use some training in delivering bad news. The room erupted into noise—Clark raised his hand to try and get them to quieten down.

"I know, I know—shut up, will you; I've got more to say," Clark said, voice annoyed. "I'm as pissed off as you are, alright? My ass is also on the line here, and there's nothing we can do about it. The decision is coming from the top; it's out of my hands, and it was never in any of yours."

"How many—or is it everyone?" Grant asked, raising his voice.

"Unknown, for now—" Clark said before raising his hand again at the outcry. "I know—you pack of vultures, let me finish before you start crowing at me!"

It took a while to get everyone under control again, and Clark looked like he'd lost the rest of his answer amongst all the noise.

"Is there some restructuring going on?" Grant said, prompting the man to continue. "We still have people in the rooms as well—are there any essential workers being kept on for that?"

Clark clicked his fingers as the questions jogged his memory.

"Right, right," Clark grunted, nodding. "I've been informed that Friday afternoon is the time we are getting the final verdict. Nobodies said anything to me about essential workers, so either they'll keep some of you on for a week or so, or we'll be giving all the guests a boot up the ass."

"Sending us all on home for the weekend," Shay said, folding her arms. "No way we can argue or stir anything up on a Friday afternoon—we're all getting the sack, may as well leave now."

"You signed a contract," Clark reminded, "Quit now, and it might affect your severance—"

"Like we're going to get shit from them," Malik said, "They're shutting down because they don't have the money to keep it open through this mess—what makes you think there'll be any comp?"

"You want to risk it? Go right ahead," Clark said, watching them. "Some of us will most likely get picked up by the affiliate companies and offered transfers—So don't go getting any silly ideas about skipping out before the end of the week if you don't want to get your name struck off the shortlist."

"Fuck," Shay grumbled. "This is such bullshit."

"This isn't going to be forever," Clark said, as something of a peace offering. "Give it a couple of months, and we'll be through all of this crap; the hotel will be back up and running eventually, and they'll be looking to pick you back up again, alright?"

"Most of us will have moved on by then, Clark," Grant sighed, "None of us are in a place to be out of work for months on end."

Bust A Bean, Saltwall City.
March 5th, 2020, 12:24 PM.

"Thanks for being so patient," Maeve said, her voice hitching for a moment. "I've finished canceling the booking; the process can take up to three weeks before you'll receive—"

"Three weeks?" Grant said, shocked. "How—there isn't a transfer on the planet that takes that long to process!"

"I'm really sorry, sir," Maeve pleaded, "Unfortunately, because of the situation, we've been forced to cancel all of our bookings; we've been dealing with far more refund requests than our business is capable of dealing with—"

Grant pinched his nose between his fingers in frustration.

"Look, Maeve, I'm fine with the booking being canceled because I was planning on calling up to cancel it myself." Grant gritted out, "The problem here is the three weeks for the refund? That is completely unacceptable."

"Sir!" Maeve burst out, voice fragile. "We are processing so, so many refunds at the moment. There is a queue, and we're working through each of them as quickly as we can, but the only way we can possibly do this is if we stagger them—"

Grant forced himself to take a deep breath—the fragility of her voice had tempered some of his own frustration. He was certain this wasn't the first conversation she'd dealt with about this; most likely, there had been hundreds of them.

"Okay, Maeve," Grant said, voice calm once more. "Look, I paid six months in advance—and I understand that it's going to take a while, but there shouldn't be any reason why it's that far down the list. What can I do to speed this up—"

Maeve interjected as if she'd answered this exact question before.

"I'm sorry, sir," Maeve said, voice wavering. "There's no way I can expedite it; you'll have to wait like everyone else."

The screen darkened to purple as his thumb pressed down against the end call button, and for a moment, he was certain the screen would crack. Somehow it survived the onslaught, and he slowly lessened the pressure.

"You've got to be fucking kidding me," Grant said quietly, eyes stinging with frustration. "When it rains, it pours."

Freeway, Saltwall City.
March 6th, 2020, 8:04 AM

Driving had always been a form of stress relief for him—just him, the road, and the car. Grant could remember when he was younger, being out late at night, driving around the city, and spotting familiar cars out doing the same.

He'd stopped doing it at some point, but he wasn't sure when it had happened; he knew why he'd stopped; he simply didn't have the time anymore. Working full days and coming home tired—it was far easier to curl up on the couch with Matt than it was to hit the streets like he used to.

Even so, driving to work in the mornings and coming home after; those times were always something he looked forward to. Grant wondered if he shouldn't get a job at a taxi service, and almost immediately, he found himself shaking his head.

Grant held the wheel with his knee and picked his phone up off the seat.

"Hey, Matt," Grant said.

"You better not be driving," Matt said, voice hesitant.

Rather than answer the old argument, he said what they'd both been dreading for several days now.

"Clark called me a couple of minutes ago—they got word a bit earlier than we expected," Grant sighed. "I'll have to start looking for another job."

"I'm sorry, Grant," Matt said quietly, "We'll figure it out, I promise—don't worry, okay?"

"Thanks, Matt," Grant murmured before shaking his head. "I have the rest of the day off at least; silver linings and all of that—"

The world rocked as something plowed into the side of his car, the window shattered instantly, and Grant tried to lift his arms up to cover his face. He felt the seatbelt pulling against his full weight as the car flipped up onto its roof. The sound of tortured metal scrapping against the tarmac washed over him, and the pressure of the belt against his chest vanished.

An indescribable pain overwhelmed him, and then everything went black.

The Fall

The mass of people moved towards the door, forced to move through the tunnel two at a time due to the width. Elliot and the others were content to wait for most of the people to leave, and it took almost three minutes before they even stepped into it.

There had to be tens of thousands of people here; it was insane.

The line moved quickly after that, as people moved away from the entrance and presumably spread out. Elliot could feel how the group was moving, almost everyone was heading directly left of the entrance, but a few dozen were standing by the right of the door.

The way everyone was walking indicated that the cracked red wall that he could see over their heads was blocking them from going straight ahead. It was strange because he could feel rocks and other debris littering the ground there.

Upon stepping outside, he realized what was going on.

The wall at the front of the entrance ran both ways, and when he followed it upwards, he had to tilt his head all the way back, as the top of the wall disappeared into pitch-black darkness that concealed the ceiling.

Almost everyone had turned left, but the line of people was not really moving, about a hundred meters ahead, the hallway turned directly right, out of view, and the flood of people was waiting for more people to move before they could continue down it.

The right path was almost empty, except for a few people milling about and sending annoyed looks at the back of the group. Thirty meters down the right passage was a hallway to the left, and another seventy meters past that was a second one.

Past that was just an endless hallway and one where the distance robbed him of the ability to make out any more details. The rocks he could feel on the ground several meters past the wall in front of him must have been sitting on the floor of another hallway.

"It's a maze," Hannah murmured, "I'm not sure if I should feel better or worse."

Elliot wasn't pretty sure it was worse. The ones heading left started were still moving forward at a crawl, and not a single person broke off from the group to go right. There was barely any room for them to maneuver if they needed to, and the people still coming out of the tunnel didn't help.

"I'm going to head right for now," Elliot said, "Stay with the group, okay? I'll come to find you guys soon for a checkup."

Hannah hugged him again before letting him go.

"Be careful," Grant said, nodding.

Elliot swapped positions with a rock next to one of the people waiting at the edge of the group on the right. The group of people stepped back from him in alarm as he suddenly appeared, and he turned to them for a moment.

"How on earth did you do that?" A man said, alarmed.

Elliot checked him over, he had no armor, and he had a metal bo-staff held awkwardly in one hand.

"You're new," Elliot said quietly. "Listen; There are monsters in this place; if you see anything that isn't a human, be prepared to defend yourself with lethal force because they will be trying to kill you."

"Truly?" The man said, bewildered.

"Stick with the group," Elliot said before turning away.

"Thank you for the advice!" The man said quickly.

Elliot swapped with a piece of the broken wall right next to the first hallway. He leaned out, just enough to see, and then turned it down. It made a right-hand turn only ten meters in, and he used his spear to slice away a part of the wall.

It fell to the ground with a crack, and he continued on, paying close attention to the edge of his swap range. He cut off more of the wall as he went, leaving himself an impossible-to-miss pathway back to the door in case he needed to move quickly.

The Maze just kept on going, and even after five minutes of swapping past walls and moving further inwards, he still hadn't encountered a single creature. He paused for a second as something larger entered his range, but when he turned to look in the direction, he could see a very faded white highlight of a chest through the walls.

Elliot swapped closer and then knelt down next to it.

Secret Found: 1/100.
Loot Gained: 500 Gold, 1 Rare Cloak, 1 Rare Ring, 1 Rare Sword.

A ring? He hadn't encountered one of them yet; He had seen a few people wearing cloaks. Elliot opened the inventory up and studied the ring;

its description held no information about what it did. He equipped it through the menu, and something about his vision changed, but he couldn't identify what it was.

He removed it and then equipped it several times before giving up and leaving it on; it had something to do with details or edges because the cracks in the walls stood out more even in the low light.

Elliot stood back up, leaving the chest behind and continuing on his way. The only sounds around were his own footsteps, echoing around him, and the sounds of stone falling in his wake as he continued to build a pathway back.

He slowed to a stop as an echoing noise caught his attention, but it was far too faint to make out. He frowned, straining his ears in an attempt to bring clarity to the noise. The hairs on the back of his neck were standing up now, and he felt something race down his spine.

Another similar sound echoed past him reached his ears again, coming from his right, and he strained to understand what it was; several more echoes from the same direction.

Strangely enough, it almost sounded like a moan and something fleshy thudding in a rhythmic pattern. The noise was growing now, not louder exactly, but overlapping? More moans reached his ears and a strange crackling noise that was entirely out of place.

The noise was growing louder now, but there were so many sources that it was just a jumble of echoes now. Other strange noises began to join the growing mess, and he couldn't begin to understand any of it.

What the Hell was he hearing?

Part of the wall to his right cracked, dropping tiny bits of stone onto the ground, and a tremor reached him as the floor began to vibrate.

Whatever the noise was, it was coming towards him from multiple directions.

It was too far away to feel with his Swap-Sense, so he wasn't exactly worried; he could easily—Elliot swapped with a rock and then the next one on his pathway without even considering stopping.

Thousands of humanoid bodies, crawling, wrenching, tearing, and climbing over each other flooded the Maze, layered so high that he couldn't even sense the top of the pile with his swap-sense. They tumbled over each other in a wave, crashing into the walls and leaving them broken and falling in their wake.

Things appeared, exploded, and vanished without rhyme or reason, strange objects appearing for scant seconds before being swallowed by the mess.

A second flood of bodies passed into his Swap-sense from further right, and Elliot forced himself to move faster. Each swap appeared like a camera shutter as the environment changed around him. A pink line of light lanced above his head, passing through walls without stopping and leaving stone tumbling down in its wake.

Elliot realized that each one of the things had powers, every single one of them. He swapped twice off his pathway to avoid the rain of falling stone before pulling himself back on track again. Seconds later, he arrived in front of the entrance to the Grey Room.

There was no one at the entrance, not a single person.

He swapped down the path the others had been moving. Did they know about the creatures in the Maze? Someone might have had a sensory power with a better range than him; if that was the case, they would have begun moving in the opposite direction to the horde.

Which way would they have gone from here?

Water surged inside of his sensory range, flooding the Maze even faster than the horde that was generating it, and it only served to move them even quicker towards his location.

Elliot made his choice, moving deeper into the unknown; he barely made it three swaps inwards before he was forced to move left again as another corridor filled with bodies were bearing down on him.

Why were there so many!?

Elliot fled again, trying to move parallel to the most recent group, but quickly started to realize that the entire right side of the Maze was simply full of the things. He wasn't sure how to even estimate a proper count of how many there were.

He was forced even further left as more of them appeared, and a fine branch of yellow light spread out, cutting everything into perfect cubes of stone. Elliot was forced to swap upwards with one of the cubes to avoid being crushed, and then he just kept going higher.

He reached the top of the Maze, the walls stretching out before him like pathways in the dark. He landed badly as the ground shook and quickly scrambled back to his feet. The noise was deafening up here, all of the sound passing over the tops of the walls with no obstructions.

Flashes of light, fire, lighting, and things he couldn't even describe light up the Maze, destroying massive sections of it as the bodies just kept on coming. They had to have been killing each other by the thousands with all of those powers going off, and it wasn't even considering how many had to have died by being crushed beneath the others or against the walls.

What kind of world could result in something like this?

Why were there so many? Why were they acting so mindlessly, throwing themselves forward endlessly, clawing, climbing, and dying?

A purple net of light hit the wall he was on, instantly disintegrating it, and he tossed the rock in his hand and then appeared in its place, running along the top of the next wall over. They weren't even chasing him, he realized, at least not really.

They were just moving across the Maze, attempting to move forward without any sense of higher thought. He finally managed to gain some distance on them as he cut a line straight across the top.

There was far less to swap with up here, as most of the debris was down below, and the thought of going back down there terrified him. Elliot threw another rock ahead of him as the wall ran out and traded places with it, keeping his speed up as best he could.

He still hadn't found any of the others, which was probably a good thing because if he did, they would most likely be overrun within a minute at the rate these things were moving—One of the things suddenly appeared on the wall in front of him with a flash of light, flopping onto the stone.

Elliot staked it to the path out of sheer panic, completing the motion before he had even decided to attack.

Loot Gained: 1 Exp, 1 Gold, 1 Lump of Meat.

It looked like an average but fit human, other than its lack of eyes, ears, and nose; just a mouth filled with white teeth, now stained with blood.

Elliot left it behind him, panting for breath as the wall below him began to tremble again. These things were only level one, which explained exactly why there were so many of them. His own team had been massive, and he had no idea what the average level had been.

There could have been millions of these things.

Elliot could see a wave of the creatures spilling over one of the walls in the distance as the entire flood began to change directions again.

What must their homeworld look like for this to happen? You only turned up in the Grey Room when you died, so why were there so many of these almost-humans dying so frequently? What was the purpose of it?

Why didn't they have eyes, or noses, or ears? It was like someone had taken a human and stripped them of all the sensory organs needed to live. Was someone making them like this? Were they grown in some kind of meat factory, used as fuel or food?

He threw another rock as his wall ran out and swapped with it, and to his horror, he found his team. Where tens of thousands had been originally mere hundreds remained, and worse than that, they had run out of ground.

A sheer cliff, the bottom of which was pitch black, ran the entire length of the Maze. A single narrow bridge crossed the chasm completely, only to run straight into the face of a cracked stone wall that stretched from the shadowed ceiling above to the darkness of the hole below.

It was a bridge to nowhere.

The bridge was packed with people, almost halfway across the gap, but they were already pressed against the wall. Most of them were facing the Maze looking terrified, while the people closest to the dead-end were using their weapons to carve what looked to be a staircase out of the wall.

Another group of three was destroying the section of the bridge that still connected to the Maze as the last of the survivors pushed their way past.

Elliot watched them work for a moment from the top of the last wall before the chasm. He wouldn't be able to make it to the bridge before the wave of bodies reached him. Instead, he took a rock and threw it as hard as he could out over the chasm.

The wall below him began to fall, and he swapped with the rock, twisting and throwing a second one, a third one—it took six rocks before he reached the other side, and as the final one bounced off the wall, he pulled his spear out of his inventory and stabbed it into the wall.

Elliot panted for breath as he hung from the spear above the endless pit below.

The horde broke through the last wall, cascading over the edge into the pit in a never-ending flood. Flashes of light, noise, and a million colors erupted throughout the mess, destroying massive pieces of the chasm wall and illuminating it as they fell.

A line of light raked across the wall above the bridge, ripping a line down through the bridge; half of the bridge broke off from the rest, falling into the chasm and sending most of the survivors to their deaths.

Elliot forced himself to stop watching and pulled another rock out of his inventory. He tossed it up into the air, above the spear, and then traded places with it. He landed on the shaft of the spear, placing a hand on the wall for balance.

He removed the Rare Sword that he'd found in the chest earlier out of his inventory, and pushed it into the wall, tip first. It wasn't anywhere near as easy as the spear had been, but he managed to cut some of the stone out. He inventoried each piece he cut out, not willing to let something fall onto the spear below him.

The sounds of chaos behind him only got worse, but he kept on cutting into the stone, widening the hole until it was deep enough and tall enough for him to sit inside. He carefully twisted, sitting on the edge of the hole, and once it supported his weight, he used his foot's contact with the spear to return it to his inventory.

Elliot sat further back into the hole, using the sword to keep cutting away at the right side of the hole, while he watched the bodies continue to surge down into the darkness below. Eventually, he was able to sit up to his full height and then turn enough that his entire body was inside it.

With his back to the wall now, he could push harder and started making way more progress, and once he'd made enough space, he switched the Rare Sword out for his Exotic Skypeircer once more. The spear cut through the stone with the same ease that it cut through everything else, and soon he was carving large scoops of stone away.

The bridge was almost entirely gone now, with only about five meters of stone left. He couldn't see well from his position in the wall, but there were at most a dozen people who had made it into a similar hole they'd cut into the stone.

A large orb of empty space made its way towards the chasm, nothing able to enter its area of influence, and the surrounding bodies were pushed away as it moved, stumbled over the broken remains of the wall littering the ground.

It walked straight off the edge of the cliff, just as mindless as the others.

A black ball of smoke-like energy flashed emerged from the flood, carving a perfect hole through everything in its path and slamming into the remains of the bridge opposite it. The bridge vanished under the attack, and the attack continued into the wall behind it, and out of sight, two more people fell as the bottom of the ledge was erased beneath them.

Elliot swallowed and turned back to his task, the hole now easily big enough to swing his spear around properly. He started a more structured attempt at carving a pathway angled downwards towards the other group.

All the while, more and more bodies fell into the chasm, and after what had to be five more minutes, the horde finally began to slow down. The front line became more scattered as the slower ones struggled to make it all the way to the edge.

Finally, a single body remained, stumbling towards the edge as best it could and diving off after the others. Almost a minute passed before a bright light appeared in the middle of the gorge, spearing up through the ceiling and bathing everything in a warm glow.

Dungeon Complete: 4,200,871/4,200,871 Enemies Defeated.

Thousands of people had been inside the Grey Room less than an hour ago; now, there were half a dozen left at most, and he was almost certain that Hannah and Grant weren't amongst the survivors. The Portal was on the other side of the chasm, almost level with the cliff wall and far out of reach of anyone without some kind of enhanced mobility.

The other survivors must have seen him cross because they were calling out to him now; he could hear the sounds of the wall being carved apart as they got closer, clearly continuing their own staircase upwards towards him.

"Hey!" A man shouted, "Do you have any way to get to the portal?"

"Yes!" Elliot called back.

Elliot could hear the relieved cries of the other four people with the man at the news, and he went to sit against the far wall; his arms were almost dead weight at this point, not at all used to the constant effort of swinging the weapons at the stone.

He felt them getting closer; six people total, three women, three men judging by the body shapes. One of the women almost slipped off the edge, and he jerked forward, almost swapping with her before one of the men next to her snatched her by the arm and pulled her back to safety.

Elliot slumped back against the wall, heart racing; the group was close enough to hear now.

"Thank you, Alex!" A woman said, clearly crying.

"It's going to be okay, Liana," Alex said confidently.

"You're getting pretty close," Elliot called, and the sound of metal crashing into stone slowed.

The tip of a thick blade pierced through the bottom of the wall before carving a massive half circle out of the wall of his hole. The mass of stone was pushed off the edge with a grunt, revealing a man with a great axe resting on the floor of the tunnel.

"You're the guy from earlier," Alex said, amazed. "What the hell is this place, man?"

He looked from each face to the next and recognized none of them; Hannah and Grant were gone.

"We don't have time to talk," Elliot managed, fist clenched by his side. "Who has the highest strength stat here?"

Most of them looked confused, but the man with the Greataxe on his back stepped forward.

"Name's Krill; My strength is at two hundred." Krill said grimly. "That enough?"

"More than enough," Elliot said, summoning a rock from his inventory and handing it to the man. "I need you to throw this hard enough that it will end up in the portal—can you make that throw?"

Krill took it and pitched it hard; the rock shot across the gap, arcing right into the Portal.

"Nice throw," Alex said, amazed.

"Looks like it." Krill nodded. "What's the plan?"

"You throw the rock into the portal; I'll trade places with it before it leaves my range and then switch with someone here." Elliot said clearly, "The person I swap with will keep the momentum and path of the rock, passing through the portal to the Grey Room."

"You'll all need to brace yourself for a rough landing inside the Grey Room," Krill said, frowning. "I'll try to put more forward momentum into the throw; rolling to a stop is probably better than crashing into the ground."

"Wait," Liana said uneasily, "I'm going to be flying through the air like a rock?"

"It's okay, Liana," Alex smiled, "I'll go first to make sure it works."

"Brave man," Krill nodded, "How are you going to get out afterward?"

"Same way I made it over the first time," Elliot said. "Ready?"

"Ready!" Alex nodded firmly.

Krill took another rock and eyed Alex for a moment and turning to the ledge. He took a moment to gauge the distance and then threw it. Elliot swapped with it as soon as it passed out of the hole, preserving the rock's momentum, and then traded places with Alex.

Elliot landed where Alex had been and turned, watching the man's arc across the chasm before he vanished into the Portal.

"Nice throw, Krill." Elliot said, "I'm ready to go again."

"Thanks," Krill grunted.

"I don't think I can do this." Liana choked out. "I'm going to fall—I can't."

Krill sent him a look that he understood completely before taking another rock from him. Liana screamed as she found herself flung through the Portal without warning. Three more rocks and three more people vanished through the Portal.

Then only Krill and Elliot remained.

"Krill," Elliot said, voice quiet. "Can you revive people in the grey room, or do you need to do it in the dungeon?"

"The Revive Token will work in the grey room immediately after the dungeon," Krill said, reaching out and clapping him on the shoulder. "What's your name?"

"Elliot," Elliot said quietly.

"Thanks for sticking around, Elliot," Krill said before taking the stone. "See you on the other side."

Krill passed through the Portal and vanished, leaving Elliot alone in the Dungeon.

He Who Devours has appeared.

Elliot tossed his own rock across, a second one ready in his hand. He swapped, and just like before, it took him six stones to cross the gap, and just as he switched with the last rock, he looked down, a splash of color catching his eye.

A pair of massive red eyes stared up at him in the darkness below, and then he vanished through the Portal.

Elliot hit the ground running, heart racing in his chest, and when he stopped, he raised his head to find the other survivors watching him.

Loot Gained: 10,001 EXP, 501 Gold.

Less than an hour on the clock, tens of thousands dead, Hannah and Grant gone, and that was what it was worth? A-rank difficulty, B-rating timer, and a new line of text explaining why he'd gotten so much experience despite only getting a single kill.

Special Objective Complete; Survive against an enemy with a significant level difference.

A significant level difference? He'd fought Svent and survived when the man was at least three hundred levels above him, and he hadn't gotten anything like that. He'd fought and killed the Five Kings with everyone in the T7 Dungeon, and he hadn't got that.

Exactly what level was 'The One Who Devours?'

Elliot shook his head, trying to drive away from the image of two red eyes following him. He opened his inventory and found the Revive Tokens he'd purchased before entering the Dungeon. He selected the use option, and a small prompt appeared asking him to enter a name.

Revive: Hannah Walker.

Elliot opened the faction menu to check he had the exact spelling and then pressed accept. Hannah suddenly appeared, curled up on the ground at his feet. She made a noise of terror, and her hand clamped down on his leg. Hannah looked around wildly before she realized he was there but made no attempt to get up.

Elliot pressed use on the second Revive Token, and the second prompts pulsed gently in the air.

"Elliot?" Hannah gasped, grabbing onto his leg tightly. "There was so many... I couldn't breathe.... I called out, I thought...."

Elliot slowly knelt down beside her and dragged her into a hug. He shook for a moment and then clutched her tighter.

"I'm sorry," Elliot managed, choking back sobs. "I thought I could do both."

"Elliot?" Hannah whispered, trying to see his face, but he just held her tighter. "Where is Grant?"

Revive: Grant Baker.
Failure: Only one revive token can be used per team.

"I'm so sorry," Elliot cried.

Elliot wondered how many others were going to die in this place because some obscure detail wasn't known. He felt like a fool; the first thing he should have done when he found out about the Revive Token was bought some and then test out exactly how they worked first.

Two hundred thousand gold would have been enough to figure this out; it would have been enough for him to know not to bring both of them into the Dungeon at the same time. Even asking around about it first would have maybe saved him; even if it probably wasn't common knowledge, someone would have known about it.

He should have known.

Hannah drew in another shaky breath as she walked beside him, trying to hold back tears. Alex and Liana followed them quietly, not quite willing to speak up yet. Krill and the others hadn't been in Hell, so they'd said their goodbyes inside the Grey Room before leaving.

"You've got questions," Elliot murmured. "Just ask."

Maybe it would take his mind off the fact that he was the reason Grant was now dead.

"This is a death game, isn't it?" Alex said quietly.

"Yes," Elliot said quietly, "And it's one you're going to have to play every single week."

Alex lowered his gaze to the road ahead of them for a moment, considering that.

"There's no way around it?" Liana managed quietly.

"Ten-thousand gold will buy you a Skip Token," Elliot said, "If you can make that much in seven days."

"Oh god," Liana murmured, "I'm going to die here."

"We were making a group help people who first arrive here," Elliot said, "If you want to join, you'll have access to food, shelter, and whatever gear I can find."

"Really?" Alex said, raising an eyebrow. "That generous of you; what's the catch?"

"Pass the goodwill along," Elliot said, "When you earn yourself better gear, donate any old stuff you don't want to the faction for other people to use in the future; that's the only requirement."

"That's all?" Alex said, blinking.

"Do you want to join or not?" Elliot sighed, turning away.

"Of course I do, Elliot," Alex said easily, "We will both join, right Liana?"

"Yes, please." Liana said quietly, "If you'll have us."

Elliot opened the menu quietly and sent them both an invitation to Excelsior.

New Faction Members: Alex Maine, Member. Liana Trell, Member.

"We have one bedroom—" Elliot cut himself off, closing his eyes for a moment before continuing. "We have two bedrooms left. You can take one each; they're both on the second floor of our building."

"Thanks, man," Alex said.

"There is food in the Faction Bank," Elliot said, "It's in the Interface menu."

"Right," Alex nodded.

Elliot eyed the tavern across from the building and saw that the woman who wasn't Koren was sitting at one of the tables.

"Thing is our building; there's one more thing you need to know," Elliot said, "We have another member you haven't met yet, she's not human, and she doesn't speak English."

"Not human?" Liana said, surprised.

"You'll see in a moment," Elliot said, watching them both, "People don't like her because she's from the dungeon if you treat her badly—"

"I wouldn't!" Liana said quickly, wringing her hands together. "I wouldn't do that."

"Neither would I," Alex nodded.

"Thanks," Elliot murmured, opening the door. "Welcome to Excelsior, make yourselves at home."

"Yeah," Alex nodded gratefully, "Come on, Liana, let's go check out our rooms—I want to meet this the other member as well."

"Thank you, both," Liana said, taking Hannah's hand.

"It's okay," Hannah mumbled, squeezing the woman's hand.

Liana followed Alex into the building, and they stepped in behind her, closing the door.

"Elliot?" Hannah said, "Can I talk to you?"

Elliot couldn't bring himself to speak, so he just nodded and steered her towards a bench. He sat down beside her, and she slumped against his arm.

"It's not fair," Hannah whispered.

"It's not," Elliot murmured, staring at the ground.

"I didn't even see where he went," Hannah said, voice shaking, "He was beside me in, and when I looked over, he was just gone."

Hannah buried her face in her hands with a choked sob, and Elliot squeezed his eyes shut, trying to stop himself from crying again.

"I just kept running," Hannah managed, "I didn't even stop to help."

Elliot swallowed.

"There was so much noise, and then I was being crushed," Hannah whispered, "Then there was nothing at all."

Crushed to death beneath the countless bodies, even thinking about it, sent a pang of fear through him.

"I'm so sorry, Hannah." Elliot managed, "I shouldn't have even brought you two with me."

"I wanted to go with you; we both did," Hannah sobbed, burying her face into his neck. "It's not your fault, Elliot; it's not."

Elliot doubted he would ever be able to believe her.

Elliot picked at the grass, wondering how he could have grown so attached to someone so fast. He reached out and touched the small wooden cross that stood straight up out of the ground.

"I'm sorry it isn't something better," Elliot said quietly. "I've never been good at making things."

This place did strange things to you, or perhaps it was the nature of desperate situations that had brought so much trust in so little time. He'd asked Grant to risk his life in that first Dungeon, and he'd done it almost without thinking.

He'd worked with him to defeat the creatures in the Dungeon; Grant hadn't even doubted him for a second. He had just slipped into the role Elliot had asked of him and done it all perfectly. He vividly remembered him rushing out into danger to save that man in the first Dungeon, fighting the pale thing and dragging the man's body back to the entrance.

Grant should have been the one to live; he was the one with a family waiting for him. Instead, Elliot was here, sitting next to a badly wrought cross, and it shouldn't have been this way. If his power had let him trade places with Grant right now, he'd have done it without a thought.

"I'm sorry, Grant," Elliot murmured, "You deserved better than this."

Elliot closed his eyes and brushed his sleeve across his face.

"I'll find a way to fix this." Elliot promised, "I will tear this place down, inch by inch, and then I'll meet the ones who built it."

Elliot pushed the Revive Token through the grass at the base of the cross until it sunk beneath the surface and out of sight.

"I'll make them bring you back," Elliot said, "Then I'll find a way for all of us to go home again. It might take me a while, so try to be patient okay?"

Elliot pushed himself to his feet and stared down at the name he'd carefully carved into the wood.

"See you around, Grant," Elliot whispered.

Hannah was waiting for him, and Elliot stopped next to her, unsure what to say.

"You better not say sorry again," Hannah murmured, a hint of warning in her voice. "I told you not to, remember?"

"Yeah," Elliot admitted quietly. "I remember."

"I heard what you said," Hannah admitted, "Do you think there's someone like that, a person who could bring him back?"

"I think it's likely," Elliot admitted, watching the grave marker. "This place isn't something that naturally occurred. There's more than enough evidence for that; the Grey Room, the Dungeons, the Interface, the Torii—all of it points towards intelligent design."

"How do you even hold someone like that accountable?" Hannah murmured. "You would need to be a god to make something like this."

A question like that had an answer that was easy to say and almost impossible to put into practice. It would take years of work, and he would probably die along the way, but he knew of one way to deal with someone like that.

Elliot just needed to figure out how to kill a god.

"Well, I am a bartender," Alex said, shrugging. "Having a bar here and not using it feels like I'm betraying my profession, you know?"

"They do have alcohol here," Elliot said in answer. "I don't know where the Taverns get it from; I'm assuming there are people with the knowledge to make it somewhere in the city."

"I'll ask around then," Alex decided, "Did you find what you were looking for?"

Elliot shook his head.

"No," Elliot admitted, "I watched the map for almost two hours, but nothing opened up; this part of the city seems to be pretty stable."

"If you describe what type of building you're looking for," Liana said gently, "I could spend some time watching it for you?"

Elliot opened the inventory and removed the Shop Token he'd bought, handing it over to her. Liana took it, surprised, and glanced back up at him.

"We're looking for space over anything else; the closer to this building, the better; if you see anything on this street, buy it regardless of size." Elliot said, "When you are looking at the map screen, be careful what you click on because it automatically buys the Grey buildings when you touch them."

Liana nodded quickly.

"I'll be careful, Elliot," Liana promised, "I know this is worth a lot of money, thank you for trusting me."

"Don't mention it," Elliot said, "It's safer this way; if everything is in my name and I die, we will lose all of the buildings; it's better to spread ownership among all of us."

"There's so much about this place we don't know," Alex sighed, "I hope it gets easier."

"So do I, Alex," Elliot murmured, standing up. "I'm going to check on Hannah; is she upstairs?"

"Yes," Liana nodded, "Tyralklivi was upstairs as well, sleeping on the table."

"Thanks," Elliot nodded, making his way to the stairs.

There was no mirror for him to check, but he was almost certain that he would find dark bags under his eyes if he looked. Sleep had been even harder to come by after what had happened, and every time he closed his eyes, he found himself within the Maze once more, desperately trying to find the others.

He reached the top of the stairs and glanced to the right; sure enough, Tyralklivi was curled up on top of the table by the balcony door. The window was open, and the sunlight poured through, illuminating her skin.

"Elliot?" Hannah said, and he turned to the door in front of him.

Hannah was sitting on the bed, with her back to the wall and a pillow on her lap, watching him.

"Hannah," Elliot said hesitantly. "Do you need anything?"

"I'm okay," Hannah said, "You can come in, you know, it's your room anyway."

Elliot stepped into the room and leaned back against the door frame, gazing at the floor.

"You can have this room if you want," Elliot said, "I'm not attached to any of them."

Hannah snorted at the comment, and he couldn't help but notice the dark shadows under her own eyes. Given what had happened to her, she was likely having just as much trouble sleeping as he was.

"Shut the door," Hannah mumbled before patting the bed next to her.

Elliot wondered if running back down the stairs wasn't the safer option after all, but after a moment of hesitation, he shut the door. He moved across the room and sat on the edge of the bed, feeling it sink slightly beneath him.

"I miss Grant," Hannah said quietly.

"So do I," Elliot mumbled.

"I only knew him for a couple of days," Hannah said, shaking her head. "But it hurts almost as much as when my mum died."

Elliot knew the feeling all too well, and he remembers locking himself away in his room for weeks when Dimitri died.

"Grant was—I don't know...." Hannah said quietly. "I can't stop thinking about it."

Elliot closed his eyes and leaned back on his hands, picturing the man in his mind.

"Grant was a bit of everything," Elliot said quietly, "He actually listened when I spoke, and he was smarter than I ever was."

Hannah shook, hands fisted into the sheets.

"He was funny too," Hannah said, crying quietly. "He won't even get to see his partner again; this is all so messed up."

Elliot allowed himself to fall back onto the bed and stared up at the ceiling above, thinking.

"Hey, Hannah," Elliot said quietly, "You and Grant were both alike in a lot of ways, you know?"

Hannah sniffled, and the bed shifted under her weight as she turned to face him.

"Were we?" Hannah mumbled.

"Yeah," Elliot said, "You and Grant were both incredibly brave; that wasn't a trait that he had a monopoly on, you know?"

"Elliot," Hannah said quietly.

"And while you may not be brilliant—" Elliot said, cracking on eye open to look over at her.

"Hey," Hannah said.

"Just a joke," Elliot said, amused, "I think you are smart and funny as well; Grant didn't have a monopoly on those traits either, promise."

"What about you, then?" Hannah murmured, "What did you bring to the table, Elliot?"

Elliot forced himself to smirk, still watching her out of the corner of his eye.

"Well," Elliot said, "At least one of us had to be pretty."

Hannah looked completely shocked, and Elliot couldn't help but laugh at her expression.

"Elliot!" Hannah said indignantly, reaching for his face with both of her hands. "That's mean."

Elliot managed to catch her by the wrists, keeping her hands away from his face. Most of his confidence fled as the expression on her face changed, and she switched to an easier target.

"Hannah!" Elliot said, mortified, "Don't grab that."

Other Works

Golden Sole: The Leaf - LitRPG, Dark Fantasy.

Felix Arlen, at twenty-four, has been stuck in a hole of depression, anxiety, and hopelessness for years, he decides to give it one last try to break free and is completely unsurprised to find that it all goes horribly wrong. It turns out there is a city hidden beneath his very feet, filled with cannibals, murderers, and things that might even be worse than that. Felix must use his wits to figure out both the glowing mark on his foot and how this insane RPG system works if he wants to survive.

The Dragons Marble - Fantasy, Myths, Magic.

A mage, a monster, and a noblewoman seek out mythical treasures in the hopes of finding something that might save them after they become enveloped in the political machinations of a power-seeking noble.

Tato's List - LitRPG, NSFW

The Tournament of King's has finally returned to Cloudhall City and Shin a member of the Monster Hunter response Unit quickly becomes entangled in a web of sex, fighting, and lewd jokes.

Reroll - Superhero, Psychological, Timeloop.

A horrific attack on a crowd ends with tens of thousands dead before Loren Parker abruptly wakes up in his bed, miraculously unharmed, two days before the explosion. Setalite City is on the brink of destruction, famous heroes and infamous villains are being systematically killed worldwide, and an unknown puppet master is pulling the strings. Lucky for him, Loren has all the time in the world to set things straight.